BOOK OF SCIENCE

*Children's Encyclopedia
of Knowledge*

BOOK OF SCIENCE

Collins

LONDON AND GLASGOW

This Edition 1971

ISBN 0 00 105107 5

© *Wm. Collins Sons & Co. Ltd.*

PRINTED AND MADE IN GREAT BRITAIN BY
WILLIAM COLLINS SONS AND CO. LTD.
LONDON AND GLASGOW

CONTENTS

CONTENTS

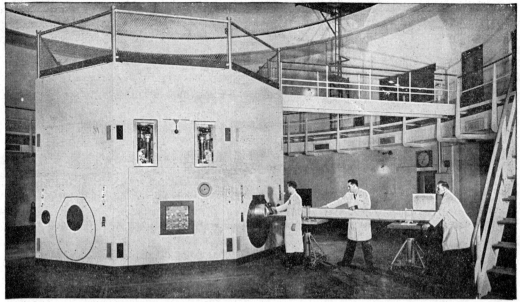

A large research reactor which is of the type being used to supply heat energy for atomic power plants that generate electricity.

ATOMIC POWER
What it is and How it can be Used

IN 1945, atomic power meant just one thing to most people in the world—a bomb that had destroyed in a flash the Japanese city of Hiroshima and 71,379 of its people.

To-day, fear of the atomic bomb is overshadowed by the even greater menace of the hydrogen bomb. But there is also a much brighter side to the picture, because the first atomic power stations are coming into use for the benefit, rather than the destruction, of mankind.

A SOURCE OF ENERGY

This is tremendously important, because we are using up our supplies of existing fuels at a high rate. In the United States alone, half the coal ever consumed has been burned since 1920, and half the oil ever consumed has been burned since 1940. In Britain, consumption of electricity will increase to four times its present level by 1975, which would mean digging an extra 60 million tons of coal each year, just to keep pace with demands for electricity. Another source of energy must be tapped, and the answer lies in the atom, because a $1\frac{1}{8}$ in. cube of uranium—the element used in an atomic bomb—weighing just one pound, can yield as much energy as 1,200 tons of coal.

92 BASIC ELEMENTS

How does this energy come to be locked up in the atom? And how can we make use of it for peaceful purposes? Before we can answer these questions, we must learn a little of what atoms are and what they are made of. If you look around you at this moment, you will see hundreds of different materials and substances —paper, leather, plastic, plants, perhaps an animal or two, china, glass, steel, wood, and so on. Yet all these things are made up of only 92 different basic substances, called elements.

Like the ingredients in your pantry at home, they can be joined together in different ways to produce different mixtures, called chemical compounds, such as water, which is made up of two basic elements—hydrogen and oxygen.

The smallest possible unit of any element is called an atom of that element, and these atoms are so small that they cannot be seen even under the most powerful microscope. In fact, the relative size of an atom compared with a cricket ball is about the same as the size of a cricket ball compared with the Earth.

THE COMPONENT PARTICLES

Until the start of this century, it was believed that atoms were solid. Then Lord Rutherford showed that they were made up of even smaller particles which themselves occupy only a part of the atom, the rest being empty space. The particles are now known as electrons, protons and neutrons and the only way of describing their size is again by comparison. In an atom of hydrogen which, as we shall see later, is the simplest of all, a single electron circles round a single proton like a planet round the sun. The two particles are so tiny that, for their size, the distance they are apart within the atom is relatively about as great as the distance of the sun from the Earth. The rest is space and, although it is difficult to believe, everything in the world, including you, contains far more empty space than solid matter, because the tiny atoms of which it is built up consist largely of space.

THE PART PLAYED BY ELECTRICITY

Before we go further, let us take a look at the three basic particles that make up atoms. The first thing that becomes apparent is that electricity plays a vital part in the structure of everything round us, because an electron has a small charge of negative electricity (the minus sign on a cycle lamp battery) in it, whereas a proton has a small charge of positive electricity (the plus sign). The two charges are equal, so that they balance each other out, otherwise atoms would repel each other and tend to blow everything apart.

To make them electrically neutral, all atoms must contain an equal number of electrons and protons. An oxygen atom, for example, contains eight of each, plus eight neutrons, which have no electrical charge. In all atoms, the protons and neutrons are clustered together as a core, or " nucleus," round which the electrons circle.

THE WEIGHT OF PARTICLES

Small as they are, electrons, protons and neutrons have mass, and, therefore, weight. It is difficult to measure, because it takes millions and millions of them to weigh an ounce. But scientists assure us that a proton has more than 1,800 times as much mass as an electron, and a neutron about the same mass as a proton.

COMPOSITION OF EACH ELEMENT

Because everything is made up of electrons, protons and, usually, neutrons, lead is different from gold, and oxygen from hydrogen, only because their atoms contain different numbers of each particle. As we have already seen, there are 92 basic elements in nature. There are also eight more which do not exist naturally but have been produced in laboratories.

Each element has an " atomic number," which corresponds to the number of protons in its nucleus. Thus, hydrogen has an atomic number of 1. Towards the other end of the scale, uranium is element No. 92, because its nucleus contains 92 protons. Although the number of protons and electrons in an atom of only one element always remains constant, this is not true of neutrons. Ordinary hydrogen, as we have seen, has a nucleus consisting of just one proton; but there is another kind of hydrogen atom which has a neutron as well as a proton in its nucleus. It is therefore called " heavy " hydrogen.

It behaves just like ordinary hydrogen in making chemical compounds like water, because the behaviour of an atom is determined only by the number of electrons it contains, and both hydrogen and " heavy " hydrogen have just one electron.

ISOTOPES

These different forms of the same basic element are called " isotopes," and one of the most important is an isotope of uranium.

The most common form of uranium is known as U-238, because its nucleus contains 92 protons and 146 neutrons, making a total of 238 particles. But there is an isotope of uranium with only 143 neutrons, and this U-235 is one of the raw materials of the atomic bomb and for peaceful uses of atomic energy.

RADIOACTIVITY

A feature of uranium and certain other elements like radium is that they are what we call radioactive. Without going into great detail, this means that they give off an invisible radiation. Some articles in common use are

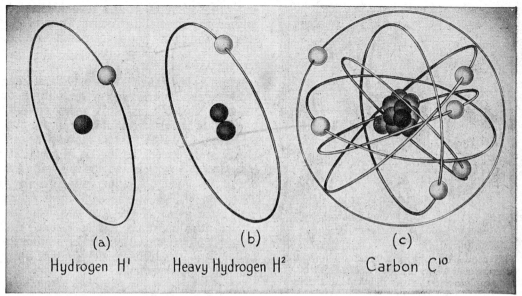

(a)   (b)   (c)

Hydrogen H¹   Heavy Hydrogen H²   Carbon C¹⁰

Atoms are like tiny solar systems with electron " planets " revolving round protons and neutrons. (a) Hydrogen is the simplest with one proton and one electron; (b) heavy hydrogen or deuterium has a neutron as well; (c) carbon has 6 electrons, 6 protons and 4 neutrons.

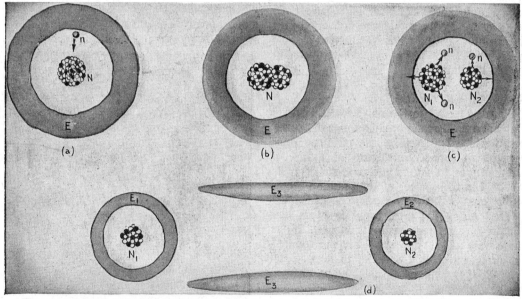

How an atom " splits." (a) A neutron (n) has passed through electrons (E) and enters the nucleus (N). (b) It makes the atom unstable, energy is released and the nucleus vibrates and divides. (c) The two fragments of the nucleus (N_1 and N_2) carry positive charges and repel each other, shedding neutrons (n) (d) As they fly apart, the two fragment nuclei take with them some of the electrons (E_1 and E_2), leaving behind half the original number (E_3).

radioactive. For instance, the paints used to mark the figures on luminous dial watches have radium in them. And, of course, radium rays are used in hospitals to save life. But, if absorbed by the body in excessive amounts, they can quickly destroy its tissues. So they have to be handled carefully.

Radioactivity was the key to atomic science, because it first enabled scientists to change one atom into another. Lord Rutherford was the

This model of part of a reactor shows the arrangement of the uranium channels through the graphite and the way they extend through the radiation shield.

first to do this over 30 years ago, when he " bombarded " atoms of nitrogen with rays from a radioactive substance. Nitrogen atoms, when struck by the rays, were converted into oxygen atoms. The work was carried a stage further in 1932 by Cockcroft and Walton, again in Great Britain.

GERMAN EXPERIMENTS

Six years later, two German scientists named Hahn and Strassmann began a series of experiments which had far-reaching results. Their purpose in shooting neutrons at atoms of uranium was to try to make some of them " stick " in the nucleus of the uranium atoms and so change them into a different element.

They knew that each uranium atom had 238 protons and neutrons in its nucleus. If one more were added, they should have produced an element with 239 particles in its nucleus. Instead, they kept on producing the element barium, with only 137 nuclear particles.

A famous woman scientist named Dr. Lise Meitner, who was an expert in atomic science and mathematics, was told about these rather surprising results. After many hours of complicated work, she decided that another kind of atom was being created at the same time as the barium and that there should also be an enormous amount of energy released. In due course, this proved to be true, and the released energy—millions of times more powerful than

any other form of energy then available— became the deadly destructive force of the atomic bombs built during the war in America.

NUCLEAR FISSION

It was at first thought that only the isotope U-235 released atomic energy by splitting, or " nuclear fission " as it is more correctly known. Scientists were able to prove that the neutron " bullet " enters the nucleus of a U-235 atom which, having as a result 236 instead of 235 particles, begins to vibrate and distort, eventually splitting into two parts. These two " fragment " nuclei fly apart, taking with them some of the electrons from the original uranium atom, and so forming new atoms. This explains why Dr. Hahn produced barium atoms, which are only one of many different fission products.

At the same time, immense amounts of energy are released, because the particles in the new nuclei are packed more closely together than in the original nucleus. As they fall in closer together, they release energy, just as a stone does if it falls to the ground from the top of a tower.

To measure piston wear, a radioactive piston ring is placed in a car engine, run 4-5 hours, and then a Geiger counter gauges the metal content of the crankcase oil.

No less important is the fact that neutrons peel off the two nuclei as they fly apart. Any one of these neutrons can lodge in the nucleus of another U-235 atom, causing a repetition of the whole process, building up what is called a " chain reaction."

It has often been feared by atomic scientists that such a chain reaction might prove so successful that it could get out of hand, spreading in a fraction of a second from atom to atom until it built up into an explosion so terrible that it would destroy all life over a vast area. Fortunately, many of the secondary neutrons miss their targets and the chain is eventually broken: but scientists have been able to produce controlled chain reactions in the laboratory with great success.

PROBLEMS WITH URANIUM ORE

At first, they were dismayed to discover that, apparently, only U-235 would undergo " fission," because when uranium ore is mined there is only 1 lb. of this isotope for every 140 lb. of U-238, and atoms of U-234 are also present. The three are not easy to separate. The method finally chosen for the atomic bomb factory at Oak Ridge, Tennessee, was to give all the atoms an electric charge and then draw them into the field of a powerful electro-magnet. They followed curving orbits but, because the three isotopes each had a slightly different mass, they had a slightly different path in the magnetic field and could be drawn into separate collectors. It was rather a slow business; but it worked.

Later it was found that U-238 itself could be " split " with fast neutrons; but its real value is as the source of a new atomic " fuel." Scientists found that when neutrons were shot into it in the normal way, they did not cause fission; but the addition of one neutron to its nucleus turned the U-238 atom into a new

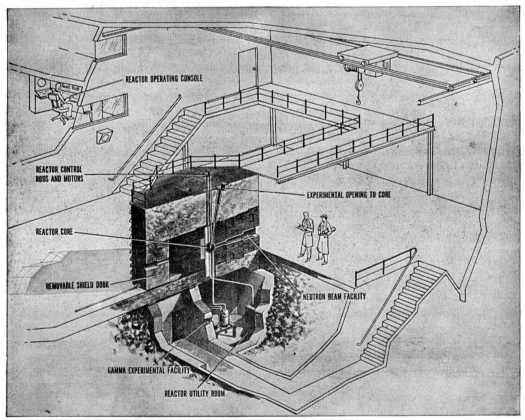

REACTOR OPERATING CONSOLE

REACTOR CONTROL RODS AND MOTORS

EXPERIMENTAL OPENING TO CORE

REACTOR CORE

REMOVABLE SHIELD DOOR

NEUTRON BEAM FACILITY

GAMMA EXPERIMENTAL FACILITY

REACTOR UTILITY ROOM

The general layout of an atomic reactor is shown here diagrammatically. The great advances which have been made in many fields as a result of these reactors is amazing.

element (No. 93), which was given the name of neptunium. This proved to be an unstable radioactive element, which gave off beta rays (high-speed electrons) and turned itself into another new element—No. 94, plutonium—which has the same fissionable characteristics as U-235.

THE ATOMIC BOMB

It was known from the start that there was a definite minimum (or critical) size for the piece of U-235 or plutonium that would cause an atomic bomb explosion. So, by dividing a little more than this amount of the element into two parts and keeping them separate inside the bomb, the scientists knew they could make it safe until the time came to drop it. Over the target, one of the two pieces was simply shot into the other in a kind of atomic gun to form a mass greater than the " critical " size, and the whole thing exploded with fantastic force, producing intense heat and radioactive rays capable of destroying the cells of a human body.

NEW ATOM-SPLITTING MACHINES

But we are more concerned with the peaceful uses of atomic energy than with bombs. Vitally important discoveries are being made almost every year by the use of the giant new betatron and synchrotron atom-splitting machines, which have supplemented the pre-war Van de Graaff accelerator and cyclotron. None is likely to have greater consequences than the confirmation in October, 1955, of the existence of a new particle, the negative proton, which can be produced at present only in the great bevatron machine at the University of California.

The existence of its counterpart, the positive electron (positron), had been discovered in cosmic radiation in 1932, and it was found that when positrons and electrons came together they disappeared, leaving a flash of penetrating radiation like X-rays.

Little is known yet about negative protons, but scientists believe that if they could be produced in large numbers and brought into contact with ordinary protons, they would annihilate each other, producing immense amounts of heat or radiation. Furthermore, they see no reason why it should not be possible to create a new " reversed " form of matter, in which positive electrons rotate round a

nucleus of negative protons and neutrons. They have no idea what the result would be; but it would be as stable as any ordinary atom until the two came into contact, when they would annihilate each other with a thousand times the efficiency of ordinary nuclear fission in uranium.

THE ATOMIC PILE

At the moment, this is speculation. Meanwhile, the main tool of " atoms for peace " is the nuclear reactor or atomic pile. This is essentially a simple piece of apparatus, in which rods of uranium are inserted into holes in a huge block of graphite which slows down the flying neutron particles, making the whole thing a sort of controlled atomic bomb. The speed of the reaction can be regulated (or

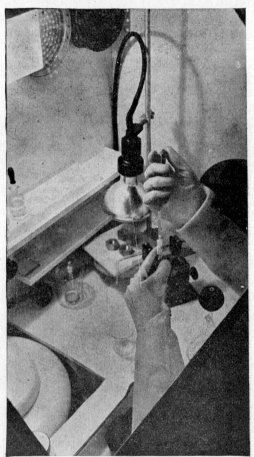

To handle radioactive substances which emit alpha-particles, the operator puts his hands through two holes in a box into rubber gloves, which are sealed to the box.

Scientists at Harwell manipulating radioactive isotopes behind heavy walls, which protect them from the dangerous gamma radiations given off by the isotopes.

stopped when necessary) by inserting rods of boron or cadmium, which absorb the neutrons before they can cause fission in the U-235.

In this type of pile, uranium can be turned into plutonium, a process that is accompanied by a great deal of heat and the emission of radiation. Both of these by-products are likely to be of immense value in the years ahead.

RADIO-ISOTOPES

To start with, scientists are able to expose quantities of elements such as carbon, iodine and cobalt to the radiation inside a pile, so that they become what are called radio-isotopes. These are already being used widely in medicine, agriculture and industry.

They can be used to attack disease directly by radiation, similar to X-ray and radium radiation. Or they can be used as " tracers " to locate disease, because their position as they circulate round the body can be detected by devices called Geiger counters, which measure radioactivity.

Danish scientists have mixed radioactive isotopes of mercury with fungicide sprayed on plants to find out how much of the spray remained on the leaves. Radioactive isotopes are also being used to measure the level of molten metal in factory crucibles, to prevent heavy presses working when the operators' hands are in the way, to detect flaws in castings and wear in tyres, to measure the thickness of paper, the wear in an engine, to ensure safer drugs and better preservation of food.

HEAT—A BY-PRODUCT

The other by-product—heat—can be used to drive turbines, and it might be used one day in rocket-motors. Already the first atomic-powered submarines are at sea, and atomic aircraft are being built. The first city has been lit by nuclear power and many more atomic power stations are being built throughout the world, particularly in Britain.

These are only a few of the ways in which the atom can be used in the service of mankind. The atom is no longer a mere weapon for the ultimate destruction of man, but a bright promise to the world of longer life, greater prosperity and lasting peace.

As the *Flying Scotsman* races along the track at Darlington, it passes the first locomotive ever made for public travel, standing on the rails on which it made its first run.

BRITISH RAILWAYS
From their Beginnings to the Present Day

THE idea of providing a track on which a wheeled vehicle could run dates back at least to the Romans, who laid long rows of flat-topped stones along their roads to make a solid and smooth path for their chariot wheels. In the late sixteenth century there were experiments in Europe with tracks formed of baulks of timber, and as early as the mid-seventeenth century these timber " rails " were common in the Durham coalfield, where it had been found that the horses which hauled the wagons of coal from the pit to the bank of the nearest waterway, for transfer to water transport, could tackle heavier loads if their vehicles rolled on these " rail-roads," as they were called. It was a short step from rails of timber to rails of cast iron, and by 1788 the forerunner of the modern railway track was in use. It was devised by William Jessop, builder of a horse tramway from a mine to a canal near Loughborough, Leicestershire, and established the principle of a track which lifts the vehicle's wheels above ground level on the upper surface of a rail, and which therefore requires the wheels to be flanged.

This arrangement also required a fixed gauge between the rails, to avoid derailments, and in the early eighteenth century the odd figure of 4 ft. 8½ in. came to be generally accepted as the standard railway gauge. Possibly this curious choice arose because the axle-width of the old " rail-road " wagons was 5 ft. overall, and 4 ft. 8½ in. the width between

the inside rims, so that the latter became the important measurement when the Jessop rail demanded the addition of flanges. Modern rails are no longer of cast-iron, which soon proved to be of insufficient strength; from 1820 wrought-iron was the material, and the modern steel rail was first laid on the Midland Railway in 1857.

TRANSPORT OF HEAVY GOODS

Railways originated as a useful means of carrying heavy goods, such as coal and iron, in bulk, which other means of land transport at the time—the stage coach and the road cart—could not do, and which otherwise had to travel by canal barge or coastal ship. Up to 1800, however, all railways had been private. In 1801 Parliament (whose authority has had to be sought, by an Act, for every new line of public railway constructed) sanctioned the building of the Surrey Iron Railway for goods traffic; opened from Wandsworth to Croydon on 26th July, 1803, this was the first public railway, not only in Britain, but in the world. Soon afterwards, in April, 1806, there was opened Britain's first public passenger-carrying railway, from Swansea to Oystermouth, which still exists to-day as the Swansea & Mumbles Railway in South Wales.

THE FIRST ENGINES

Horses hauled the trains on both these

This first-class carriage, built about 1850, was used on the Midland Railway. The seating
space was very limited and, of course, there was no corridor.

railways, as they still did on the private lines, but the steam locomotive was taking shape. Steam had first been used to rotate the wheels of a vehicle by a Frenchman, Cugnot, who produced a steam-driven road carriage in 1769. The world's first railway engine was built by a Cornishman, Richard Trevithick, and demonstrated on the tramway of the Pen-y-darren ironworks at Merthyr Tydfil, Wales, in February, 1804, when it is said to have hauled 10 tons of iron at 9 m.p.h. But it was not entirely successful, for it was too heavy for the light rails of its day, and little was heard of other engines Trevithick built.

A third-class coach of the early nineteenth century. Comfort was non-existent; there was
no roof and the seating was of hard wood.

The London and North Western Railway's 2–4–0 No. 790 *Hardwicke*. It took part in the Race to Aberdeen in August 1895, when it ran the 70-ton West Coast route train from Crewe to Carlisle during the 540 miles London–Aberdeen journey which was covered in 512 minutes.

Another engineer, John Blenkinsop, felt a steam engine needed more than its smooth-running wheels to take a grip of the rails, and built a colliery locomotive with an additional toothed rack-wheel that engaged a toothed rack-rail outside the running rails. A third, William Hedley, thought this needless, and proved his case, with the assistance of Timothy Hackworth, by producing for his colliery at Wylam, Northumberland, the first outstandingly successful British railway engine—the famous *Puffing Billy*, now preserved in London's Science Museum.

A young engineer at Killingworth Colliery, not far from Wylam, saw *Puffing Billy's* success and in 1814 produced his own first engine. This was George Stephenson. By 1823 he had set up his own locomotive works at Newcastle with his son Robert and had secured the job of building the track and locomotives for Britain's first steam-worked public railway, the Stockton & Darlington, opened on 27th September, 1825. The first train was hauled by Stephenson's *Locomotion No. 1*, a locomotive now displayed at Darlington (Bank Top) station. Steam had not yet completely convinced the public, however, and after this inaugural run, the Stockton & Darlington reverted to horses for its passenger trains, entrusting goods only to its steam locomotives.

THE LIVERPOOL AND MANCHESTER RAILWAY

The turning point for steam was the Rainhill Trials, organised by the promoters of the Liverpool & Manchester Railway in 1829. In these Stephenson's famous engine *Rocket* won convincingly, and as a result the L. & M.R., opened on 15th September, 1830, and adopted steam locomotives based on Stephenson's ideas for both passenger and goods traffic; it was the first public railway in Britain to do so.

The Liverpool & Manchester was an immediate success; not only was its goods traffic greater than expected, but passenger traffic became its main activity, whereas its sponsors had expected the latter to be a subsidiary business to freight. Its prosperity soon inspired schemes for railways in many other parts of the country, but at first not without strong opposition. Landowners across whose property it was hoped to route a railway would not sell the necessary ground because it would spoil their amenities, or because they had monetary interests in rival forms of transport, such as the canals, whose owners were naturally antagonistic; many newspapers encouraged the public to regard railways as unsafe, even though no train was travelling faster than 20 m.p.h.; and there was widespread fear of the steam locomotive and its noise, sparks and smoke, which many considered would kill plants and trees, frighten cattle to death, and do all kinds of mischief. Often the surveyors of new lines of railway had to fight pitched battles with local people attempting to frustrate their plans, so much did they fear the ill-effects the railways would have.

THE SPREAD OF THE RAILWAYS

Nevertheless, in the years 1830–50 the backbone of our railway system was laid. In 1837 the first British main line, the Grand Junction Railway, engineered by George Stephenson's pupil, Joseph Locke, was opened to connect Birmingham with the Liverpool & Manchester, and in the following year the London & Birmingham was ready; in 1841 Isambard Kingdom Brunel had completed the first of his superb railway works, the Great Western main line from London to Bristol. By 1845 you could travel by train from London to Dover, Brighton, Southampton, Exeter (via Bristol), Birmingham, Lancaster, York (via Derby), Cambridge and East Anglia, or you could go across country from Hull and Leeds to Manchester and Liverpool.

In the mid-1840's the craze for railways reached a peak. By then these early railways had achieved astonishing success, and the country was clamouring for more. Hundreds of dubious schemes were promoted and invested in, and inevitably this " Railway Mania " ended in a financial crash which destroyed confidence temporarily and slowed down the extension of railways to a more reasonable pace. The most famous casualty in this crash was George Hudson, the " Railway King," a York draper who had promoted many of these " Mania " schemes and had appropriated much of the money invested in them to buy control of most of the railways in the North of England. Nevertheless his drive led to the forging of the first London-Edinburgh rail link, via the Midland Railway from the capital, by 1848 and the building up of a great railway network in the North-East.

PASSENGER COACHES

At the start of railways only first-class passengers travelled in fully-enclosed vehicles, and even these were without any heating other than footwarmers, and lit by foul-smelling

The London and North Eastern Railway's 4–6–2 locomotive No. 2509 *Silver Link* drawing the pre-war streamlined " Silver Jubilee " express. This train covered the 268 miles between King's Cross and Newcastle in 4 hours. On a trial trip *Silver Link* touched 112½ m.p.h.

oil lamps. Second-class passengers usually rode in open-sided coaches, though they did have the benefit of a roof, whereas third-class passengers were herded into roofless open trucks, without any protection, until an Act of 1848 ordered that all passenger vehicles must be roofed. At first all vehicles were four-wheeled. Improvement in accommodation was gradual, but for many years third-class passengers were not catered for by the best trains; it was not until 1872 that the Midland and Great Eastern Railways established the precedent of providing third-class accommodation on all their trains, both fast and slow. In 1874 Pullman cars, offering superior accommodation at a supplementary fare, made their first appearance in Britain on the Midland Railway, and it was a Pullman car that provided the first restaurant car service on a British railway, working between King's Cross and Leeds on the Great Northern Railway from 26th September, 1879.

SAFETY MEASURES GRADUALLY INTRODUCED

Provisions for the safety of trains were improved. At first trains were operated purely on a time-interval basis. At a certain period after a preceding train had departed, the next was allowed to leave; between stations or junctions there were no signals and it was left to the driver to see that his track was clear of obstruction. From about 1850 onwards there appeared the beginnings of the modern block signalling system, which by 1870 had become established on most British main lines. Under this system the responsibility for ensuring the line was clear passed to signalmen controlling " blocks "—sections into which a line is divided for signalling purposes—and a driver was forbidden to move until he saw a signal ordering him to do so. By 1870, too, the familiar semaphore signals were in general use. The first British application of automatic signalling —trains setting signals to danger behind them by short circuiting a current run through their rails—was made by the London & South Western Railway between Woking and Basingstoke in 1904–7, while after the 1914–18 war British railways began to adopt the colour-light signal in place of the semaphore arm.

THE STRUGGLE TO ACHIEVE A STANDARD GAUGE

Just before the turn of the century the " Battle of the Gauges " came to an end. Although 4 ft. 8½ in. had been accepted as the standard gauge by the great majority of British railways, I. K. Brunel disagreed, maintaining that a broader gauge was safer and more suitable for high speeds; as engineer of the Great Western, he had had that railway laid to a gauge of 7 ft., and companies associated with the G.W.R. had followed suit. Brunel believed that other railways would ultimately come round to his belief, but they did not. At places like Gloucester breaks of gauge greatly hindered traffic and other big companies fought to prevent G.W. acquisition of railways that would introduce the broad gauge into their territory. The G.W.R. eventually had to yield and begin a long programme of conversion; the last 7 ft. gauge track, between Exeter and Penzance, was replaced in 1892.

SPEED

The first notable example of rivalry between railways for speed occurred in 1888, when the partners of the East Coast route from London to Scotland—the Great Northern, North Eastern and North British Railways, went into fierce competition with the West Coast companies, the London & North Western and Caledonian, for London-Edinburgh passenger traffic. Within two months the schedules of the 10 a.m. trains from King's Cross and Euston were cut from 10 to 8 and 9 to 7¾ hours respectively. Peace was agreed, but the contest was resumed in the 1895 " Race to Aberdeen," whose climax came on 21st and 22nd August. On the first night G.N. 4–2–2s Nos. 668 (from King's Cross to Grantham) and 775 (from Grantham to York), and N.E. 4–4–0s Nos. 1621 (from York to Newcastle) and 1620 (from Newcastle to Edinburgh) took a 105-ton train from London to Edinburgh, 392¾ miles, in 6 hours 19 minutes, a time not beaten until 1937; Aberdeen, 523½ miles from London, was reached in 520 minutes. Next night L.N.W. 2–4–0s *Adriatic* (from Euston to Crewe) and *Hardwicke* (from Crewe) ran a 70-ton train over the 299 miles from London to Carlisle in 4 hours 33½ minutes, and this train was eventually brought

British Railways standard Class "7" 4–6–2 locomotive No. 70004 *William Shakespeare*
drawing the "Golden Arrow" express between Victoria (London) and Dover. The British
and French flags are always carried on this train.

into Aberdeen, 540 miles from London by the West Coast Route, in 512 minutes, an excellent time for the distance.

In 1904 the Great Western & London & South Western Railways were also involved in a race, this time from Plymouth to London in competition for traffic from Transatlantic liners. In this contest the highpoint was reached on 9th May, when the G.W. 4–4–0 *City of Truro* reached a speed claimed at the time to have been 102.3 m.p.h.; later research suggests the maximum may just have reached 100 m.p.h., but not more. If accurate, this was the first three-figure speed recorded on a British railway.

Up to the end of the 1914–18 war Parliament had generally resisted any attempt by the big railway companies to amalgamate for more efficient working. The advantages of co-operation were realised during the war and this attitude changed. As a result, there took place in 1923 the grouping of British railways, involving all but a handful of companies and amalgamating some 120 railways into the "Big Four"—the London Midland & Scottish, the London & North Eastern, the Great Western and the Southern Railways.

THE BETWEEN WARS PERIOD

The years between the two wars were the heyday of the British steam engine. Express passenger train weights had grown from the less-than-100 tons of the 1850s to 400 or 500 tons, and the size of engines increased to match. From the small-boilered types with a massive single driving-wheel, designers progressed from four-coupled to even bigger six-coupled classes, and in 1922 the latter-day style of heavy express passenger locomotive, weighing in the region of 100 tons, was set by Nigel Gresley's first 4–6–2, or Pacific locomotive, for the Great Northern Railway, later the L.N.E.R.

In the 1930s British steam power did its best to hold off the challenge of the diesel engine, which was beginning to take a grip of U.S. railroads and to attract Europe as the power of new German high-speed trains. At the beginning of the decade the G.W.R. accelerated its *Cheltenham Flyer* to run the 77.3 miles from Swindon to Paddington at an average of 71.4 m.p.h., then the fastest start-to-stop booking in the world, and on 6th June the engine *Tregenna Castle* covered the distance at an average of 81.7 m.p.h.—still the fastest journey ever made in Britain. Then the L.N.E.R., inspired by the German flyers, laid plans to operate high-speed stream-lined expresses—but steam-powered. After tests in which the Pacific engine *Flying Scotsman* touched 100 m.p.h., in November, 1934, and its sister *Papyrus* 108 m.p.h. in March, 1935, the fully streamlined " Silver Jubilee " express was put on a four-hour booking for the 268 miles between King's Cross and Newcastle in September, 1935, its streamlined Pacific *Silver Link* touching 112½ m.p.h. on a preliminary trial trip and running at 100 m.p.h. or more for 25 miles on end.

In 1937 both the L.M.S. and L.N.E.R. marked the Coronation of King George VI by introducing streamliners between London and Scotland. On a trial run of the L.M.S. " Coronation Scot " the engine *Coronation* raised the British speed record to 114 m.p.h.; in regular service the train linked Euston and Glasgow, 401½ miles, in 6½ hours, while the L.N.E.R. " Coronation " took 6 hours for its 393-mile King's Cross–Edinburgh run. Finally, on 3rd July, 1938, the L.N.E.R. Pacific *Mallard* raised the speed record to 126 m.p.h. on a special test run, a world record for steam that still stands. But by then scores of foreign diesel- and electric-hauled expresses were ahead of the steam-hauled British flyers, so far as *average* speeds for start-to-stop journeys were concerned.

NATIONALISATION

The 1939–45 war terminated this high-speed running and the streamliners were never re-introduced after it, for the railways were far too run-down after their great war effort to resume just where they left off in 1939. Moreover, on 1st January, 1948, they were reorganised by nationalisation, which placed them under State control, abolished the

A British Railways multiple-unit diesel train, which is used for cross-country services. This train is used on the Newcastle to Middlesborough route. Trains such as this are cleaner than steam trains and, being lighter stock, are able to give a rapid service.

An example of electrification of the overhead type in use on the Manchester–Sheffield line, with electric locomotive No. 27003 passing Penistone on an up express. Overhead electrification at the high voltage industrial frequency is to be adopted for future British electrification outside the Southern Region of British Railways.

"Big Four," and established one national system—British Railways (divided into six Regions)—as part of a British Transport Commission. One result of nationalisation was standardisation, amongst other things, of liveries, design and manufacture; twelve standard types of steam locomotives were evolved, and it was intended that these should ultimately replace the 20,000 or so locomotives of well over 200 different types inherited from the private companies.

Gradually wartime arrears of maintenance and new construction were tackled—but slowly, for successive Governments restricted British Railways' capital expenditure and use of scarce materials, like steel, so that we fell behind countries such as France, whose railways were given scope to modernise extensively. Expresses on mile-a-minute schedules returned, though not in so many numbers as before the war, like the Western Region "Bristolian," now Britain's fastest train, timed between Paddington and Bristol at an average of 67½ m.p.h.; and a pre-war world record for the longest non-stop run was taken up again by the resumption of summer running without a stop between King's Cross and Edinburgh, now made by the "Elizabethan" express in 6½ hours.

COMPREHENSIVE MODERNISATION

At length, in 1955, British Railways were given authority to spend over £1,200 millions on an overdue plan of comprehensive modernisation. A principal feature of it is the death sentence on the steam locomotive, due to the shortage of good quality coal necessary to fire it, the dirt it creates (and in consequence the difficulty of attracting men to drive and maintain it), and the greater efficiency possible with diesel and electric traction, for locomotives of the latter type do not have to be stopped between long journeys for servicing; moreover, their powers of acceleration are greater and will permit of higher average journey speeds. Steam locomotive construction for B.R. therefore terminated early in 1958.

The twin diesel-electric locomotives Nos. 10000 and 10001 hauling the " Royal Scot " through the Lune valley gorge on the long climb from near sea-level at Carnforth to Shap summit, 916 ft. above sea-level in the Westmorland fells. These locomotives were completed for the L.M.S. in 1947 by the English Electric Co., and were the first main line diesel locomotives to be introduced in Britain. Each is a 1,600 h.p. machine.

With the possibilities of atomic power stations, electrification offers the best prospects for main lines of high traffic density, but the amount of work involved in the overhead type of electrification B.R. has selected for future conversion outside the Southern Region (where the third-rail system adopted before the war is to be continued) makes it a lengthy business. Present electrification plans therefore concentrate on two trunk routes out of London —Euston to Crewe, Birmingham, Liverpool and Manchester; and King's Cross to Leeds and York—apart from some subsidiary routes and suburban schemes. Diesel traction will take over in other parts of the country, until resources are available for further electrification.

The modernisation plan aims to increase considerably the average speed of all trains. With passenger trains and their new motive power the track will be prepared to permit speeds of 100 m.p.h. in ordinary running, while goods trains will travel at a mile a minute. This last will be made possible by the fitting of all goods wagons with continuous brakes operable by the driver, whereas hitherto this has been the case with a minority only, so that the speeds of all but " fully fitted " freight trains—those in which all wagons have continuous brakes—have to be severely restricted.

Henceforward British Railways are evidently to concentrate on the job for which they are best fitted—the long-distance haulage of passengers and freight in bulk; their modernisation schemes are mainly directed at routes and installations involved in this job. Many rural services and routes, conceived in days before road motor transport, which is now able to do the job more economically, no longer pay their way and are being gradually closed down.

MEDICAL MARVELS
OF YESTERDAY AND TO-DAY

MODERN scientific medicine dates only from about 1880, when Pasteur began to show that infectious disease was due to minute living microbes which could only be seen through a microscope. Before that, the treatment of disease was a matter of guesswork and folklore. Indeed, the old belief was that disease was either a punishment for sin or a possession by devils, so that doctors starved people, purged them and bled them to get these evil spirits out of their systems and, indeed, many people were much safer without a doctor than with one.

Nevertheless, throughout the ages, there have been brilliant men who thought for themselves and refused to accept all the old beliefs and superstitions. More than 400 years before the time of Christ, there lived a Greek called Hippocrates, who is still called " The Father of Medicine." He had the original idea that diseases were things which could be studied. He made careful notes about all his patients, and was often able to tell which complaints would yield to treatment, and which would be fatal, and he studied simple remedies to see if they really did good or not.

He practised in an island called Cos, and people came from distant lands to be treated by him. He used to do his work under a large tree, and either that tree or its descendant is still pointed out to tourists.

Hippocrates made his students take an oath that they would only work for the good of their patients and never give them any treatment which might harm them, or give away their secrets, and this oath is still held binding by some doctors to-day.

Many centuries followed, of quacks and witch-doctors, while just now and then a man of genius added something to real knowledge. One of these was William Harvey, who, in the time of Charles II, showed that our blood circulates round the body, from the heart, through the arteries, and back again by the veins. Before that there was a vague idea that it just sagged about in the veins, while the arteries were actually supposed to carry air from the lungs—hence the name artery, or air tube. But it still took another three hundred years for blood transfusion to become the commonplace life-saving thing it is to-day.

THE MILKMAID WHO HELPED MEDICINE

Still nobody knew in the least what caused the plague, cholera, smallpox, leprosy and all the other horrid things people died from. But there was a man, called Jenner, long before germs were discovered, who found out how to prevent smallpox. Actually, it was an unknown milkmaid who gave him the tip. She said to him one day that she could not catch smallpox, because she had had the cowpox. This was a fairly mild disease, rather like chicken pox, which cows used to suffer from, and the milkmaids caught it in milking the cows. Jenner inquired and found it was a firm belief on the farms, that those who had had cowpox could not get smallpox. So he experimented, and inoculated some volunteers (very plucky people they must have been!) with cowpox, exposed them to smallpox, and, true enough, they didn't catch it. And that was how vaccination started, more than a hundred years ago, before it was discovered that smallpox is due to a virus.

If medical knowledge over all these centuries was in a primitive state what about surgery? The people who needed surgeons were the armies in the field, who had to have someone to care for their wounds. If you have read or seen Shakespeare's *Henry V*, you will know a lot about that monarch's campaign in France. He took 2,500 men-at-arms and 8,000 archers to France, and the medical stores for the whole lot of them were conveyed by one cart with two horses. If this seems incredible, it is still more strange that in the Peninsular War in 1808, much nearer our own time, the medical stores for Wellington's army were conveyed in two carts drawn by bullocks. More soldiers in these campaigns died of disease than of wounds, but when they

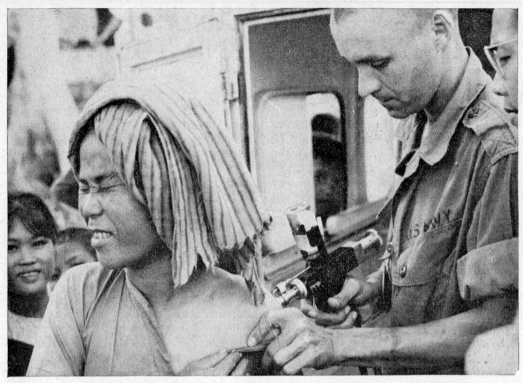

The use of inoculation has led to the prevention of many serious epidemics, particularly in the underdeveloped areas of the world. Here, using a modern injector, a U.S. doctor inoculates an apprehensive Vietnamese woman against cholera.

were wounded their prospects were grim. Amputations were done without any sort of anæsthetic, and the great majority of the patients died.

So it was a very great marvel indeed when, on the 21st December, 1846, the first operation under an anæsthetic was done in this country, and the patient declared he had felt no pain and was quite willing to have it done again. This operation was under ether. Chloroform was introduced the following year, and surgeons were now able to operate when necessary without hurting their patients.

Marvellous as this was, it came very near to becoming a great disaster. Before anæsthetics were invented, it was only possible to operate very quickly, and the best surgeon was the speediest one who didn't go on hurting for more than a few seconds. But now all this changed, and surgeons began to tackle bigger operations and take a lot longer over them. But remember they still didn't know anything about germs and infection. While the speedy operations gave little time for germs to get in, so that many people recovered, the longer ones all got infected, and the poor patients mostly got blood-poisoning.

Things got so bad that people dreaded to go into a hospital, thinking quite rightly that they were unlikely to come out alive. This state of affairs went on for forty years, through most of Queen Victoria's reign, and nearly finished surgery for ever.

Tragedy was prevented by the marvel of the introduction of antiseptics by Lord Lister. He had studied Pasteur's work on germs, and Pasteur's idea that they might be the cause of infection. He said, if all this blood-poisoning is being caused by germs getting into the operations, let's kill them before they can get in. So he introduced a pump with a carbolic spray, which was kept working all the time he operated, and must have been very unpleasant for all concerned. But his patients all healed

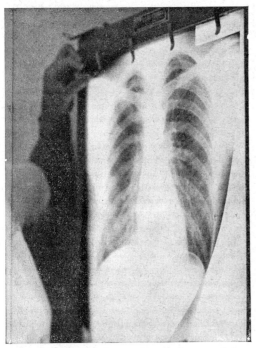

X-ray photographs provide a picture of the internal condition of patients.

first things tackled. Pure water stopped the epidemics of cholera which occurred in this country up to a hundred years ago. Apart from occasional accidents, it has stopped epidemics of typhoid fever, because the germs of cholera and typhoid are mostly carried in water. But things were different in war-time, when thirsty soldiers would drink from any old stream or puddle, and in the South African War typhoid was so bad that far more soldiers died of it than from wounds.

It was then that Sir Almroth Wright asked himself: Can't people in some way be made immune to these infectious diseases? He noticed that often if you had a disease once, you didn't get it again, and assumed that the body manufactured some antidote during the illness, which stayed there afterwards. His idea was that if you took some disease germs and killed them, they would not be able to multiply, so couldn't do much harm, but might still have the power to cause a person

up and got well, without any blood-poisoning. That was in 1887 and it really started something.

WAGING WAR ON GERMS

After some years it was discovered that there was no need to kill germs in the operating theatre unless someone took them there. By being perfectly clean, and boiling everything used, the wounds would still heal up all right without spraying the carbolic all over the place. This was called aseptic surgery (a-septic, without germs—anti-septic, against germs) and is the method still used to-day, when operations are not only painless, but free of infection too, and people are no longer frightened to go into hospitals.

But while it was perfectly possible and sensible to keep germs out of a hospital operating theatre, it just was not possible to keep them all out of ordinary rooms, and trains and cinemas, so people went on catching things. It should be possible to keep them out of our food and water, but that still isn't always done, and people did and do catch things from what they eat and drink.

Actually, germ-free water was one of the

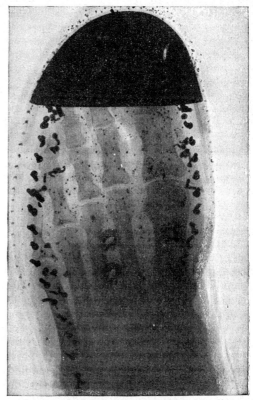

How to find where the shoe pinches. An X-Ray picture of a foot through its encasing shoe. The black dots are nails fastening the sole.

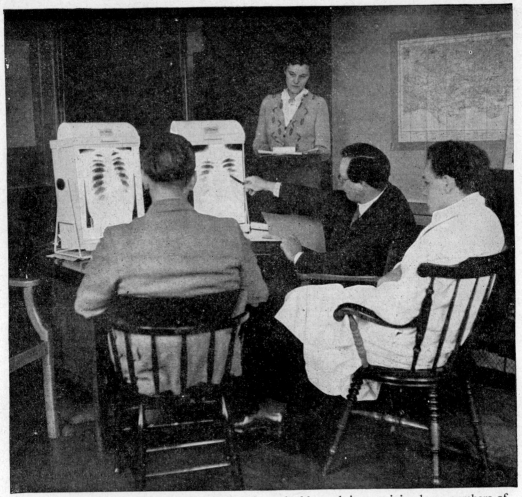

In the war against T.B., Mobile Units are doing valuable work in examining large numbers of people by Mass X-Ray. 1% of all X-Rays taken by the Mobile Units reveal chest abnormalities. These subjects are re-photographed and doctors confer over the re-takes.

to form the antidote. In this way he made anti-typhoid vaccine, and it worked so well that, although it was a bit too late for the South African War, it cut down typhoid in the First World War to a negligible amount, and typhoid vaccine has been used by the Army ever since. All soldiers, as soon as they join up, are inoculated.

It was hoped at the time that the same method could be used to protect people against all infections, but it did not work out quite as easily as that, and various modified methods had to be discovered before we had our present inoculations against diphtheria, tetanus, yellow fever, rabies, and so on. Even now we are still searching for really effective vaccines against diseases like influenza and mumps.

So the position at the outbreak of the First World War was that we could prevent infection of clean operations, kill germs in our water, disinfect things which were covered with germs, inoculate people against typhoid; but once the germs had got into people, we were still rather helpless, because the sort of antiseptics we used, like carbolic, were just as poisonous to people as they were to the germs, so it was no use giving them as medicine.

THE MIRACLE OF A CHANCE DISCOVERY

It was then that doctors began to dream of

The late Sir Alexander Fleming, discoverer of penicillin, at work in his laboratory in St. Mary's Hospital, Paddington, London. Before him are type specimens of the common mould, *penicillium notatum*, from which the wonderful drug is extracted, growing on culture plates. The discs on his right are specimens of the same mould being used in experiment with other drugs.

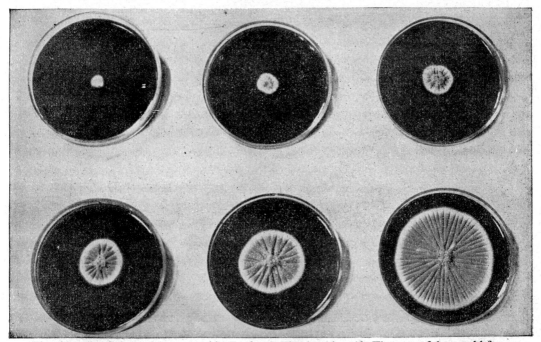

The above specimens were prepared by Professor Fleming himself. They are of the mould from which penicillin is extracted, growing in culture dishes on agar-agar jelly. From top left to bottom right the rate of growth is shown from one to ten days.

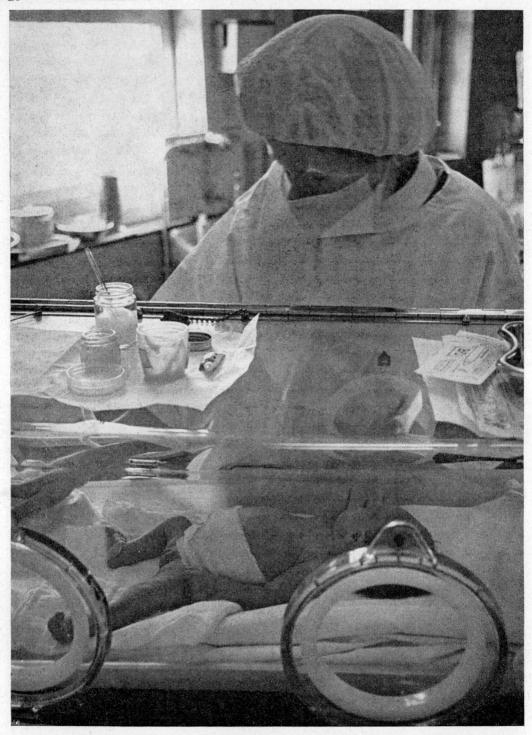

A nurse attending a baby requiring special care in an incubator. These units admit absolutely germ-free air only to the baby with, if necessary, additional oxygen. Many babies who formerly would have died are now saved by the use of incubators.

some wonderful substance which people might be able to take which would kill the germs without injuring the patients. There was an inkling that this might be possible, because, for instance, quinine would kill the malaria germs without killing the patient, but it was a long search. The marvellous thing was that it was not the men searching for drugs who found the answer, but men looking for new synthetic dyes. Many dyes are antiseptics, that is they will kill germs, but it was found that some of them would not only kill germs but were fairly harmless to us.

Trypan blue was developed in this way as a cure for African Sleeping Sickness, and later on it was found that a red dye called prontosil would kill blood-poisoning germs, and that a white powder obtained from this red stuff, which wasn't a dye at all, was even better. It was called sulphanilamide and was the first of the many " sulpha " drugs which are now used by doctors in all sorts of infections.

The discovery of penicillin was another marvel in the fight against the germ. In every bacteriological laboratory, germs are grown in test tubes or in little circular glass dishes, on some sort of jelly mixture on which they thrive. The bacteriologist wants to study one kind, and does his best to see that only one kind gets into each dish. But germs, especially moulds, float about in the air, and every time the cover is taken off a dish, there is a risk of an outsider getting in and spoiling the experiment.

This happened one day to Sir Alexander Fleming, and he was on the point of throwing the spoiled dish away, when he noticed that the mould which had got in was killing off the germs in the dish. From that one accidental speck of mould has been grown and made all the tons of penicillin since used all over the world.

But, of course, germs aren't the only troubles doctors have to cope with. A good deal of their time is taken up with accidents and injuries resulting in broken bones. When a bone is broken, the limb goes a funny shape and hurts a lot. Unless it is handled very, very gently, the broken ends will move about and grate on each other. In the old days, the doctor had to judge from the change in shape and so on, what bone was broken, how badly, and how much it needed setting into place. How

often he must have longed to be able to look inside and see just what he had to deal with. This seemed a very vain wish indeed, till that very marvel happened by the discovery of X-rays.

THE DISCOVERY OF X-RAYS

It was a German called Roentgen, who was experimenting with electric currents passed through tubes from which the air had been pumped, and found that some photographic plates on his bench got fogged. Still better, he found that if he put his hand between the tube and the plate and gave a long exposure, he got a picture of the bones inside. Incredible, but true! X-rays are of the same nature as the rays of light, heat and wireless waves, but they have a very short wavelength, and hence greater penetrating power. The modern X-ray tube is a finely finished piece of mechanism which will produce beautiful clear pictures with an exposure of a small fraction of a second, compared with about twenty minutes which Roentgen had to use. But his was the marvel of it all.

And it was around the same time, fifty years or more ago, that Madame Curie, experimenting with an ore called pitchblende, extracted tiny quantities of a material which glowed in the dark, and she called it radium. From that new marvel came not only the use of radium in medical work, but the whole of modern atomic science.

During the last thirty years, new medical marvels have come on us in increasing numbers, and this is not due to chance. It is due to the abandonment of the old guesswork and superstition, and the substitution of scientific experiment, of trying things out for oneself, as recommended by Hippocrates over two thousand years ago.

Probably the first thing that happens is that someone gets a " hunch." Lots of hunches lead to nothing. Some prove gold mines. The man who gets a hunch has to experiment to prove if there is anything in it or not, and this is often the beginning of much laborious work.

It is not, for example, good enough to have a hunch that a drug will cure measles, and then give it to fifty children with measles, watch them get better and proclaim that it works. Because the fact is that children with measles get better anyhow and the drug may have made no difference. So everything of this kind has to be the subject of what is called a controlled experiment: the people having the stuff have to be compared with an equal number of similar people who are not having it.

Even this is not as easy as one might think, because it is terribly hard to make sure they really are quite similar, and because it is terribly easy to delude ourselves into thinking what we want to think.

A HUNCH THAT CAME OFF

One hunch that did come off was the treatment of diabetes by insulin. Up till about 1923, people who had diabetes usually died of it fairly soon. It is a disease in which people cannot use in their bodies the food they eat. Some of it even turns to poison inside them. Some people had an idea that the trouble lay in an organ called the pancreas, or the sweetbread, which is just behind one's stomach. It was thought that this produced a chemical which enabled the food to be used, and that diabetics hadn't got this chemical.

All attempts to find such a chemical failed, till a man called Banting tried a new method, succeeded, called the stuff he got insulin, and now all diabetics have a daily injection of insulin and keep as well as other people. Strictly speaking, they are not cured, because they have to take it all their lives, but they no longer die of diabetes.

One last medical marvel—or rather a surgical one. It used to be said that doctors were in a much worse position than garages, because garages could fit new spare parts to cars, but doctors just had to patch up what people had got. That isn't quite true any longer. Some unlucky people get arthritis of the hip joint—a painful complaint in which the bones of the joint become misshapen and past repair. Until recently, it wasn't any use attempting to replace them with anything else, because "foreign bodies," as we call them, act as irritants and work loose.

First of all a new metal was discovered called vitellium, which did not irritate at all. It could be left inside someone indefinitely, and was still smooth and shining. Then plastics were found which also could be left inside people. Now a new joint is made out of a metal cup and a plastic " head " to go in the cup. The diseased bone is removed and a nice new spare part fitted, which really works, so that all the pain goes and the patient strides about as he hasn't been able to do for years. But the greatest medical marvel of all time, surely, is the transplanting of spare, or rather new, hearts. First achieved in South Africa, hearts are being transplanted in ever greater numbers, bringing new life and hope to people who would otherwise have died.

DO YOU KNOW?

When is the shortest day?

All days are the same length, but when we speak of the " shortest day " we mean the day when we have least daylight. This falls on 21st December. Daylight lasts for only 7 hours 45 minutes. After that we talk of the days beginning to lengthen, until at last we reach the " longest day," which falls on 21st June. On this day daylight usually lasts for over 16 hours 30 minutes.

When winter days are short in our land, the people at the other side of the earth are enjoying many bright hours of sunshine. Their winter comes when we are having the benefit of our " longest day".

How far can a kangaroo leap?

The kangaroo is the star leaper in the animal world. He can jump 30 feet without effort, and has been known to clear a 15-foot fence.

The springbok, a member of the antelope family, is another clever jumper. He will leap 12 feet into the air, with the greatest of ease.

Lions, tigers and leopards are all fine jumpers. Even the Morocco goat can clear a fence 12 feet high.

Although horses are known to be good jumpers, their record falls far behind that of the kangaroo. The longest recorded jump by a kangaroo is 42 feet.

The *Empress of Britain* steams over the measured mile during her acceptance trials.

SHIPBUILDING

A Masterpiece of Engineering

TO DESIGN and build a ship and launch her is the greatest "combined operation" in the world of engineering. A great deal happens from the time when the shipowners decide to order a new vessel, to the time when she is delivered, and a large number of specialists take part in the work.

First of all there is the shipowner who requires a new vessel; then there is the Naval Architect who designs the new ship, and the Engineer who designs the machinery, after being informed by the Naval Architect of the power required, the space available and the type of machinery preferred. The chief ship draughtsman and his assistants draw the detailed plans of every part of the ship's structure, and the engineering draughtsmen, under their chief, do similar work for the machinery.

THE NAVAL ARCHITECT'S DRAWINGS

The form of a ship must be designed in such a way that the hull shall be large enough to carry the weight of structure, cargo, passengers and stores and yet be fine enough to be easily driven through the water. The shape of the hull is indicated by a "lines" drawing or "sheer draught" plan which shows the shape fore and aft; also various vertical and longitudinal sections to give the exact height, width and depth of the ship at various points along its hull. In addition there are buttock, and sometimes diagonal, lines drawn to ensure that the sheer, water-lines and the sections agree, or are "fair."

FULL-SIZE DRAWINGS

A series of measurements called offsets are taken from these drawings and are used to

31

draw the lines again to full size on the Mould Loft floor.

The floor is of wood, blackened, and the lines are drawn with french chalk. During this process they are " faired " again, to an extent which is not possible in the small-scale drawing.

Moulds and patterns for the vessel's hull are taken from these full-size drawings on the Mould Loft floor. Such patterns include thin iron bars bent to the shape of the frames and called " sets "; these are used by the frame squad and are taken to the bending slabs. These slabs consist of a large platform of thick cast steel, pierced with a number of round or square holes rather like a "Meccano" plate. The purpose of the holes is to hold the " dogs " which are short pieces of round or square iron, bent at right angles and dropped into the holes to hold down the bar which is being made into a frame, when it arrives red-hot from the furnace.

FITTING THE STEEL PLATES

The platers, with their various helpers, are next on the scene, for it is their job to cut out and fit the steel plates which form the skin of the hull: they also drill or punch holes in the plates and in the frames and beams, so that the shipwrights' erection squad may bolt together the various parts of the ship prior to their being riveted together.

Before World War II almost all ships were riveted, but to-day many ships are welded, and large parts are built in workshops and then taken to the berth to be joined up by welding. In cases where ships are riveted, however, there are caulkers, who, by means of a special powered tool, force the edges of the over-lapping plates against the inside plates, thus making the ship water-tight.

The blacksmiths and angle-smiths, (with whom are included the frame benders) are concerned with the fitting of any special or awkwardly shaped parts of the ship, such as the oxter plates, which are those between the rudder post and the stern, and the bossing plates, which occur where the propeller shafts leave the hull. This department, however, is more concerned with the fitting-out stage, making such parts as rail stanchions, boats' davits, etc.

LAUNCHING THE SHIP

Once the hull of the ship has been built, under the supervision of the shipwrights, who

The last keel plate is about to be swung ceremonially into position.

ensure the accuracy of all parts, arrangements have to be made for the launching. The ship has been built on specially made-up sloping ground, called a slipway (or the old word " stocks "). There is nothing slippery about the slipway until the shipwrights have finished and then it is very slippery indeed. What happens is this: the ship has been built on bilge and keel blocks on the slipway. It is then necessary to get the ground-ways beneath her. These consist of large baulks of timber laid under and along the length of the vessel and resting on their own blocks, port and starboard of the middle line of the ship. A thick coat of tallow and grease is applied to the top surface of these ground-ways and then similar baulks of timber called the sliding-ways are laid on top, the whole being arranged as close as possible to the bottom of the ship, and packed up with wood chocks to the shape of the hull. The top keel blocks are then split or hammered out, so that the vessel settles on the sliding-ways. At the fine ends of the ship, large timber and steel cradles are built up from the sliding-ways, and are known as the fore and after poppets.

Amidships there is a rectangular hole in both the ground and sliding-ways. This is to accommodate a heavy wood or metal trigger pivoted in the timber of each of the ground-ways. The upper ends of these triggers are in close contact with the timber of the sliding-ways and the lower ends are held up by hydraulic rams (one or more port and starboard), thus preventing the ship from moving after the last blocks and shores have been removed.

FITTING OUT BEFORE OR AFTER LAUNCHING

Now we have the completed hull of the ship on the ways ready for launching. She will be completely plated (or planked in the case of a wooden ship) with all framing, girders, beams, decks, double bottom, engine seatings, rudder, propellers and shafting, but will usually not have her machinery or deck fittings on board. In some foreign yards vessels are sometimes launched completely fitted out and ready for sea, sometimes even with steam up. One of the reasons for this is that such yards do not have docks for fitting out and have nowhere to put the ship after launching. A great disadvantage of this practice, however, is the

length of time a slipway is occupied and the extra work entailed in bringing the heavy machinery and deck equipment to the berth. Another disadvantage is the difficulty of ensuring sufficient stability (that is the resistance a vessel has to turning over or " turning turtle "). Many vessels require ballasting in some way, and this considerable extra weight has to be allowed for in building the slipways and launching-ways.

LAUNCHING SIDEWAYS

It is also possible to launch a ship sideways, and though this method is sometimes used for quite large vessels, it is mainly used for barges, tugs and trawlers. The kind of shipyard which builds these craft is often on the side of a narrow river or a canal, where there would not be room to launch endways. The launching-ways are similar to those for a conventional launch, except that there are more of them and they are much shorter. The results are much more spectacular, the ship sliding faster than usual due to the greater slope, hitting the water with a great splash, rolling nearly to her beam ends, and causing a tremendous spray.

THE TRADITIONAL CEREMONY

Now to revert to our launch. A platform having been erected under the bows of the ship, visitors arrive for the occasion and the launching party, including the lady who is to perform the ceremony, take their places on the platform. Shipwrights knock away the last blocks and shores, whilst others are ready at the hydraulic rams to release the triggers and also to give the vessel a push if required. The only things now preventing the ship from sliding down the ways are these triggers. A bottle of champagne, decorated with coloured ribbons, has been hung over the stem of the vessel and when the right moment arrives (that is when the state of the tide gives the right depth of water over the end of the slipway) the bottle is taken in hand and thrown against the bows of the vessel. At the same moment the rams release their pressure on the triggers and, perhaps with a little push from the rams under the bows, the vessel begins to move and in a few seconds enters her native element.

It has already been mentioned that in very narrow rivers or canals side launching is used,

The hull of a passenger ship gradually takes shape in the yard. The river into which she will be launched is on the left.

may be much more. A great deal of work now takes place at the same time. The boilers, main engines and the numerous auxiliary engines, such as pumps and generators, are hoisted on board and engineers busy themselves with aligning the main engines to the propeller shafting, securing boilers and engines in place and bending and fitting the piping in connection with the machinery. The plumbers are working on the piping connected with the ship's services, such as pumping, flooding and draining, wash-basins, baths, etc.

Most of the trades who take part in the work on the slipway have little to do with the actual fitting-out, with the exception of the shipwrights, who will now be busily employed in laying wood deck planking and arranging positions for the various fittings, making spars, boat chocks, awning rafters, etc. The riggers, too, are engaged in preparing and fitting the rigging, which is considerable even in a modern ship, comprising shrouds, backstays, stays, boat falls, halyards and derrick gear.

The painters have also a great deal to do as may be imagined, for there is much of it that cannot wait until the other trades have finished

but there are many other shipyards, on rivers wide enough for end-launching, where special precautions have to be taken to prevent the vessel from hitting the other bank. These precautions consist of drag chains coiled down at intervals along the length, with their ends secured to the ship's side and so positioned that their weight and drag take effect as the ship moves down the ways and enters the water. The effect of these drags can be calculated so exactly that ships may be launched in rivers very little wider than their own length.

The vessel, now afloat, is taken in tow by tugs to the fitting-out basin.

THE WORK OF FITTING OUT

As has already been explained, most ships are launched without their machinery, though it will have been constructed at the same time as the ship was built. The seatings for the engines and boilers are already in place and very soon after the arrival of the ship in the basin, the boilers and machinery are being lifted into place by the giant cranes on the dockside. The machinery installation comprises very heavy weights totalling something like 1,000 tons in a large merchant ship and

The ship is nearly ready for launching. She will enter the water stern first.

The ship has been launched and is just entering the water. The chains which prevent the vessel from getting out of control lie on either side of the slipway in the foreground.

(as the painters would naturally prefer). Consequently the unfortunate painters are continually dodging shipwrights, welders, riggers, joiners and others as they work to complete the ship. Much of the joiners' work will have been prepared while the ship is building, and during the fitting-out period they have to install cabin bulkheads and doors, bunks, staircases, panelling and furniture of all kinds.

THE SHIP'S TRIALS

All this work culminates in the ship's trials. A trial of the main machinery takes place in the fitting-out basin before the acceptance trials and in this first trial the boilers are put under steam and the engines turned at slow speed. At this stage various minor defects are usually found, such as leaky joints, etc., and all such things are corrected before the acceptance trials.

The acceptance trials include making several runs over a measured mile to ascertain the maximum speed, turning trials to test steering gear and turning ability, and anchor trials to test the windlass. Derricks with their gear and winches would have already been tested during the fitting-out stage. The really important part of the acceptance trials, however, is to confirm that the engines deliver the power stipulated and the vessel attains the speed for which she was designed.

In the main the foregoing description applies to the building and launching of a merchant ship, there being a number of differences in warship construction. The trials of a warship, too, are different. They often take several weeks, for every piece of equipment in the ship must be thoroughly tested. Submarines, for instance, are of very complicated design, with all the problems of a normal ship as well as others peculiar to themselves. The stability of a submarine, while adequate, is comparatively small and consequently special attention must be paid to ballasting before launching. Often machinery is installed prior to launching and ballast fitted in lieu of batteries.

It has not been possible to go into detail about the work of all the various craftsmen who help to build a ship, but this short description will show you how a large complex team can work together to produce a masterpiece of engineering.

THE ROMANCE OF
THE MICROSCOPE AND TELESCOPE

TWO scientific instruments which have enabled us to probe into the mysteries of nature are the microscope and the telescope. Although these two instruments are similar, for they both contain lenses, they are concerned with very different worlds. The microscope is the instrument which enables us to look at very small things, while the telescope is mainly concerned with immensely large things, which are so far away that they appear small, as, for example, stars and planets.

These two great instruments of research had their origin many centuries ago in the magnifying glass. The Greeks knew a good deal about magnifying glasses, and the Athenian playwright, Aristophanes, mentioned one in a play. In those days people wrote on wax tablets, and Aristophanes explained how the wax could be melted with a big magnifying glass, thus erasing the writing on the wax.

Magnifying glasses can be made very easily. If a glass flask, rather like those used in chemistry laboratories, is filled with ordinary water, the flask will act just like a big magnifier. The Romans used water-filled flasks as magnifiers, and the Roman author Pliny said that this sort of magnifier, when held in the sun's rays, could sometimes create so much heat that it would set clothes on fire.

ROGER BACON

No advance was made until the middle of the thirteenth century. It was then that Roger Bacon began making experiments with magnifying glasses. He studied at Oxford University, which had recently been founded, and later spent a good deal of his life in Paris, eventually becoming a Franciscan monk. His experiments and writings on magnifying lenses and other scientific subjects were condemned as magic during his lifetime and he was imprisoned for many years. It is not known whether he knew how to make a telescope, but he did know how the magnifying glass worked, for he wrote that one could make lenses which, when placed at the correct distance from the eye, would enable one to read small letters from a long way off, and that they could make a boy as big as a

giant and a man as big as a mountain. Scientists referred to his writings for many centuries.

THE INVENTION OF SPECTACLES

Although in use in China much earlier, spectacles were invented in Europe shortly after Bacon's time, and it may well be that his work made their development possible. Most spectacle lenses are really magnifying glasses, though some of them do not magnify, but make things look smaller. The need for spectacles meant that there had to be craftsmen to make the spectacle lenses, and the business of grinding and polishing lenses began in earnest.

The spectacle-makers of the seventeenth century were largely responsible for the development of both the miscroscope and the telescope. Although there may have been one or two telescopes made late in the sixteenth century, the first one of which we have details was made in Holland in 1608 in the town of Middleburg.

HANS LIPPERSHEY'S TELESCOPE

There was a spectacle-maker at this time in Middleburg whose name was Hans Lippershey. One day he was working at his lens-grinding bench while his children were playing in his workshop. The children were looking through the lenses that their father had made, and quite accidentally they held two lenses in a line and looked through them. Their shouts of delight brought the game to their father's notice, and he too looked through the two lenses. He was amazed to find that when he looked at the weather vane on the top of a distant church steeple it looked very close and very large. In fact Hans Lippershey was using not two spectacle lenses but a real telescope.

In a few weeks Lippershey had produced two telescopes which he placed side by side so that one could use both eyes at once, and the first pair of binoculars had been made.

Hans Lippershey's telescope was a very simple instrument. The first lens was a double convex lens so called because it bulged out on both sides, and the lens near to the eye was a double concave lens. Concave means hollowed

Galileo (1564–1642) the Italian scientist who produced the first practical telescope.

out, or like a cave. These two lenses were placed at the right distance apart in a tube, and nowadays it is called the Galilean telescope, after another famous scientist, Galileo.

GALILEO

Galileo, an Italian, was born in Pisa, Northern Italy, in 1564. He produced his telescope shortly after Lippershey had produced his, but apparently independently. Galileo wrote: " Guided by the laws of optics I hit upon the idea of fixing two lenses to the ends of a tube, one lens being plano-convex and the other plano-concave. When I brought my eye near to the latter lens, objects appeared to me only about one-third their actual distance away and nine times as large. As I spared neither pairs nor expense I was so successful that I obtained an excellent instrument which enabled me to see objects almost one thousand times as large, and only one-thirtieth of the distance in comparison with their appearance to the naked eye."

Galileo made many telescopes and gradually improved their design. One day he decided he would turn his telescope towards the sky. He already knew a good deal about the moon, the stars and the planets, but his knowledge increased rapidly when he used his telescope.

On 7th January, 1610, he turned his telescope to look at one of the planets which revolve continually round the Sun in the same way as our Earth, the planet Jupiter. When he could see Jupiter clearly he was amazed to find that he could see four little planets very close to it, and what was more astonishing was that they kept on getting nearer and nearer to Jupiter, then disappearing, and then reappearing on the other side of the planet. Very quickly Galileo realised that Jupiter had moons just like the Earth, but whereas the Earth had only one Moon, Jupiter had four.

Galileo was delighted with his discovery and he began searching the night skies more and more with his telescopes (a favourite one of

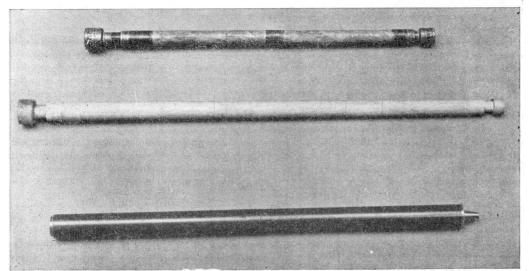

Replicas of the telescopes of Galileo and Torricelli, successive professors at Florence.

which he called " Old Discoverer "). He looked at the Moon and the Milky Way, and he wrote down the results of his observations.

TELESCOPES WITH MIRRORS

About the middle of the seventeenth century the telescope and the microscope began to part company and became very different. At this time Sir Isaac Newton discovered that ordinary sunlight was really made up of light of many colours or wavelengths, and he was able to explain why the images seen through the telescopes which had been made up to that time were rather indistinct, due to rainbow-coloured fringes round the images. Newton, therefore, developed a new kind of telescope which had no chromatic aberration, as this blurred image defect is called. To achieve this he used mirrors, and as the light was only reflected from the surface of the mirrors and did not actually pass through the glass lenses as before, there was no chromatic aberration and the image was very much clearer. His telescope had one large concave mirror at the bottom of the main tube, and a small flat mirror near the other end of the tube which reflected the light to the side. That meant when using the telescope the user had to

An ornate silver microscope made by George Adams in the 18th century.

A replica of Newton's original reflecting telescope. The eye-glass is on the side.

look into the side of the tube where there was an eye-glass.

This type of telescope is called a reflector, to distinguish it from telescopes made from a number of lenses which are called refractors. Many reflectors were made in the eighteenth and nineteenth centuries, one of the principal makers being Sir William Herschel, who discovered the planet Uranus in 1781.

To-day nearly all the big telescopes are very similar to that of Sir Isaac Newton. The concave mirrors have become larger and larger until at the present time the largest telescope in the world, at Mount Palomar in California, has a mirror nearly 7 ft. in diameter. This mirror was made from a giant piece of glass which was ground to shape very carefully and then polished and silvered, and it was so large that it took several years to make.

Many of the larger observatories have both reflectors and refractors, and these are the instruments by which we are extending our knowledge of the stars, the planets and other heavenly bodies.

THE DEVELOPMENT OF THE MICROSCOPE

The progress of the microscope since the beginning of the seventeenth century is no less interesting than that of the telescope. Another Dutchman, Antony van Leeuwenhoek, who was born in 1632, became one of the greatest users of the miscroscope who has ever lived. Leeuwenhoek made his own lenses and, strangely enough, he made only single lens microscopes, which were simply small lenses of very high magnification. He made a great number of these small microscopes and looked at all sorts of objects with them.

Leeuwenhoek was probably the first man to see bacteria, and actually watched blood circulating in arteries. He looked very closely at objects such as rabbits' ears, bats' wings and tadpoles, all the time discovering fascinating things about how animals and human beings live. About the same time as Leeuwenhoek was using his tiny microscopes, an Englishman, a friend and contemporary of Newton's, began making microscopes, which were the fore-

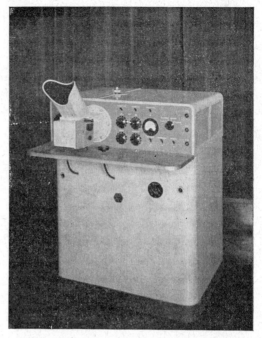

Another electron microscope showing the operating desk and power supply cubicle.

runners of the microscopes of to-day. This man, Robert Hooke, wrote a book, which was published in 1665, called *Micrographia*. In this book he tells us all about his Compound Microscope. It was called compound because it contained a number of lenses and not just one, as in a simple microscope or magnifying glass. The design was so good that nearly all the microscopes made for the next 100 years were based on it.

THE ELECTRON MICROSCOPE

Quite recently another kind of microscope has been invented. This is the electron microscope which one cannot use like an ordinary light microscope, for a beam of electrons is used instead of a light beam. Scientists have discovered that a beam of electrons is in many ways very similar to a beam of light, except that it is much more powerful in that it enables us to probe more deeply into tiny things. Objects have to be photographed with this instrument for we cannot see electrons, and we have found that we can obtain magnifications up to 100,000 times with this new microscope. This is a considerable advance since the days of Lippershey and Galileo.

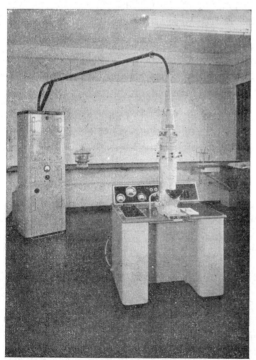

One type of electron microscope.

7th October, 1903. Langley's *Aerodrome* in position on its launching catapult.

Conquest of the Air

THE GREAT RACE

For centuries Man dreamed of flying. Then, as the twentieth century approached, the ingenuity of Man was about to make the dream reality. Our story concerns the ingenuity of three men: Samuel Pierpont Langley, a professor of Astronomy, and Wilbur and Orville Wright, bicycle makers.

IT is not known just what aroused Professor Langley's interest in aeroplanes. His main interest was astronomy and, in 1867, he had become Professor of Physics and Astronomy at what is now the University of Pittsburg. There he worked for twenty years and by 1886, at the age of fifty-two, he was well known. People respected his views and took note of the things he said.

And then, in that year, Langley became interested in aerodynamics. At first he was not so much interested in actually flying, as in testing one of Sir Isaac Newton's Laws concerning the relationship between the resistance of a flat board and its inclination in an air stream.

To help him in this work Langley designed a special whirling machine. This had arms 30 feet long and in Langley's own words: " was of unprecedented size, mounted in the open air and driven round by a steam engine, so that the end of its revolving arm swept through a circumference of 200 feet at all speeds up to 70 miles an hour."

The machine started whirling in 1887. Plates, attached to the ends of the arms, were swung around at various speeds and varying angles of inclination, and measurements taken.

The experiments showed that the air resistance was only $\frac{1}{20}$ of that indicated by Newton's Law. From the results, Langley deduced that less power would be required to support a thin surface in the air at high speeds than at low speed. Langley also calculated that one horsepower could support more than 200 lb. in the air at the speed of an express train.

The cable was cut and with a roaring, grinding noise Langley's aircraft fell.

Based upon this Langley came to the following conclusions: " So far as the mere power to sustain heavier-than-air bodies in the air by mechanical flight goes, such mechanical flight is possible with engines we now possess, since effective steam engines have lately been built weighing less than 10 lb. to 1 horse-power."

Although this was not strictly true, this statement had far-reaching effects. Here was a learned man, who obviously knew what he was talking about, saying, in effect, " powered flight is possible."

Coming when it did, at a time when there were some people only too ready to ridicule attempts to fly, it gave encouragement to many, including the very men who later were to succeed so soon after Langley himself failed —two bicycle makers known as the Wright brothers.

In 1889 Langley went to the Smithsonian Institution, the famous American Museum which had started collecting aeronautical exhibits as long ago as 1876. There he continued to study and experiment both in aeronautics and his old love astronomy.

FLYING MODEL AEROPLANES

He built a small model aeroplane, powered by a rubber band. It flew for about 6 seconds —half as long as the French model on which it was based! Undaunted Langley went on to build some 40 rubber-driven models and from these there developed a long line of models powered by all kinds of tiny power plants, running on steam, compressed air, carbonic acid—even gunpowder! The models grew

After the crash rowing-boats go to pick up the pilot and salvage the wreckage.

bigger and bigger as the years passed but none was really successful until, in 1895, it was decided to use two pairs of wings, one behind the other. By 6th May, 1896, two models had been completed to this form, Nos. 5 and 6, each weighing about 26 lb.

First off was Model No. 6, but a wire got caught somewhere and broke the left wing. Next came the launching of No. 5. Off it went and, much to everybody's delight, it stayed up. 1,000 feet, 2,000 feet it flew, up to a height of about 100 feet, on it chugged for 1 minute and 20 seconds, to land nearly 3,000 feet from the take-off point. A second flight of 2,300 feet was made the same day and, in November, 1896, No. 6 flew a distance of 4,200 feet at about 30 m.p.h.

For Langley, these flights meant success. His main interest was in demonstrating the practicability of powered flight, not in actually flying, and this he had done. Had it not been for the Spanish-American war, it is probable that he might well have withstood the longing to take the final step of making a man-carrying machine.

However, the war came and with it an invitation from President McKinley " to construct a flying machine with possibilities as a weapon of war. . . ." And so Langley set about scaling up his most successful model and making it big and strong enough to carry a man.

LAUNCHING A FULL-SIZE AIRCRAFT

Work started in 1899 and a large house-boat was made ready for the day when the aircraft would be completed. On top of this was an impressive turn-table weighing some 16 tons. It incorporated a spring-operated catapult and permitted heading the 80-ft. long rails into the wind, whatever the direction from which it might be blowing.

By the summer of 1903, the full-size machine, measuring 48 ft. in span and 52 ft. long was ready. On 14th July, the final balancing tests were completed and the house-boat was towed down the Potomac River, to a point opposite a place called Widewater. As can be imagined, the river was packed with small boats of every description, containing sight-seers and newspaper reporters. What Langley was about to do, of course, was big news.

But as happens with even the best of aircraft, last-minute snags cropped up. A wire needed tightening here, a piece of canvas repaired there, an oil leak mended here and so on. The days lengthened into weeks, and the weeks into months. The sight-seers departed, leaving only the now impatient reporters bobbing up and down near the house-boat.

To make things worse the weather turned bad, but finally, on 7th October, all was ready. The *Aerodrome*, as it was called, was hoisted on to the catapult, the pilot climbed aboard, the engine was started. A mechanic cut the cable releasing the catapult, there was a roaring, grinding noise—and the aircraft tumbled off the end of the launching rails into the river some 16 ft. below. By sheer bad luck a piece of the launching gear had failed to fall clear as it should have done and its extra weight had pulled the machine to disaster. However, the engine proved to be quite undamaged and the airframe easily repairable and by the middle of November the machine was again ready. The weather, however, was not—and got worse day by day.

The weeks dragged by until, on 8th December, it was decided to make a " do or die " attempt, although the river contained large blocks of floating ice several inches thick.

Take note of the date—8th December, 1903. The official report of the launch records: " The car was set in motion and the propellers revolved rapidly, the engine working perfectly . . ."

THE WRIGHT BROTHERS

But let us now leave Langley for a while and see how the other contestant in this great " race " was faring. Unlike the case for Langley, we know what aroused the interest of the Wright brothers in flying. First it was the report of the death of the great gliding pioneer Otto Lilienthal in 1896, followed about 3 years later by—a flight of buzzards! Watching a number of these birds closely, Wilbur noted " that they regained their lateral (sideways) balance when partly overturned by a gust of wind by a torsion (twisting) of the tips of the wings." This simple observation led Wilbur to his vital idea of wing twisting to give lateral control to aircraft. This idea, perhaps more than any other, led the Wright brothers to ultimate success and it is not often that the birth of so great an invention is so clearly recorded.

This brilliant inspiration led the brothers to read every book on flying that they could lay their hands on. They studied these carefully, noting the reasons why previous attempts to fly had failed. They paid particular attention to the numerous flights made by Lilienthal—and noticed something that less observant men would have missed! In a period of 5 years Lilienthal had made about 2,000 flights some covering distances up to 1,200 ft. Two thousand flights seems quite a lot, but what struck the Wright brothers was the shortness of the glides. They estimated that his total flying time was only about *five* hours. Coupling this with other reports the brothers concluded: " the main reason why the problem (of flying) had remained so long unsolved was that no one had been able to gain any adequate practice."

Wilbur Wright then went on to explain: " We thought that if some method could be found by which it would be possible to practise by the hour instead of the second, there would be a hope of advancing the solution of a very difficult problem."

They proposed to do this by building a machine that would fly at about 18 m.p.h. and then finding a place where winds of this speed were common. Then the brothers intended to do something clever, they planned to attach a rope to the machine and fly in it as a kite so that : " it would be possible to practise by the hour and without any serious danger, as it would not be necessary to rise far from the ground, and the machine would not have any forward motion at all."

EXPERIMENTS WITH THE TRAINER GLIDER

So the brothers set to work building their trainer glider. The result was a biplane, with a controllable elevator carried forward on outriggers. There was no tail unit and the pilot lay flat on the lower wing in order to reduce wind resistance. Perhaps the most important feature was the fact that lateral control was provided by twisting the ends of the wings. The brothers hoped that this would prove better than Lilienthal's method of shifting one's body, which " did not seem quite as quick or effective as the case required."

The glider was ready by the summer of 1900.

Wright glider No. 1 being flown as a kite at Kitty Hawk in 1900. The Wright brothers used it to measure the lift and drag at various wind speeds.

The 1901 glider had an improved elevator and almost twice the wing area of the previous glider so that it could support a pilot when flown as a kite.

The windy site for the flights had already been chosen—a place called Kitty Hawk, in North Carolina, a little settlement located on a strip of land that separates Albemarle Sound from the Atlantic Ocean.

The first " flight " was made as a kite with cords reaching to the ground and the brothers suffered their first disappointment. Instead of the estimated 21 m.p.h., to sustain it, a wind speed of about 30 m.p.h. was required!

Undaunted the brothers continued to fly their machine as a kite, as shown in the historic photograph appearing on the previous page making a series of measurements of the lift and drag at various wind speeds. This was apparently the first time this had been done with a full-sized machine and gave quick and accurate results.

In addition, about a dozen successful glides were made from the nearby Kill Devil sand-hills and the brothers returned to their home in Dayton, Ohio, well satisfied.

Commenting on the results of the first year's gliding, Wilbur concluded: " Although the hours of practice we had hoped to obtain finally dwindled down to about two minutes,

we were very pleased with the general results of the trip, for, setting out as we did, with almost revolutionary theories on many points and an entirely untried form of machine, we considered it quite a point to be able to return without having our pet theories completely knocked on the head by the hard logic of experience, and our own brains dashed out into the bargain."

A NEW GLIDER CONSTRUCTED

A new glider was constructed for the following year. The main difference was an increase in wing area from 165 sq. ft. to over 300 sq. ft., so that it could support a pilot when flown as a kite.

After several preliminary hops to get the centre of gravity in the correct position relative to the centre of pressure—achieved by the pilot sliding himself backwards and forwards on the wing, a flight of 300 ft. was made. But it was clear that something was wrong.

The wing curvature was reduced and a number of successful glides made, but still the glider was not behaving as it was expected to. For one thing, the lift was only a third of what

Lilienthal estimated. So the brothers returned home once more, convinced that the figures laid down by Lilienthal and others were dangerously wrong.

They set about finding the correct ones. To help them they knocked the ends out of a starch box and placed a fan at one end to make a simple wind tunnel—one of the world's first! In this they tested over 200 model wing sections, and so laid the basis for their third—and most successful glider.

This was made in the summer of 1902, and incorporated all they had learned about wing sections and pressures. It had one new feature—a tail—consisting of two vertical fins, and is shown in the second photograph on this page.

The fins were sometimes found to be " seriously in the way " and so they were changed for a single surface, made movable like a rudder. At the same time the control wires for warping the wings were linked with the rudder control. This had the effect of permitting smoothly banked turns.

With this change came success. Wilbur

Nearly there! The Wright brother's glider of 1902. This shows the machine with the original twin fixed rudders.

reported: " With this improvement our serious troubles ended."

They went on to make nearly a thousand glides, nearly 375 being made in the last six days, the longest covering 622 ft. and lasting 26 seconds. Highly elated the brothers returned home, now ready to start on a powered aircraft!

THE BUILDING OF A POWERED AIRCRAFT

Two major problems faced them, the engine itself and the all-important propellers. Work on both had begun at the end of 1902 and the Wrights' work on propellers is another story of brilliant achievement paralleling that of the aircraft itself, and also that of the engine.

The propellers they built, designed entirely from their own calculations, turned 66 per cent of the power of the engine into useful work— a good third better than those of Professor Langley.

The brothers would have been only too pleased to buy the engine they required, but

To compare wing shapes, a test wing (right) was mounted on the rim of the freely-mounted bicycle wheel, then adjusted until its lift balanced the resistance of the flat plate on the other side when the bicycle was pedalled.

nobody could give them one with the desired power-weight ratio. After writing to various firms they gave up the search and laboriously built their own! This they did in *six weeks*, at a time when other people had spent years in trying to design a suitable engine for aeroplanes. For comparison, the engine used by Langley had taken *seven years* to develop.

Construction of the powered machine started in June and by mid-September all was completed.

Notice the month—September 1903. At this time, remember, less than 400 miles away the finishing touches were being put to Langley's *Aerodrome*, as it bobbed up and down on the house-boat in the Potomac River.

The brothers set off for Kitty Hawk on 23rd September, 1903, taking with them their *Flyer* as they called it, and the 1902 glider to practise on.

Confidently they assembled their precious craft. In appearance it looked very similar to the 1902 glider. It was slightly bigger, with a wing span of 40 ft. instead of 32 ft., and it had twin rudders. The engine was mounted on the bottom wing and turned, by chains, two pusher propellers, mounted on the wing

8th December, 1903. Final Catastrophe—the Langley *Aerodrome* plunging into the Potomac river for the second time.

struts. The weight of the engine was counterbalanced by the pilot who lay on the wing on

17th December, 1903. Final Success. The *Flyer* made a perfect take-off. Orville Wright, with admirable forethought, arranged that this photograph would be taken of the first controlled, sustained and powered heavier-than-air flight.

his stomach to the other side. The all important wing warping device was worked by wires attached to a movable cradle which the pilot wore round his body.

The *Flyer* was nearly ready when they heard of Langley's unsuccessful attempt on 7th October. Spurred on by this news, work progressed apace on the *Flyer* but, on 8th December it was still not quite ready, when Langley made his " do or die " attempt. Recall the opening words of the official report: " The car was set in motion and the propellers revolved rapidly, the engine working perfectly . . ." Unfortunately the report continued: " but there was something wrong with the launching, and a crashing, rending sound, followed by the collapse of the rear wings, showed that the machine had been wrecked in the launching." Once again part of the launching gear had fouled the aircraft, as can be seen on the previous page.

THE FIRST FLIGHT OF THE "FLYER"

The news of Langley's final disaster reached the Wright brothers a few days before the *Flyer* itself was ready for flight. The date was 14th December, 1903. The *Flyer* did not have a wheeled undercarriage, but rested on skids and for take-off was placed upon a little trolley which ran along a rail.

A coin was tossed to see who was to make the first flight and Wilbur won. Witnesses in the form of friendly coastguards were called. The engine was started and set the whole aircraft shuddering. Suddenly, it went gliding down the rail, took off, climbed too steeply, stalled, and crashed into the sand. The witnesses disappeared, while the brothers began the repairs.

By 17th December the repairs had been completed and once again the witnesses were obtained. The engine warmed up, as Orville, whose turn it now was, lay in position on the wing. At 10.35 a.m. he released the slip wire and down the rail he sped. The machine quivered, rose into the air, and then flew at 30 m.p.h. for 120 ft. before coming down in the soft sand.

" This flight lasted only twelve seconds," wrote Orville later, " but it was, nevertheless, the first in the history of the world in which a machine carrying a man had raised itself by its own power into the air in full flight, had sailed forward without reduction of speed, and had finally landed at a point as high as that from which it started."

THE FOUNTAIN

Into the sunshine, full of the light,
Leaping and flashing from morn till night!
Into the moonlight, whiter than snow,
Waving so flower-like when the winds blow!
Into the starlight, rushing in spray,
Happy at midnight, happy by day!
Ever in motion, blithesome and cheery,
Still climbing heavenward, never aweary;
Glad of all weathers, still seeming best,
Upward or downward motion thy rest.
Full of a nature nothing can tame,
Changed every moment, ever the same.
Ceaseless aspiring, ceaseless content,
Darkness or sunshine thy element.
Glorious fountain! Let my heart be
Fresh, changeful, constant, upward like thee!

J. R. Lowell

HOW YOUR DAILY NEWSPAPER IS PRODUCED

The Miracle of the Daily Press

PROBABLY you've noticed that the word "news" is composed of the cardinal points of the compass, and that's exactly where news comes from; every direction, every corner of the globe, at every moment of the day and night.

That is why when you open your newspaper each morning, you see stories and pictures of a score of countries. An earthquake happens on the other side of the globe, even while you sleep, but you expect, and you find, a report and a picture in your paper next morning.

It is a miracle; a miracle of science, engineering, organisation and distribution, but you take it for granted, just as you take the miracle of your body for granted, because it is always there.

Probably the only time you really appreciate the newspaper is when it fails to arrive, and that perhaps has never happened to you; for even during the heaviest days of the blitz, the presses never failed to turn, and aeroplanes, trains and swift cars brought the daily newspapers to their customers.

How is it done? The gatherers of news span the globe, penetrate the sound barrier, descend to the depths of the ocean.

In the wind-swept, lonely isle, in the seething city, men and women wait and watch and listen for news. To serve its readers a newspaper's staff face death daily; the terrors of forbidden territory, the privations of uncharted regions, the murderous menace of rioting hordes, the indescribable dangers of fevered fanatics, the perils of earthquakes, plagues

The newsboy, last link in the chain.

Messages from all over the world coming in to the newspaper Tape Room where they are automatically tapped out on recording machines and sent to the editorial offices.

and pestilence. The mightiest cables are commanded, the latest aircraft are held in readiness, communications satellites are utilised that news may come with lightning swiftness and its urgent message be imprisoned in the fastest presses.

The finest writers and photographers reveal the news and through them that epic story lives again in pulsing print and vivid picture; that great sporting contest holds you tense, that pastoral scene unfolds with gentle beauty.

THE PULSE OF THE PEOPLE

You see, a national newspaper is like the great heart of a nation; its pages reflect the pulse of the people. It has its main arteries extending to the capitals of the world, its veins reaching even to the smallest village.

Look in your newspaper to-day and you will find not only world events but records of human endeavour in isolated hamlet or lonely village.

A daily newspaper office never closes, day or night; every telephone call, every letter is investigated, each caller interviewed. Sometimes the most remarkable news has been uncovered by a hint from an unknown person, and occasionally news is so important that a newspaper's doors are locked until the presses have started running, lest any chance word should give away the secret to a rival. There is fierce rivalry for news, but the friendliest of rivalry, and if one newspaper meets disaster —as several did by bombing during the war— its rival will be the first to offer the victim every facility and help.

It's a strenuous life, and unless you are very fit and adaptable, you won't survive it for long. There's no nine-to-five business, no guarantee that you will get your lunch-time, no certainty that even your summer holidays will be undisturbed.

INK IN THEIR VEINS

Your paper has the first claim on you, and no one can predict what news will " break," or when; or who will be involved. But I've never heard good newspapermen complain. It is said they have ink in their veins, and maybe it's true, but they certainly live very exciting lives.

You can observe from the chart on page 55 just how news comes into a newspaper office; now let's see how it is dealt with. Generally when a person is asked what he thinks is the size of a national daily newspaper staff, he says: " Two or three hundred? " You can multiply that by ten. The garage staff alone is large enough to run a substantial business, for it is no good getting hot news unless the papers are swiftly distributed. You know yourself how quickly news goes " cold." You are not interested in the morning's paper when the evening paper has come out, and yesterday's paper seems as stale as an old sandwich, and about as appetising.

First, then, there is all the administrative side which is common to any big organisation: the directors, managers, accounts department, electricians, firemen, cleaners, canteen staff and a host of others.

Then there is every type of news-gatherer, from the distinguished war correspondent to the ordinary reporter in the remote village. The News Agencies have representatives all over the world, and their stories come tapping out of the machines in the Tape Room; the ticker tape, as it is called. There are the specialists in City and finance, the literary

The metal blocks of the photographs have been made and here is an engraver working on a block to bring out the picture to the best advantage.

Now the reading matter (made up of Linotype slugs) is being made up into columns and pages, and the blocks of the illustrations are put into place in each page.

experts, book reviewers, theatre, film, radio and television critics, the cartoonist, the gossip writer, the experts on gardening, law, medicine, art, music; anything about which there may be a story of interest to readers.

There are men and women in the House of Lords and the Commons, visiting the Law Courts; the News Editor watching the whole of the British Isles, the Foreign Editor responsible for the rest of the world, and probably talking by telephone each day to half a dozen of the capitals of Europe. There are special correspondents at all the key points of the globe and hosts of expert cameramen, ready to give you the news in pictures; and often a brilliant photograph can tell you more than any writer could in the equivalent space.

Never imagine that a newspaper doesn't have sufficient news; it can never have enough important news, and sometimes the trouble is to accommodate it all, but every night the editorial staff is faced with enough material to fill five or ten times the space of to-morrow's paper.

DIGESTING THE NEWS

That is why the vast mass of news has to be co-ordinated and " digested " by the various departments which select, edit and arrange it before it gets to the printers.

The reporters and the sub-editors and the pictorial side have two remarkable libraries to help them. A newspaper library has a wonderful reference section; far better and more extensive than that which you can visit unless you live in one of the great cities. It also has millions of newspaper cuttings, from the world's press, all indexed and cross-referenced. Every subject has its envelope; every facet of every subject, and each person of fame or notoriety has his or her envelope of cuttings.

Ask a newspaper librarian what plays were produced in 1890, the name of a famous man's

A battery of Linotype machines in a big London newspaper office. On these machines the news is set in lines of type called slugs. Proofs are then pulled, to be read by sub-editors.

This is the camera room where huge process cameras photograph the pictures needed for the paper. From the negatives so produced, metal blocks of these pictures are made, and these are printed, with the text, in the paper.

dog, the import of matches last year, the last man to score six goals in a professional Soccer game, the rainfall in Guatemala, or how to make chop suey—and the information will be in front of you in a minute. And minutes, even seconds, are vital in journalism; the speed is terrific and everything goes to a split-second schedule.

A national newspaper picture library has millions, yes millions, of photographs of every subject and person under the sun; all indexed and cross-referenced so that any print required can be produced on demand.

Now what happens when the " copy," as we call it, gets to the printers?

The bulk of the reading matter is set by Linotype machines, though there may still be some hand-setting on complicated advertisements. Some of the lettering in displayed advertisements may be incorporated in the blocks and all the headings of the news items, which you will see are in different, larger types, will be set on separate Ludlow machines. But let's look at the Linotypes, which eat most of the " copy."

The machine has a keyboard rather like an enlarged typewriter. As each key is pressed it releases a brass die, or mould, of the letter concerned. The operator sets almost as quickly as a competent typist strikes out the letters, but in this case the dies of the letters fall from the magazine above and assemble in a line, making the line you will eventually read in the newspaper.

When the line of dies is complete it is moved over, mechanically, to the casting portion of the machine. Each has its own electrically heated furnace holding over 30 lb. of molten metal, and if you look at the picture on the previous page you will see the refills that keep the furnace fed. They are ingots weighing 25 lb. each, and one " stick," you will notice, is already half-way into its furnace.

HOW MOLTEN METAL MAKES NEWS

Automatically the molten metal is pumped into contact with the line of brass moulds and a line of type is cast, cooled and ejected in as short a time as it takes for you to read these words. The line toddles along into its place behind the previous line and an arm descends and picks up the dies which have just finished their work—for the moment. They are distributed automatically, each into its own particular magazine, ready for re-use when the operator presses the key.

This vast mass of type, pouring from many machines, goes to the makers-up on the " stone," or flat steel tables. The right headings have to be brought from other machines, some of the lines may have to be re-set to go round pictures, proofs go for reading, and the arrival of fresh news may not only alter the page planned for an item, but completely alter its length. What started early in the evening as a full-column story with a picture, may, by the time the newspaper goes to press, be reduced to a few lines.

Now swift though modern printing is, it is impossible to distribute everything in time from London, so the national dailies have offices in Manchester and Scotland, where printing is simultaneous.

When proofs come from the first setting they go to the Wire Rooms, where operators work at standard typewriter keyboards, but their tapping produces not a sheet of typing but an endless perforated tape. This is passed through transmitters which telegraph the news at 200 words a minute. The office, in Manchester or Edinburgh, receives the messages in the form of perforated tape, which is swiftly transformed into normal letters.

HOW PICTURES ARE MADE

But in following the news we have forgotten the pictures, and they are most fascinating. It is impossible here to describe all the processes, but briefly the operation consists in transferring the picture to metal which will " print." The simplest form is the black and white, or " line," block; a bold, " unshaded " cartoon, for instance. The picture is photographed on to metal, the white parts are etched away with acid, leaving the lines of the picture. These are now raised in relation to the rest of the surface, and will take the ink and can be printed from, much in the same way as if you made a lino-cut and smeared it with ink.

The half-tones, those that look like normal photographs, are copied through a screen, and if you examine any newspaper picture with a magnifying-glass you will see it is composed of thousands of tiny dots, which are really the mesh of the screen.

WHEN PIGEONS BROUGHT NEWS

But how, you will ask, can you radio or telegraph a picture? Such are the miracles of modern science and engineering that whereas not so long ago newspapers used to employ homing pigeons to bring news swiftly to the office, now an event that happened in Australia can be photographed and appear in London in a few hours.

You know how a gramophone needle travels over a record with microscopic undulations in the track which have been made by sounds. The needle and the diaphragm translate those markings back into sounds. Well, it's something like that with light, which can be transformed into pulses or waves. These are transmitted by radio or cable and then transformed at the other end into light or dark.

Imagine a cylinder (which was the first shape of gramophone records), and instead of a needle a pin-point of light playing on it as it revolves, following the " grooves " just in the same way as a needle does in the musical instrument.

Now put on that revolving cylinder the simplest picture in terms of black and white—the check pattern of a draughts board. Right, the cylinder revolves and the pin-point of light starts to take its impressions, a hair line at a time, just as the gramophone needle takes each minute groove in its progress, creeping across the face of the disc.

What does it pick up? Two inches of black, two inches of white, two inches of black; going on and on until it has moved along the cylinder and covered the whole of the first line of squares. The pulses are transmitted across the world and the receiver begins to translate them into light and dark—two inches of black, two inches of white, two inches of black, the cylinder spinning round and round until gradually the first line of the squares and then the whole draughts board design is built up.

That's the principle, and you can see that the most delicate machines can go further and register, transmit and re-register the black, white, grey, white, black, grey which—when you come to look at it—you will see are the ingredients of every photograph.

You may not understand it completely from this brief description, but if you have a chance see one of these miracle machines at work.

THE WONDERFUL "MANGLE"

Then, of course, the transmitted photograph has to be made into a block. The block is fitted into the page, the page is locked up and ready for printing. Of course, it's far, far too heavy for any man to lift and it has another great disadvantage; it is flat. You can run an ink roller over it, place a sheet of paper on it and get a rough proof. A machine would get a better and a quicker proof, but the best machine in the world would not be able to produce proofs or prints at a thousandth of the speed that is essential for newspapers. If they were printed flat, they would have to start printing the week before. So then comes the vital stage, from flat to circular, or rotary. So the page of type and pictures, locked up and perfectly tight and every inch of the surface level, is slid from the "stone" to a trolley and transferred to what we call a "mangle." It is one of the matrix presses; very wonderful machines.

Over the prepared page is placed a "flong" of papier mâché and other ingredients. It looks rather like a large sheet of boracic lint that has been ironed out and polished. This is placed on the surface of the page and over it are placed blankets of wool and rubber. Thus prepared for the big squeeze, the page passes into the machine, where it is subject to a pressure of 500 tons. In seconds the page emerges on the other side, and when it is undressed the result of the intense pressure is seen to be that the papier mâché has been forced into every crack and crevice of type, into every line and letter. It is an exact replica of the page, except, of course, that it is now a positive and not a negative. The letters are readable in the normal way and the pictures the right way round, instead of "back to front."

GOING DOWN THE CHUTE

These moulds go down a chute to the Stereotypers' Department, generally well below ground, on a level with the giant presses, which are far too heavy to be placed on raised floors.

In the foundry are many tons of metal at a

The flongs of the pages are placed in this Auto-plate machine, bent round, and then molten metal rushes in, making a plate.

temperature of over 550° F., so it's not exactly refreshing. Each Autoplate machine has its own furnace containing 7½ tons of molten metal. The papier mâché moulds are bent to semi-circular shape and are fitted round the casting cylinder. The machine is closed, molten metal is pumped between the flong and the central cylinder and floods every crevice of the page. The metal sets swiftly, though it is too hot to handle without protection, and is placed on an automatic runway, where it passes through water sprays so that it is cool enough to touch by the time it reaches the presses.

These machines each cast four plates a minute. Think of it! The "boracic lint" impression of the type and pictures is placed in the Autotype, it is closed, the molten metal floods up, and in half a minute a plate has been made and set and can be removed—and that plate bears every letter in the page, every dot in the photograph.

These semi-circular plates of bright, aluminium colour are assembled on the presses in the right position for printing.

At one end of the presses stand the paper feeds. You have probably seen the great reels of paper being delivered. They weigh three-quarters of a ton each and contain five miles of paper. So marvellous is the machinery that when one reel runs out, like an emptying cotton reel on a sewing machine, the next is joined on so that the presses never stop.

WATCHING A MIRACLE WORKING

You can stand in the gallery of a daily newspaper and watch the whole process, and incredible it is. Not a hand touches it, but at one end of the great room the white paper scurries off the whizzing reels, leaps through the presses at a rate which makes it impossible even to grasp the general impression of the pages which that battery is printing. Not only printing, but drying instantly, so that there shall be no blur, bringing the pages together, folding, cutting, and delivering the finished paper as you know it in a dazzling stream at the other end.

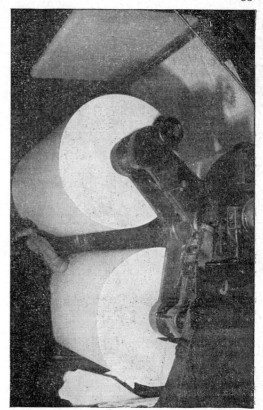

Each reel of over 5 miles of paper will soon be swallowed up in the machine, to become printed newspapers.

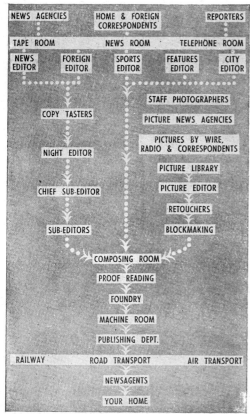

This chart shows the processes through which the news passes in the making and delivering at your home of your daily newspaper.

As the papers emerge in an endless band they pass the eye so quickly that it is difficult to grasp the detail even on the continually recurring front page. Over 30,000 an hour from each battery; work it out for yourself; printed, dried, assembled, folded, cut, even counted automatically.

The streams of copies wind like snakes along conveyors to the various publishing departments, where swift vans dash to get them to airports and railway stations for delivery to wholesalers, retailers, and then to your letter-box.

Every morning, without fail, you can open your newspaper and find it a mirror to the world. To-morrow morning, when you pick it up, you will not take it for granted; you will understand a little of what goes on in its production and take your daily newspaper for what it is, a miracle of science, engineering, organisation and distribution. Then you'll enjoy reading it all the more.

WINGS ACROSS THE WORLD (I)

After the Wright Brothers at Kitty Hawk came the pioneers of Britain, France and other European countries. Within a few years men were hopping into the air all over the world. But the world had to wait four years for news of the Wright Brothers' exploits.

ON THE day, 17th December, 1903, they made the first flight in the history of the world, the Wright brothers also made three more flights. Then a gust of wind overturned their precious *Flyer* and the resulting damage was too serious for it to be repaired.

One would think that news of this historic event would soon have flashed round the world. But, in fact, this was not so. Little news of the first flights got through and what did was disbelieved. The Wrights built a second aircraft in 1904, and another further improved machine in 1905. Flying from a small field near Dayton, Ohio, they made many successful flights, including one of 38 minutes during which they covered 24 miles. But still the world refused to believe the reports—at a time when anyone interested in the rumours could have seen what the Wright brothers were up to from the roads bordering their " airfield." In fact the sight of the *Flyer* buzzing round the

This Parachute Aeroplane was built by optimists early this century, but needless to say it never flew.

field became so familiar to local farmers that they soon stopped looking up when it passed overhead.

So the story continued through 1906 and 1907. Then, in 1908, the world at large learned of their stupendous achievement. In that year Orville astonished his countrymen at home with a public demonstration, whilst Wilbur caused a sensation in Europe—four and a half years after the first flights at Kitty Hawk.

EARLY EUROPEAN MACHINES

One result of the delay of proper news of the Wright machines was that European designers continued to work on original lines. About this time, all sorts of odd " flying machines," typified by the " Parachute Aeroplane " illustrated on this page, began to appear, most of which failed even to hop.

A novel machine deserving special mention was the glider, pictured opposite, developed by a young Scotsman named Preston Watson in 1903. As can be seen from the illustration, the aircraft had a low wing, on which the pilot sat, a box-kite type tail and a smaller top wing. This small wing could be tilted to bank the machine and was an ingenious solution to one of the most difficult problems confronting the early pioneers—the provision of suitable lateral control. Preston Watson's solution was entirely different from the wing warping developed by the Wright brothers.

Watson produced a succession of powered aircraft based on this glider, one of which is thought to have made short hops in 1908-1909. His 1910 aircraft, fitted with a 30 h.p. Humber engine was flown many times at Errol by Watson, his brother James and Archie Dickie. In 1914 a Preston Watson biplane powered by a 60 h.p. Anzani took part in a safety competition near Paris. Soon after this Watson was killed while serving with the Royal Naval Air Service.

As it is, the first proper aeroplane flight on this side of the Atlantic is officially credited to Santos-Dumont, who was also connected with

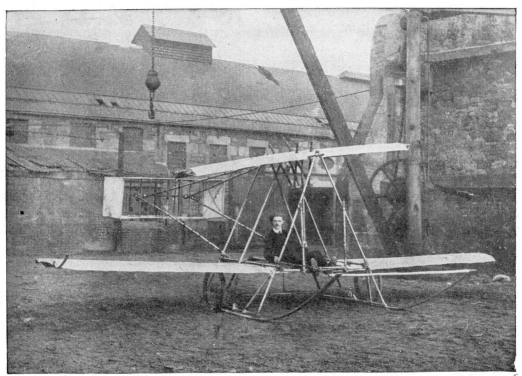

The Preston Watson glider of 1903. This early British aircraft was a praiseworthy effort, and differed radically from the Wright *Flyer*.

This powered Preston Watson aircraft may have made short hops in 1908-9. Later machines flew well.

the development of airships. This was made on 23rd October, 1906, in a 14 bis, an ungainly, tail-first biplane.

At the forefront of the European experimenters were the Voisin brothers, Louis Blériot and Robert Esnault-Pelterie. The Voisin brothers were developing a biplane based largely on the huge man-lifting box-kites which had been perfected by the Australian pioneer Lawrence Hargrave, whilst Blériot and Pelterie were in favour of " engine first " monoplanes.

These men were all Frenchmen; but the first really practical flight in Europe was made by English-born Henry Farman who, in a Voisin biplane on 13th January, 1908, made the first European circular flight of more than a kilometre. For this he won the Deutsch-Archdeacon prize of £2,000.

THE FIRST FLIGHT IN GREAT BRITAIN

In Great Britain the first official flight in a piloted aeroplane was made on 5th October, 1908, by the famous American-born " Colonel" S. F. Cody. Cody, flying his own aircraft, covered a distance of nearly 500 yards at a height of 50 to 60 ft. over Laffan's Plain, now famous as the scene for the great annual Society of British Aircraft Constructors' air shows at Farnborough.

Farnborough's part in the air story of this country had begun three years earlier, when the Balloon Factory, created to equip the Balloon Section of the Royal Engineers formed in 1890, was moved from Aldershot to Laffan's Plain. Consisting of a single shed, the Factory was used for experiments with man-lifting kites and balloons.

" COLONEL " S. F. CODY

Instructor-in-chief on the kiting side was American-born S. F. Cody. Cody, who had spent many years as a buffalo hunter and Indian scout in Texas, followed by years of organising a lavish Wild West Rodeo show, was one of our most colourful pioneers. This was in spite of competition from the superintendent, who had the unusual habit of taking his wife shopping in a caravan towed by a 10-ton traction engine!

Cody usually travelled astride a white horse, wearing a Stetson hat, cowboy boots and a goatee beard. The resulting resemblance to the

The old salutes the new. A Hunting Percival Pembroke comes in to land over the remains of Cody's tree at Farnborough during a recent S.B.A.C. exhibition.

even more famous Col. W. F. " Buffalo Bill " Cody caused considerable confusion which still exists to this day.

As he watched his huge kites swaying in the breeze, Cody became convinced that other ways could be found of harnessing their tremendous lifting powers. The first step was a biplane glider, followed by the fitting of a 12 h.p. engine into one of the man-lifting kites. This made several short unpiloted flights and Cody was all ready to go ahead with the construction of a full-size machine, when the War Office refused to allocate the necessary money.

For a while Cody devoted his attention to the *Nulli Secundus* Britain's first military airship, which was then being built. 122 feet long and displacing 50,000 cu. ft., this was powered by a 50 h.p. *Antoinette* engine driving a pair of metal-bladed propellers. The cumbersome engine was started by giving a series of sharp tugs to a wheel fitted to the crankshaft, no easy task. Being one of the strongest men available, this unenviable duty usually fell to Cody.

WAR OFFICE SUPPORT

The War Office then had second thoughts about Cody's proposal for a full-size aeroplane and made a grant available—of £50! The result was a sturdy biplane, known as the British Army Aeroplane No. 1, weighing over a ton and with a wing span of 52 ft. To measure the thrust of the engine Cody tied the aircraft to a spring balance attached to a tree. It is the gnarled remains of this tree which has become a meeting place for aviation enthusiasts. Standing at the northern end of what is now the main runway, protected by iron railings and specially treated to preserve it from the weather, a tablet at its base records:

"Col. S. F. Cody picketed his aeroplane to this tree and from this spot on May 16, 1908, made the first successful officially recorded flight in Great Britain."

Another early pioneer was Lt.-Col. Dunne, who believed that the bogy of instability in flight could be overcome by a swept-wing tailless type of aeroplane. Tests with paper models in 1904 gained him official support two years later and the construction of a full-size machine was started. " Official support " also meant official secrecy and, after being made behind locked doors at Farnborough, the aircraft was sent in great secrecy to the Duke of Atholl's estate in Scotland for testing, where the Duke's notoriously tough private army guarded it from prying eyes. Engine trouble marred the tests, but flights made as a glider with the engines removed were sufficiently promising to justify the development of similar aircraft.

OFFICIAL SUPPORT WITHDRAWN

On test the second machine proved to be underpowered and before it could be improved the War Office, on checking through its 'aviation accounts up to the year 1909, was suddenly horrified to find out that a small " fortune " had been spent on aeroplane development—to be exact, a total of £2,500. This is put in its true perspective when one realises that Germany spent over £400,000 on

military aviation alone that year! However, the War Office ordered an immediate end of all experiments with heavier-than-air machines at the Balloon Factory.

Fortunately this incredible decision had little effect on British aeroplane development. Dunne and Cody continued their work privately and other new designers began to enter the new business of aeroplanes.

A. V. ROE'S PIONEER WORK

One of these was a young man named Alliot Verdon Roe. Roe's interest in flying started when, during voyages to and from South Africa as a marine engineer on the S.S. *Inchanga*, he used to watch albatross gliding over the ship with their lovely wings outstretched. He started making model aeroplanes and eventually built some that would glide quite well.

In 1906 Lord Northcliffe offered, through his newspaper the *Daily Mail*, a series of prizes ranging from £250, for models capable of mechanical flight, to £1,000 for the first airman to cross the Channel, and £10,000 for the first flight between London and Manchester within 24 hours. A rival answered sarcastically that he would give ten *million* pounds to anyone who flew between the two cities—little knowing that at that time the Wright brothers had already flown up to 24 miles in America.

Roe entered for the model contest and was rather disheartened when he learnt that there were more than 200 entrants. However, during the tests, held at Alexandra Palace, his 8 ft. span, rubber-driven pusher biplane turned out

The Roe biplane, which was made by A. V. Roe under the most difficult and disheartening conditions in 1908, at Brooklands, where his work was hampered by petty restrictions.

Here you can see Roe's incredible little 9 h.p., brown-paper-covered triplane (shown here without the engine). In this fragile aircraft he became the first pilot to fly an all-British aeroplane, which he had built himself.

A French-built Voisin biplane being prepared for a flight. It was in a biplane of this type that J. T. C. Moore-Brabazon made the first official flight in Britain by a British pilot in May, 1909, at the Isle of Sheppey.

to be the only one to cover the qualifying distance of 100 ft. and he won £75.

BUILDING A FULL-SIZED MACHINE

This he used to build a full-size machine and, as the authorities at Brooklands had offered a prize of £2,500 for the first person to fly round their track before the end of 1907, he decided that was just the place to start building. The authorities, however, in spite of the fact that they had offered such a prize, were not exactly enthusiastic about this proposal. First of all, he was told to put up his shed near the finishing straight; then he was told to move it somewhere else, and later still to paint it green. At last he was allowed to stay—provided he offered his shed as an extra refreshment room during races. It took him two hours to get his

This was the first aeroplane built by Geoffrey de Havilland in 1910. It crashed on its first flight, but de Havilland himself was fortunately not hurt seriously.

machine out of it and on to the track, and he had to be off before the first car arrived, and yet he was forbidden to sleep in the shed. Roe got round this stupid order by saying " Good night " to the gatekeeper, walking out—and then climbing back over the fence!

In spite of these hindrances the aircraft was at last finished. It had a span of 36 ft., and was 20 ft. long. Unfortunately its first engine, a 9 h.p. *J.A.P.*, proved insufficiently powerful to lift it off the ground. Roe then lived on *five shillings'* worth of food a week until he had saved enough to hire a 24 h.p. *Antoinette* engine from France.

With this engine fitted he made several taxying runs until, one day in 1908, he suddenly felt the machine lift into the air— not just the front wheels as in the past, but all four. He suddenly realised that he was actually flying and later wrote: " Those few

Louis Blériot lands at Dover on 25th July, 1909, after making the first successful Channel crossing. This important flight, which roused public interest in the conquest of the air, might have failed if Blériot had not flown through a rain shower which cooled his engine.

The snappy little Sopwith Tabloid which, with a speed of 92 m.p.h., helped to establish the supremacy of the biplane for nearly 20 years.

Europe's first flying-boat. The Sopwith Bat Boat of 1913.

seconds of life gave me a most exhilarated feeling of triumph and conquest, which more than repaid me for all my previous trials and disappointments."

This exciting flight was too late to win the £2,500 prize, and it was not long enough to constitute officially a properly sustained and controlled flight. And so the honour of the title of the first British airman to fly in this country went not to Roe, but to J. T. C. Moore-Brabazon, who made a flight of nearly 500 yards in a French-built Voisin at the Isle of Sheppey in the spring of the following year. Cody, of course, was American at the time of his earliest flights.

Nevertheless, Roe stands out as one of our

greatest British pioneers and, at Lea Marshes on 13th July, 1909, he made certain of one important " first " by making the first official flight in an all-British aeroplane. This was made in a remarkable little triplane, covered with brown paper to save cost and weight so that it would fly on only 9 h.p. This aircraft is now one of the prized exhibits of the National Aeronautical Collection, London.

Even this triumph did not end Roe's troubles, for the authorities at Lea Marshes were just trying to take him to court as a " public

Rheims flying meeting was followed by similar events at Blackpool and Doncaster. From the latter Cody made a cross-country flight of 47 miles in his biplane which, because of its imposing appearance, was usually known as the *Cathedral*.

In 1910 the *Daily Mail* prize of £10,000 for the first flight from London to Manchester was won by Louis Paulhan, who completed the 183 miles in 3 hours 47 minutes flying time after an exciting race with another famous pioneer—Claude Grahame-White.

The famous Avro 504 K biplane in which thousands of people learned to fly.

menace " when Louis Blériot flew the Channel. The authorities could hardly charge Roe with the " crime " of wanting to fly, when the same ambition had brought world-wide fame to a Frenchman, and the charges were dropped.

THE WORLD'S FIRST FLYING MEETING

In August, 1909, the world's first flying meeting was held at Rheims. More than a quarter of a million people flocked to see the 40 or so aircraft on show. The star turn proved to be an American, Glen Curtiss, who flew at the astonishing speed of nearly 50 m.p.h. in a development of his *June Bug* biplane, with which in 1908 he had won the first aeroplane prize awarded in the United States. The

Names that are now world famous began to become known. Robert Blackburn had flown his first aeroplane, T. O. M. Sopwith taught himself to fly, and Short Brothers at Eastchurch, the British and Colonial Co. at Bristol, Handley Page Ltd. at Barking and A. V. Roe & Co. at Brooklands were building aircraft of their own design.

THE FACTORY AT FARNBOROUGH

In 1911, the War Office, realising that aircraft were here to stay, thought that it might be cheaper to have all its machines built at the Factory at Farnborough. Thus followed the long series of aircraft and engines, some of which were to be produced in great numbers and do sterling work in World War I which was then but three short years off. Later, however, as the air war grew in intensity it became all too clear that to have all aeroplanes designed at one factory was not the way to obtain the best fighting aircraft. To encourage private companies the Factory ceased to design and construct aircraft and concentrated on research and advice, for which now, as the Royal Aircraft Establishment, it is world famous.

The Bristol Fighter, a successful aircraft of World War I.

AIRCRAFT FOR THE ROYAL FLYING CORPS

In 1913 two aircraft appeared that gave Britain a lead over the rest of the world. One was the A. V. Roe Type 504 biplane, the other was the little Sopwith Tabloid, which could fly at 92 m.p.h. The appearance of these two aircraft, combined with a ban on monoplanes following a series of accidents, established the superiority of the biplane which was to last for something like twenty years.

Small numbers of these types contributed towards the 179 aircraft which comprised the total strength of the Royal Flying Corps when World War I started on that fateful day in August, 1914. By comparison, Germany had 1,000 military aircraft and France 1,500.

All British warplanes were unarmed because, although tentative experiments in dropping bombs and firing machine-guns from the air had already been made, nobody was quite sure

exactly how they could be used in war. The Army thought that they might have a use now and again for reconnaissance work and the Navy had suggested in 1911 that they might be useful for anti-submarine patrols, spotting for naval guns and reconnaissance of enemy harbours.

AIRCRAFT IN WORLD WAR I

Four years later pilots in " fast," heavily-armed fighters were shooting it out with enemy pilots in aerial battles known as dog-fights; aircraft by the score were being used to photograph and report every movement of armies locked in muddy battle across shell-torn fields; bombers were showering down high explosive, incendiary and fragmentation bombs, Zeppelins had bombed London, a dive-bombing technique had been evolved against men in trenches, torpedoes launched from the air had sunk ships, carrier-based fighters had escorted battleships into action; long-range flying-boats had scored their first successes against U-boats. The warplane had arrived. The newly named Royal Air Force now stood on its own feet, a separate fighting service under a special Ministry, fed and sustained by a civilian army of 350,000 workers churning out aeroplanes at the rate of 30,000 a year.

De Lana's prophecy made in the 17th century—that aircraft might " kill men and burn ships, great buildings, castles and cities, by artificial fireworks and fireballs "—had come true in a really terrifying manner.

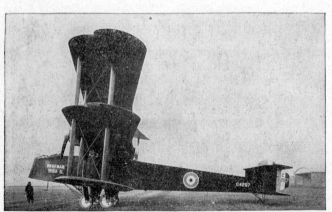

The Bristol Braemar, specially developed for bombing Berlin in World War I was completed too late to see action.

WINGS ACROSS THE WORLD (2)

With the Armistice of 1918, all government contracts for aircraft were cancelled. Companies expanded for war production found themselves with big factories, thousands of workers—and little to do.

THE miseries and horrors of World War I (1914-18) had been made bearable for the Allies because of the sincere belief that they were fighting a " war to end war." And so, with the war won, there would obviously be no need for new military aircraft. As there was little money to be made in civil aviation, many firms closed down. Some went bankrupt. A few, such as the companies headed by great pioneers like Handley Page, Fairey, the Blackburn and Short Brothers, A. V. Roe and De Havilland, struggled on, building one aircraft here and two there, where a few months previously they had been making hundreds. Some kept busy by making pieces of motor cars, kitchen utensils and garages.

But aircraft were built and the story of aviation in the ten years following the war is a record of great achievements. New pioneers began a series of exploits which made front-page news in the papers of the world. First was the crossing of the Atlantic in 1919. This vast ocean, cold, forbidding and stormy, stretching unbroken for nearly 2,000 miles represented the most formidable " barrier " to flying. The first attempt to cross, made by the airship *America* in 1910, had ended in disaster. An attempt by a special flying-boat was put off owing to the outbreak of war, but in May, 1919, three American Curtiss N.C.4 flying-boats made the attempt, one of which, 11 days later and via the Azores, completed the journey.

THE FIRST TRANSATLANTIC NON-STOP FLIGHT

A month later, the much more important first non-stop crossing was made. The aircraft was a Vickers Vimy, a modified bomber, fitted with extra fuel tanks and powered by two Rolls Royce 375 h.p. Eagle motors. The pilot was Captain John Alcock, and the navigator Lieutenant A. Whitten Brown. Their base was at St. John's, Newfoundland, the starting point

of many gallant transatlantic flights. This is the nearest point to Europe on the American continent, the west coast of Ireland being less than 2,000 miles distant, and from no other point could airmen cross non-stop over a shorter expanse of open sea. The historic flight lasted 15 hours 57 minutes and the 1,890 miles were covered at an average speed of 118 m.p.h. This speed seems low in these days of turbo-props and jets, but even that speed was largely due to a strong helping wind and the record remained for 13 years as the fastest ocean crossing. When landing in boggy land at Clifden, Galway, in Ireland, the aircraft sank into the soft ground and tipped on to its nose. This mishap prevented Alcock and Brown from continuing to London as they had planned, but this in no way detracted from the fact that for the first time an aeroplane had spanned the great Atlantic Ocean.

ENGLAND TO AUSTRALIA BY AIR

Before the end of the year another historic flight had been made—from England to Australia. For the first time the Motherland was linked by air to one of her farthermost Dominions. The flight was made by two Australian brothers, Captain Ross and Lieutenant Keith Smith, and the aeroplane was another Vickers Vimy, similar to the one used by Alcock and Brown. Taking off near London on 12th November, they landed at Port Darwin, 11,130 miles away, on 10th December.

Now that the journey is regularly made by big airliners in a few days this flight may seem nothing out of the ordinary, but at that time things were quite different. Many experts did not think that one aircraft and one set of engines could possibly make such a flight, and its successful completion was hailed throughout the world as one of the greatest achievements in flying history. The Australian Government had offered a prize of £10,000 for the first such

Conquest of the Atlantic. Capt. J. Alcock and Lt. A. Whitten Brown leaving Newfoundland on 14th July, 1919, for the first non-stop flight over the North Atlantic.

Unfortunately, after crossing the North Atlantic, Alcock and Brown's plane landed in Ireland on soft ground and the aircraft was badly damaged. This did not detract in any way from a really great achievement. Here you can see their damaged plane.

flight to be completed in less than 30 days and this was without doubt worthily won and gladly paid.

A SERIES OF MISHAPS

In 1920 another main airway of the Empire was pioneered—from England to Cape Town, South Africa. Once again a Vickers Vimy was

heat, the air is therefore considerably " thinner" than it is in colder places nearer sea level. The ill-fated *Silver Queen II*, burdened by a heavy load of fuel, failed to take-off properly and crashed. But still the gallant crew refused to accept defeat. A De Havilland D.H.9 biplane was sent to meet the expedition and in this, the third aircraft of the trip, Cape Town was

Charles Lindbergh's Ryan monoplane the *Spirit of St. Louis* in which, in May 1927, he flew alone non-stop the 3,600 miles from New York to Paris in 33 hours.

used, but this flight was only completed after a series of misadventures. Named the *Silver Queen*, the machine first flew south to Africa and then followed the north coast towards Cairo. At Sollum, the last halt before Cairo, the aircraft ran into a boulder when landing and repairs to the undercarriage delayed the flight for a day. Then, some 500 miles south of Cairo, a tap on one of the radiators suddenly opened and out poured all the water, necessitating a forced landing. In the darkness the machine hit some rocks and was completely wrecked, although happily the crew escaped unhurt. Another machine was obtained, and, fitted with the motors salvaged from the wreck of the *Silver Queen* and carrying the same name, the journey recommenced. Bad luck still dogged the flight and at Wadi Halfa water, instead of petrol, was put into one of the tanks. This meant that the fuel tank had to be drained and the fuel pipes thoroughly cleaned before the aircraft could continue. All then went well, apart from an encounter with a number of rather frightening whirlwinds, until Bulawayo was reached. Here the aerodrome is nearly 5,000 ft. above sea level and, in the tropical

reached at last on March 20th. The distance covered was about 8,500 miles and the flying time totalled 4 days 13 hours 30 minutes.

ROUND THE WORLD FLIGHT IN 174 DAYS

Naturally, British pioneers were not the only men to make these thrilling flights. In the same year as the flight from England to Cape Town, two Portuguese Naval Officers made the first crossing of the South Atlantic in a Fairey seaplane. Two years later American Air Force pilots completed the first round-the-world flight of 27,534 miles in four Douglas World Cruisers. This historic journey took 174 days!

NEW YORK TO PARIS NON-STOP

One of the most famous flights of all time was made in 1927. In that year, Charles Lindbergh, then a comparatively unknown American pilot, leapt into fame when he flew, non-stop, the 3,600 miles from New York to Paris. This long flight was made in bad weather in a little single-engined Ryan monoplane named the *Spirit of Saint Louis*. It was not, of course, the *first* flight across the Atlantic; nearly 100 people had crossed by the time Lindbergh made his flight. But Lindbergh's achievement appealed somehow to ordinary men and women and he became a popular hero overnight. His spectacular accomplishment placed him in the front rank of the world's aviators and rewards and honours were showered upon him.

AN AFRICAN SURVEY

Another thrilling event of 1927 was the beginning of a big survey flight round Africa by Sir Alan Cobham. Sir Alan had already made himself famous by a series of long distance survey flights, in a comparatively fragile De Havilland D.H.50 biplane. The flight round Africa was the climax to these earlier eventful flights, made to demonstrate how air transport could link together the countries of the Commonwealth. The important difference of the African survey was that for the first time Sir Alan used an aircraft that did not require special airfields, or landing facilities—the Short Singapore I flying-boat.

The trip, as can be imagined, was not without its share of excitement and mishaps. The whole venture nearly came to ruin at the start when, during the outward flight, bad weather caused an emergency landing at Malta. Alighting on a rough sea, a big wave tore off one of the wing-tip floats, causing the machine to lurch dangerously to that side. She would almost certainly have capsized but for the bravery of the crew who clambered up the opposite wing to keep the aircraft on an even keel, and then clung on despite great waves which crashed right over them. Later, when the machine was being towed to safety, the storm broke out afresh and a gigantic wave smashed her down on to a concrete slipway. There, to avoid complete destruction, she was dragged over a sea wall, further damaging the port wing.

A new wing was built and rushed out from England and fitted, together with new floats and tail surfaces, and the flight continued. On 23rd January the big flying-boat alighted at Aboukin, and early in February, after a journey up the valley of the Nile, Kisumu was reached. Here, Sir Alan made a circuit of Lake Victoria and then returned to Khartoum. On 12th February, the Singapore again turned its nose south and, via Mongolla, Beira and Durban, reached Cape Town on 30th March.

The return journey was made up the West Coast of Africa, through Freetown, Bathurst,

Handley Page Hannibal. These somewhat ungainly aircraft may be something to laugh at now but in the 1930s these airliners, more than any other, made air travel comfortable and popular. They achieved records of safety unsurpassed in the history of aviation, and as a result gained the confidence of the travelling public.

Cabot, one of Imperial Airways' great fleet of Short " C " class Empire flying-boats which introduced new standards of safety, reliability and comfort to world airline travel.

Gibraltar and back to Rochester, the starting point. Altogether the Singapore had covered 23,000 miles, a tribute to the sturdiness and reliability of flying-boats. The flight provided much valuable information about flying conditions in Africa and, together with other long-distance flights, proved the success of the Singapore, which became the forerunner of a fine line of Short flying-boats.

THE EMPIRE FLYING-BOATS

Seven years later the experience gained on this flight played its part in helping Imperial Airways to make the bold step of ordering, " off the drawing-board," twenty-eight Short flying-boats, to be used exclusively on all their Empire air routes. This was a most unusual step in those days for the order totalled £1,750,000 and the design was for a revolutionary four-engined monoplane lay-out with a hull of advanced design.

The decision was little more than a gamble, yet events were to prove it more than justified, for the Empire 'boats, as they were called, covered over 40,000,000 miles, many of them under dangerous war-time conditions. Each 'boat was powered by four 910 h.p. Bristol Pegasus engines and could carry seventeen passengers, their luggage, and two tons of mail

and freight. Cruising at 164 m.p.h. they had the useful range of 810 miles. They gave Britain a leadership on the civil air routes of the world such as she had never known before and has not yet recaptured.

THE FIRST ATLANTIC AIRLINE FLIGHT

It was flying-boats too, that were destined to make the first airline flights across the Atlantic—the most difficult air route in the world. Two Empire 'boats were adapted to carry additional fuel, giving a range of 3,780 miles. One of them, the *Caledonia*, made the first crossing on 5th-6th July 1937, completing the 1,993 miles between Ireland and Newfoundland in 15 hours 8 minutes.

During the summer of 1939 'boats based on the Empire series operated a transatlantic air-mail service. For this the big 'boats were refuelled in mid-air—the first time such a scheme had been attempted commercially. From these came the biggest and best 'boats of all—the " G "-class 'boats, the now famous *Golden Hind*, *Golden Fleece* and *Golden Horn*. These were designed from the start for the Atlantic route and, weighing 33 tons, combined a range of 3,200 miles with a luxury unknown in earlier airliners. Unfortunately, the " G "-class did not have the chance to

In March, 1936, the prototype Spitfire flew for the first time. So impressive was its performance that three months later the Air Ministry ordered 450 of them; a momentous decision which was to save these islands from invasion and determine the course of the war.

show their paces for shortly after the *Golden Hind* had been launched, Britain was once again at war with Germany.

HURRICANES AND SPITFIRES

Tragic as this was, it was by no means unexpected. In fact, some people had realised that war was inevitable since that fateful day in 1933 when Hitler seized power. Only one year later a Government specification for a new fighter was issued, the answers to which, eight years later, were to save Britain and the world. Perhaps the outstanding feature of this specification, which called for a retractable undercarriage and an enclosed cockpit to improve performance, was the requirement for *eight* machine-guns. This big increase over the two guns usually fitted to fighters was called for because it was realised that the fighter pilot would, at the high speeds envisaged, have an enemy bomber in his sights for a matter of seconds only.

And so, to meet this specification the immortal Hurricane and Spitfire fighters were born. The Hurricane flew first in 1935 and the Spitfire in March, 1936. By September, 1939, there were a total of 22 squadrons of these fighters in service. They had little to do during the first months—so little that this period was christened by some the " phoney war." But, behind the scenes, there was feverish activity and in May, 1940, the storm broke. First Denmark and Norway, then Holland and Belgium and then France fell before the dive-bombers of the Luftwaffe and the tanks of the Wehrmacht. By June, 1940, only twenty-two miles of water lay between Britain herself and the German panzer divisions, twenty-two miles of water—little wider than a big river—but protected by patrolling squadrons of Spitfires and Hurricanes. Behind the patrolling fighters highly-trained technicians peered at a new form of horizon—pale green lines across the circular faces of cathode ray tubes—part of an incredible device developed before the war by

British scientists—radar. Invisible wireless waves emanating from tall, mysterious, lattice-work masts, rising at strategic points round the south-east coast, reached out and detected enemy bombers while they were still many miles away, and not only detected them but gave their speed, height and numbers.

Ignorant of this, the Germans were supremely confident, as is shown by these words of a broadcaster, recorded in the summer of 1940—" We of the Luftwaffe are ready with our plan to eliminate the British Royal Air Force. Its destruction will take two—maybe four weeks. Fighter Command comes first—four, maybe eight days."

THE BATTLE OF BRITAIN

On 8th August, the sporadic attacks began to take on a more sinister character. In the morning no less than sixty enemy aircraft attacked a single convoy off the Isle of Wight. In the afternoon the same convoy was attacked by more than one hundred bombers, while a further one hundred and fifty attacked another convoy off Bournemouth. A few days later, three hundred and fifty aircraft made mass attacks. From then onwards the attacks continued, gathering momentum day by day. But things did not go quite according to the German plan. The Royal Air Force proved a tougher nut to crack than the small, ill-equipped, air forces of the countries the Germans had previously attacked. Four days later the Royal Air Force was very much in evidence and, after about eight days, when according to the plan its destruction should have been complete, no fewer than 147 German aircraft were shot down, their twisted, blackened frames littering the fields of southern England. Four weeks later the fateful battle reached its climax and, on September 15th, although it was estimated at the time that a record number of enemy aircraft had been shot down, subsequent corrected figures give the

Dunkirk! Out of sight from the beaches, far behind the enemy lines, Hurricanes and Spitfires held the vaunted Luftwaffe at bay until over 300,000 soldiers had been rescued.

THE BATTLE OF BRITAIN

These historic photographs typify the days of the Battle of Britain when Hurricanes and Spitfires of the Royal Air Force shot the vaunted Luftwaffe out of the skies over southern England to win this vital battle of World War II. The photographs show: *top*, German Dornier raiders approaching; *centre*, Spitfire pilots " scrambling " and taking off to intercept them; *bottom*, a blazing victim, the German insignia clearly visible.

total as fifty-six German planes destroyed. Nevertheless it was certainly enough to break the spirit of what had been the most terrible air armada the world had ever seen. Although the attacks continued until the end of October, they no longer seemed part of a co-ordinated plan and the Luftwaffe lacked the skill and determination that had carried it to victory in Poland and France.

The Battle of Britain indeed marked the whole turning-point of the war, a fact which the Prime Minister, Winston Churchill, fully appreciated and which he expressed in the following words: "The gratitude of every home in our Island, in our Empire, and indeed throughout the world, except in the abodes of the guilty, goes out to the British airmen, who, undaunted by odds, unwearied in their constant challenge and mortal danger, are turning the tide of world war by their prowess and by their devotion. Never in the field of human conflict was so much owed by so many to so few."

THE ALLIES BOMB GERMANY

In the years following the Battle of Britain, the Royal Air Force set out to do to Germany what the Luftwaffe had failed to do to Britain. A mighty bomber force was gradually built up. At first there were only about 50 aircraft available to venture over the blacked-out German cities, but by 1943, massive raids of up to a thousand heavy four-engined bombers were launched against selected targets. Hitler had promised that ten bombs would be dropped on England for every one dropped on Germany; but it was Bomber Command,

Lancasters of Bomber Command. After winning the Battle of Britain the Royal Air Force built up a big force of bombers to make devastating raids on German war factories.

Secret Weapon. The German flying-bomb, officially called " Reprisal Weapon No. 1," was fired against England during the closing stages of the war.

backed up by heavy raids in daylight by the United States Army Air Force, that returned the bombs, not ten, but one-hundred fold.

Four bitter years passed after the Battle of Britain before the Allies were strong enough to attempt in June, 1944, an all-out attack on Hitler's Fortress, as the Germans called gun-encircled Europe.

PHOTOGRAPHIC RECONNAISSANCE

As far as aircraft were concerned, their preparations began over a year before the actual landing. The photographic reconnaissance squadrons started the immense task of photographing the coastal areas from Denmark to Spain and of building up an air portrait of France. Then, as " D-Day " approached, hundreds of bombers and thousands of fighters began to attack the lorries, tanks and troop trains of the German Army. Nearer still to zero hour, the Allied Air Forces concentrated upon the heavy defensive guns emplaced along the Atlantic Wall and upon the network of carefully camouflaged radar sites, with which the Germans were hoping to track the Allied invasion fleet as soon as it left England.

THE NORMANDY INVASION

At sunrise on 6th June, 1944, the great Allied assault on the Normandy beaches began. This was the invasion of all time—this was the beginning of final victory. Because of the clever planning of the air attacks by Allied aircraft—for every five targets attacked in the area where the landings eventually took place

ten were attacked elsewhere. The invasion was almost a surprise to the enemy and Allied troops were well ashore before the Wehrmacht was able to do much about it. Within a few hours of the initial landings fighters were touching down on hastily prepared landing strips, refuelling and re-arming, and taking off again. The immense part played by aircraft can be imagined when it is realised that during the first three days of the invasion the Allied Air Forces flew more than 31,000 sorties.

THE FLYING-BOMB

Two days before D-Day, the Germans had used the first of several secret weapons against England which, they believed, could still win the war for the " Fatherland." This was the Flying-Bomb, the V-1, or Reprisal Weapon No. 1. For several months they made life most uncomfortable in south-east England and, crashing down in the thickly populated suburbs of London, caused many casualties and much damage. But, as the attack mounted, so more and more of them were destroyed. First, some were intercepted over the Channel and shot down into the sea. Then, near the coast, they were decimated by radar-directed guns, and survivors were then brought down in hundreds by an almost solid belt of barrage balloons. The few which managed to pass through this line of defence were pounced on by more fighters, the pilots of which, if they had used up all their ammunition, used to fly alongside the flying-bombs and tip them over with their wing-tip, thus making the bombs fall down

Secret Weapon. A unique picture of a battery of three German V-2 rockets, known as " Reprisal Weapon No. 2," whilst they were being prepared for firing.

out of control, to explode harmlessly in fields.

V-2 LONG-RANGE ROCKET

As the Allies enlarged their beachhead the Germans unleashed their second secret weapon —Reprisal Weapon No. 2—the V-2 long-range rocket. Fired vertically from sites in northern France and Holland, these 45 ft. long, 12½-ton missiles climbed 60 miles into the air before crashing down at speeds in excess of 3,000 m.p.h. As a long-range bombardment weapon the V-2 represented a frightening introduction to the push-button warfare of the future. But, in 1945, it appeared too late and in insufficient numbers to affect materially the outcome of the war. It was no answer to the mighty power of Bomber Command, which could drop with greater accuracy, five, six, or even seven thousand tons of bombs on any target in Germany.

THE ADVENT OF JET ENGINES

Towards the end of the war, a new sound, the shrill whine of jet engines, was rapidly becoming commonplace. Gloster Meteor aircraft joined battle over England with the flying-bombs and, as the Allied Armies threatened Germany itself, Messerschmitt Me.262 jet-fighters began to make things a little unpleasant for our air forces as they could out-pace all Allied fighters. However,

A new sound. The shrill whine of a jet engine was heard over England for the first time on 15th May, 1941, when the historic Gloster-Whittle E. 28-39 took to the air.

Another new sound. The nose of *Enola Gay*, the B-29 Superfortress used to drop the first atom bomb on Hiroshima, in Japan.

these formidable aircraft, like the V.1s and V.2s appeared too late and on 7th May, 1945, the German armed forces surrendered.

THE FIRST ATOM BOMB

On the other side of the world the Allied net of bomber bases was closing rapidly on the homeland of the remaining Axis partner, Japan. In this area, as in Europe, air power had played a dominant part in military operations, whether allied or enemy, ever since the Japanese had attacked and sunk some American ships in Pearl Harbour in 1941. Now, nearly four years later, mighty forces of American bombers flew northwards, day after day, from little island bases to burn and blast cities on the Japanese mainland.

And then, on 6th August, 1945, a lone B-29 bomber took off and set course for its target— Hiroshima. A few hours later another new noise was heard by the people of that part of the world. The first atom bomb exploded. In a single blinding flash the whole force of air power was multiplied a million times. In thirty-five years air power had grown into a potential destroyer of the world.

CHEMISTRY AS A CAREER

AS recently as the eighteenth century chemists were feared because their work seemed like witchcraft to the ignorant, who burned laboratories and put chemists to death. To-day, however, the chemist is respected as an essential member of the community. No longer, it is true, do we look to him, as in the alchemy days of the Middle Ages, to transmute base metals into gold; but we know that he transforms polymers into yarn of synthetic fabrics which are made into clothes. We no longer expect the chemist's shop to supply us with such queer concoctions as unicorn's horn and balsam of bats, as the apothecary did of old, but on the doctor's prescription the chemist will give us a drug such as a sulphonamide which will control a disease that previously had to be left to cure itself.

When one thinks of a chemist one may picture the pharmacist, who dispenses medicines in a shop or hospital, or the man or woman in the laboratory with his test tubes. These two main branches of chemistry have different appeals, and within them there is wide scope. Both require a high standard of general education before the student is admitted to the special courses.

HOW TO BECOME A PHARMACIST

To become a pharmacist it is necessary to pass the examination of the Pharmaceutical Society of Great Britain. The student has to undergo three distinct periods of study, occupying a total of four or five years. Two of these, occupying three years, are passed by attendance at a recognised school as a full-time student, and the third, under approved conditions, in a chemist's shop, hospital pharmaceutical department or manufacturing pharmaceutical laboratory. In his training the student learns about drugs and their preparation and the law relating to them. The choice of the place at which he takes his practical training will depend to some extent on the kind of career in pharmacy which he proposes to follow, although working both in a hospital and in a retail pharmacy is valuable experience no matter what branch is eventually adopted. Whilst the majority of pharmacists train in this

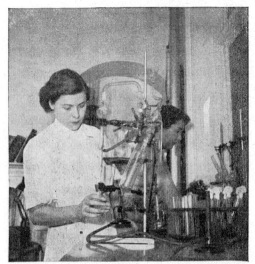

Laboratory work calls for patient attention to detail, and any intending chemist should like this type of work.

way, it is possible to obtain the diploma of the Society through a university degree in pharmacy.

Qualification entitles one to the letters M.P.S. (Member of the Pharmaceutical Society). It is important to remember that the practice of pharmacy is primarily a branch of the Health Service with standards of knowledge and conduct that have to be observed irrespective of financial gain. As with doctors, pharmacists have a professional discipline.

AN ADVISER TO DOCTORS AND PUBLIC

A pharmacist does more than dispense and supply drugs and poisons. He is an adviser— to the doctor on the latest pharmaceutical advances, and to members of the public who often ask him about simple preparations for minor ailments. The last is an interesting survival of the time when the pharmacist was an apothecary, giving medical advice.

TYPES OF PHARMACEUTICAL PRACTICE

There are three main types of pharmaceutical practice—general, hospital and manufacturing. At present, with the growth of corporate and group ownership of pharmacies, about half of the pharmacists in general practice are managers or assistants. The cost of purchasing a business of one's own is considerable, although it varies; there are ways

In some large commercial firms there is almost " an army " of chemists at work on experiments and tests. The work, much of which is done by teams of chemists, is naturally very varied, and always of absorbing interest.

by which financial assistance can be obtained. Before owning his own shop or becoming a manager, a pharmacist needs to have gained sufficient commercial knowledge. In hospital the pharmacist does not work in a commercial atmosphere, being concerned with pharmacy only and not with incidentals like selling toothpaste, and is in close touch with the medical, nursing and other staff who make up the hospital team. The British pharmaceutical manufacturing industry is one of the largest in the world, and pharmacists are employed in it in many capacities.

TRAINING TO BE A CHEMIST

The best preparation for a career in chemistry is a full course at a university or higher technical college. A course for an Honours Degree in chemistry includes the ancillary subjects, physics, mathematics and biology or geology. It is interesting to note that the Chemical Society was founded in the same year

—1841—as the Pharmaceutical Society, but it is purely a learned society and does not hold examinations. Associateship of the Royal Institute of Chemistry, whether gained by examination or through the holding of a university degree or other similar qualification, confers professional status on the holder.

THE VARIETY OF WORK AVAILABLE

Since there is no facet of modern life into which chemistry does not enter, there are many and varied fields of activity for chemists. Chemists are soil technologists, fuel technologists and food technologists, for example. Chemists have prevented epidemics by evolving insecticides like D.D.T. and they saved many lives in the Second World War by devising a simple process which rendered sea-water drinkable. Chemists are consulted in the making of paints, and of cosmetics.

In academic institutions the chemist is generally engaged in fundamental research to find

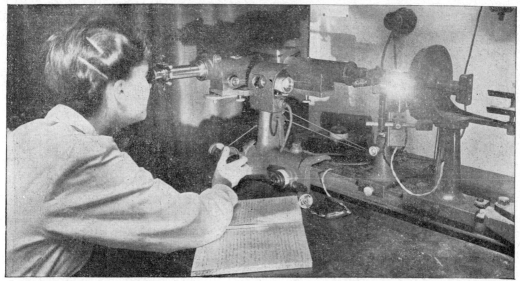

An industrial spectrophotometer being used in connection with the manufacture of dyestuffs.

new basic facts; the chemist in industry is more commonly concerned with applied research, to solve the practical problems of putting fundamental knowledge to use. The division, however, is by no means a hard and fast one. Both types of investigation are carried out in industrial laboratories, and now universities have departments specialising in various branches of technology, such as glass at Sheffield, leather at Leeds, textiles at Manchester and fermentation processes at Birmingham. Chemists are employed by local authorities as Public Analysts, who deal with such matters as the adulteration of foodstuffs. The Forensic Science Laboratories, of which there are six under the Home Office, have chemists carrying out investigations on behalf of the police. Problems associated with the storage of meat, the preservation of timber and the disposal of radioactive and other waste are matters which call for the skill of the chemist. There is also plenty of scope in the teaching of chemistry in technical colleges and schools.

CHEMISTS IN INDUSTRY

When Priestley discovered oxygen he was, incidentally, able to lay the foundation of the soda water industry. The study of coal-tar carbons by Hofmann and Mansfield at the Royal College of Chemistry, London, laid the foundations of aromatic chemistry, leading to the great coal-tar industry. To-day more than half the qualified chemists are working in industry. In many divisions of Imperial Chemical Industries, for instance, the men who manage the plants are graduate chemists. Other chemists are directors of research and development departments. Chemists whose bent lies in administration and commerce may become managers or directors of companies.

The world to-day certainly does not smash laboratories or behead chemists. It wants more of both, and there is scope and opportunity for men and women.

A microscope in use to check results.

Smoothly and efficiently, the long assembly-belt brings boxes of biscuits to be checked.

THE MASS-PRODUCERS
The Planned Use of Machinery

DURING the last 150 years we have come to depend more and more upon machinery in our daily lives. In this period there have been developments in science and engineering which have transformed the way in which we live, and for most of us it is difficult to imagine a normal existence without such things as trains, motor cars, motor buses, aeroplanes, wireless sets, telephones and so on.

All these things are " machines " in the true sense of the word, but if we look about us in our homes it will almost certainly be difficult to point to anything which has not been produced by machinery and, moreover, produced *in quantity* by machinery. The carpet, for example, is almost certainly made on a giant loom; the vacuum-cleaner, although an intricate piece of mechanism, will be one of hundreds of thousands of similar ones; so will the wireless set and the electric iron, the pins in the wife's work-box and the nuts and bolts in the husband's tool-shed.

All these things are needed—or at least wanted—in great quantities. As a result of this demand, they are produced in quantities. They are, as we say, mass-produced.

WHAT MASS-PRODUCTION MEANS
Before we go on to see how mass-production has come about, let us be quite clear about the meaning of the two words. Mass-production means, briefly, the making of very large numbers of identical articles at the lowest possible cost by the planned use of machines. This definition holds good so far as *single* articles are concerned—the common or garden pin for example. But a complication arises (and this is the real key to modern mass-production) when we turn to articles which are made up of more than one part.

Take the case of the nut and bolt. Both can be mass-produced—the nuts on one machine and the bolts on another. But every nut produced must be capable of fitting every bolt produced. No one is going to have time to try every nut on every bolt to make sure that it will fit properly. The machines making the nuts and bolts must be set up so that they will work accurately enough for the makers to be sure that, say, every quarter-inch nut produced will fit *any* quarter-inch bolt produced.

This is what the production engineer calls *interchangeability*. It is the most important factor in modern mass-production and it applies to the whole range of things consisting of more than one simple part made by mass-production methods—from nuts and bolts to motor cars, from electric light bulbs to television sets.

DEVELOPMENT OF MACHINE-TOOLS

Mass-production was made possible by the machine-tools which were developed during the nineteenth century. During this period the lathe and the milling machine, the grinder and the shaper and the die-stamper were improved and developed continuously, mainly with the object of increasing the amount of work that one workman could do in a particular time. At the same time, in Britain and in the other industrialised countries of the world, populations were increasing and so the stage was set for the introduction of mass-production as the best method of meeting the demand for relatively cheap articles of all kinds in great numbers.

MASS-PRODUCTION METHODS APPLIED

It is not easy to point to the earliest example of mass-production as we know it because the idea occurred to many people from time to time—and even before the Industrial Revolution introduced the steam-engine to transform factory organisation. A Swedish manufacturer, Christopher Polhem, was mass-producing a number of iron articles such as hammer-heads, ploughshares and teeth for harrows as early as 1700, using machines powered by water (via a water-wheel). In 1808, 44 special machines were installed in Portsmouth Dockyard for mass-producing wooden pulley-blocks for the Navy's ships. In those days a frigate needed something like 1,500 of these blocks, and their sheaves, and every year more than 100,000 were needed by the Admiralty. Before these machines were devised by Henry Maudslay,

and installed by Sir Marc Brunel and Sir Samuel Bentham, six dockyards were constantly at work turning out the pulley-blocks by traditional and slow methods, using highly skilled men to do it. Maudslay, Brunel and Bentham studied the production problem involved and " broke down " the process of manufacture into separate stages. The 44 machines were designed to cope with each stage of manufacture successively and the result was an output of about 130,000 pulley-blocks a year, using only 10 unskilled men to operate the machines.

That *could* have been the beginning of the development of mass-production in Britain but, in fact, the ingenuity of the English and Scottish engineers was concentrated on " heavy " engineering—forging, rolling, steel working and so on—and it is an American who is regarded as the " father " of modern mass-production.

THE MOVING ASSEMBLY LINE

In 1913 Henry Ford set up in a factory near Detroit in America the first "moving assembly line " for producing motor cars. It was a new idea. Or at least it was a new version of the idea of " breaking down " the stage of manufacture of an article, such as was used for making pulley-blocks in Portsmouth Dockyard 100 years earlier. The principle of Ford's assembly line was the use of gangs of men moving down the line fitting some particular component. Take the engine for example: engines would have been delivered at points along the line by other gangs of men, who also delivered parts like wheels, rear axles, frames, etc.—so that at the end of a working shift a line of completed cars would be ready to be driven to the factory's " delivery point."

Nowadays, in British and American factories making cars by mass-production methods, the system has changed to the extent that the men on the job stay in one place and the assembly line itself moves. Automatic machinery is used for making the component parts of the finished car, and electronic control is used to regulate the speed of the various moving conveyer belts. But Henry Ford must be regarded as the first man to see how a complicated piece of machinery could be made and assembled cheaply and in quantity so that it could be bought by millions of people. Henry Ford was also the first man to make history in a slightly

Henry Ford, whose mass-production methods revolutionised the motor industry.

who built early steam-engines considered that they had done a good job if an old shilling would not pass between a piston and its cylinder! It was Sir Joseph Whitworth who invented a system of close measurement and introduced it into the factory about 1850. Without his work, mass-production would probably have been much slower in developing.

Of course, while Ford was the pioneer, he was not the only mass-producer of motor cars in America. He was quickly followed by Chrysler, the Dodge brothers and others. In Britain William Morris, now Lord Nuffield, used mass-production methods after World War I to build his first cars, and another industry in which mass-production methods were used more than 50 years ago was bicycle-making (four million bicycles were on the road by 1896). Even earlier than this, in the 1850's, the sewing-machine was being produced in large numbers in America, and, earlier still, fire-arms were being made on the principle of the interchangeability of parts—although in

different sense by offering to pay a "minimum wage" to his workers: this was a year later, in 1914, and his offer of five dollars a day was so much higher than the average daily wage of American workmen that he was called every sort of name from "madman" to "Communist." The Ford company has sailed many stormy seas since these early days but is now re-established as one of the major car-making concerns of America—and throughout the world.

INTERCHANGEABILITY

You will see how important is the principle of interchangeability in this example of the making of a motor car. It does not matter *which* engine from the pile, or from the moving assembly line, is fitted into any particular chassis. All the engines are identical. They will all fit. All the holes previously drilled in the chassis and in the engine mountings will line up. All the bolts which hold them together are precisely the same so that there is no question of trying a bolt in a hole to see if it will fit.

Naturally, this would not be possible without exact measurement—or, at least, measurement exact enough for the purpose; and for mass-production purposes the measuring is close enough to make no difference. In the days of the first steam-engines one of the greatest difficulties was in producing parts for the engine which would really fit; in fact the men

Sir Joseph Whitworth, the inventor of a system of accurate measurement.

The final inspection on a motor car assembly line ensures perfection of workmanship throughout.

this case the intricate working parts were made by hand by skilled workmen, not machines.

THE PRESENT-DAY NEED FOR MASS-PRODUCTION

Many people tend to deplore mass-production and the gradual disappearance of the skilled man who made articles with his two hands and a few simple tools. In some people's minds, mass-produced goods means shoddy, badly-finished goods.

But, in fact, while the disappearance of the craftsman may be rather sad, it would not be feasible for craftsmen to produce the enormous variety of goods required to-day in the great quantities needed. In addition to the fact that men making articles entirely by hand simply could not keep pace with the demand, the articles themselves would cost at least two or three times as much as their mass-produced equivalents.

It is true that in the early days of widespread mass-production much shoddy stuff was produced; but this was largely due to the fact that machines were not then nearly so accurate as they are now, and engineers were forced to allow wide margins of error to make sure that parts would be interchangeable. Now, however, with greatly improved methods, mass-production has brought a wide range of articles, once considered luxuries and only available to the well-to-do, within the means of the ordinary working man's pocket.

See also page 84.

ROBOTS IN THE FACTORY

IT IS often said that we live in a "machine age" and to a large extent this is true. It would be difficult to imagine life to-day without machines, and especially without the machine tools which produce so many of the things which we use in our daily lives.

We have used machines in one form or another to produce the goods we all need for more than a hundred years. The coming of the machine in its earliest form, the steam engine, is generally called the "industrial revolution"; the great change was that whereas before the introduction of the steam engine into the factory all articles were made by hand, with the introduction of machinery the work of one man could be multiplied many times. Instead of using his two hands to make an article, the workman used his hands to operate a machine which could do the job much more quickly.

THE SECOND INDUSTRIAL REVOLUTION

To-day we are going through the first stages of what has been called "the second industrial revolution," because we can now do away with the workman altogether in making some articles, and allow the machines to run entirely by themselves. The name usually given to this idea of using fully automatic machinery is "automation."

EXAMPLES OF AUTOMATION

If you walk round a modern oil refinery, with its maze of pipes and towers, you will probably be puzzled at the absence of human beings. You may see an occasional man, but he will probably be doing nothing more strenuous than looking at a bank of dials. The process of refining crude oil to produce petrol and many other by-products is largely a chemical one in which things like temperature, pressure, rate of flow and so on are vitally important. These factors can be controlled by men of course; but they can be controlled more efficiently, more speedily and more accurately, by machinery guided by electronic controls.

The electronic unit which takes the place of

After receiving its instructions the electronic brain can solve a wide variety of problems or do complicated calculations for industry.

the workman is, basically, a very complicated set of wireless valves; these "thermionic" valves are very sensitive to tiny changes in an electric current flowing through them. This sensitiveness to electrical change can be changed into a sensitiveness to physical change, to variations in temperature, pressure, thickness, weight and so on.

Another example of automation is the "electronic brain," or giant calculating machine, which can work out mathematical problems many hundreds of times faster than a human mathematician.

So, within limits, the machine tool allied to an electronic unit, can be left to work on its own. All that is required from human hands is that the machine and its electronic control should be switched on and switched off again. We have mentioned oil refining as one example of an industry in which this sort of automatic process is widely used: it was, in fact, one of the first industries in which automation was introduced. There are also a number of other industries in which chemistry is important where automation is used: making nylon, plastics, distilling and milling are some of them.

AUTOMATION IN ENGINEERING

In other industries, where production is not a smooth chemical process but a series of engineering processes, the automatic machine is, so far, only used at certain stages. In a famous car firm in the Midlands, for example, cylinder blocks are machined by a series of " automatic transfer " machines. They are received from the foundry in a rough state at one end of the line of machines and after $3\frac{1}{4}$ minutes, during which they are passed automatically from one machine to the next, they emerge at the other end of the line almost fully machined, faced, drilled and tapped and ready for the cylinder head, sump and pistons, etc. to be added.

Such machines, and their electronic apparatus, are enormously expensive. One such set of three automatic transfer machines for making cylinder blocks cost £90,000 to install. But only six technicians are needed to watch over the whole line of machines. And the automatic transfer process is more than twice as fast as the former men-plus-machines method, where the part being made had to be passed by hand from one machine to the next at each stage in the manufacture. So you can see that, in cases where thousands and tens of thousands of identical articles are being made, the great cost of such automatic machines can eventually be recovered in a saving in wages, and a greater number of articles made in a given time.

HOW LABOUR IS AFFECTED

Quite clearly, the day will come when some kinds of factory can be run without human workers at all. In fact there is already a factory in Britain making wireless components which is entirely automatic; there *are* human beings working in it, but they are highly-skilled technicians whose job it is to keep an eye on the working of the automatic machinery, and to maintain it and repair it if necessary.

This brings us to the great problem connected with automation—the fear of unemployment. If men, or women, working on the assembly line in a factory hear that at least one similar factory has already changed over to automatic machinery, it is not surprising that they will worry about what will happen to them if automation comes to their factory.

SOLVING THE PROBLEM

The answer to this problem is not simple, but there are a number of cases which show how it can be solved. The radio industry provides one such case: the demand for radio and television sets to-day is greater than it

An electronic brain used for calculating wages. *Left:* the control panel where a light goes on if a mistake is made. *Right:* the code is passed through a tape reader.

A recently developed metal, titanium, has proved to be of considerable use to industry. Distillation of crude titanium is controlled largely from this panel by remote control.

ever was. Formerly manual workers were hard to find and the automatic factory was (in one case) the answer to a shortage of suitable labour and the increasing demand.

A similar thing happened, even before 1939, in the G.P.O. when the automatic telephone exchange was introduced. Quite naturally, many of the telephone staff wondered if they would be thrown out of work; but what, in fact, happened was that the demand for telephones went up, more or less as a direct result of the increased efficiency that the automatic exchange provided, and at present there is still a great shortage of skilled people to install and maintain telephone apparatus.

In America, where automation in factories has gone a good deal further than it has here, a similar process has taken place: the demand for goods which can be produced by automatic, or even semi-automatic machinery, has risen because, in this way, they can be produced more cheaply and more efficiently. This has meant that men who can design, produce and maintain such machinery are wanted in greater numbers. In other words an "economic

balance" can be achieved—although no one can be sure what the position might be in a slump, when the demand for mass-produced goods falls.

There have been temporary spells of unemployment of course; but the point that emerges most clearly from all this is that it is the *skilled* man or woman who is wanted in the industries of to-day and, even more important, of to-morrow. Unskilled workers cannot be turned into technicians overnight. But, from what we can see happening, there is no need for a sudden transformation. If, bit by bit, as our factories change over from the old men-plus-machines process to the new automatic process, there can be a corresponding change in the training of workers in industry so that they can take their proper places as skilled *overseers* of these "robot" machines, there need be no fear of sudden and catastrophic unemployment. And we should remember that there are some articles which cannot be made by automatic machines; automatic machinery is probably one of them.

See also page 80.

The Aswan dam on the Nile, an engineering masterpiece, regulates the flow of that great river so that land, which is otherwise desert, can be irrigated and grow fine crops.

ENGINEERING
A Profession Working for the Present and the Future

FIRST of all, what *is* engineering? Perhaps the classic definition is still the best: engineering means " directing the great sources of power in Nature to the use and convenience of man." Engineering is, in short, the supreme example of applied science, and it has been aptly called the art that makes science useful. It is sometimes claimed that the engineer is a man who can make with one ton of steel what any fool could make with two tons; and certainly, by knowing the exact scientific basis of what he is doing, he can develop safer structures, faster aircraft, or stronger machines without wasting an ounce.

PROFESSIONAL QUALIFICATIONS

In engineering, the recognised professional qualification is membership of one of the three major Institutions—of Civil, Mechanical, or Electrical Engineers. Full membership, which carries with it the right to use the initials M.I.C.E., M.I.Mech.E., or M.I.E.E., is reserved for those who have not only qualified as professional engineers in terms of education, training and experience, but have held positions of " superior responsibility " for a number of years. The newly qualified engineer will normally become an Associate Member of his chosen Institution: this grade of membership entitles him to describe himself as a Chartered Civil, Mechanical or Electrical Engineer, and to use the initials A.M.I.C.E., A.M.I.Mech.E., or A.M.I.E.E. after his name.

The three major Institutions publish details of their own conditions of membership in the form of Examination Regulations, which can be obtained direct from the Secretaries, or through schools or public libraries.

Their requirements are not identical, but they all insist on a high standard of theoretical knowledge, balanced by plenty of practical experience. Broadly speaking, there are three ways in which this can be acquired. For some, the theoretical side comes first in the form of a full-time University course. An engineering degree requires three years of study, after which the graduate may spend one or two years in practical training, perhaps as a graduate apprentice, or—if he is lucky—go straight into a responsible job.

STARTING AS AN APPRENTICE

In the second approach, the emphasis is on the practical side right from the start. By becoming an apprentice, or an articled trainee, the would-be engineer can start earning his keep while he is learning his job. The essential theoretical side, however, will have to be acquired by spare-time study, either by evening classes or by an approved correspondence course. It is likely to take up to five years to reach the necessary standard, and this means a long, hard slog, with little time to enjoy the lighter side of life; but the apprentice who perseveres and qualifies will prove not only that he has the high standard of knowledge required, but that he possesses the strength of mind, self-control and determination to stick at a tough job and see it through to success.

The third method is the so-called " sandwich " scheme, which is an attempt to combine the advantages of the other two. Theoretical studies occupy the normal term times at a University or Technical College, and the vacations are spent on practical training in works or factory. The time taken to qualify in this way will normally be four years.

TRAINING AS AN ENGINEERING TECHNICIAN

A word of warning should be given here. If anyone seriously doubts his ability to reach the very high academic standard of the professional examinations, it would be far better for him not to attempt them, but to aim from the start at becoming an engineering *technician*. These men, whose training is at once more practical and more specialised, occupy a vital place in the industry. Their work lies between that of the craftsman and the engineer: in many cases it involves the highly skilled use of delicate and

In Holland, engineers build dykes to prevent the sea from inundating the flat land.

complicated instruments, and requires a reasonable knowledge of theory in some particular and limited subject.

A WIDE VARIETY OF WORK

Within each branch of engineering, whether it be hydraulics, radar, aerodynamics, mining, or transport, there are several different kinds of work for the engineer. There is, for instance, applied research, the aim of which is to find out more and more exactly how and why things happen, and how they can be controlled. Next comes the stage in which the findings of research are applied to the design of a practical structure or machine; it is here, perhaps, that experience and ingenuity, theory and practice must be most closely allied.

The production of equipment, whether it be the construction of a single enormous unit—a turbo-alternator, perhaps, to convert 150,000 horse-power into electricity—or the manufacture of small precision items by the hundred thousand, is another process which requires engineering management. Engineers travel to all parts of the world to supervise the building of dams, bridges, harbours and railways, and the installation of technical plant. Finally, engineers and technicians are needed to run the mines, power stations, refineries, radio transmitters, telephone networks, and all the other technical services of civilisation: this comes under the heading of operations and maintenance.

AN IMPORTANT CAREER

Engineering offers a high degree of security as a career, as civilisation comes to depend more and more upon its services. It can safely be said that one who enters the engineering profession can be sure of playing an important part in running the world of to-day and in building the world of to-morrow.

To give just a few examples of the important work to be done: the whole British Railways system is being modernised, at a cost of hundreds of millions of pounds; the mines are being mechanised; a new electrical " supergrid " will soon span the country with overhead lines working at 275,000 volts; aircraft are being developed to fly faster, higher, and

Road-building problems in Switzerland. Labour has to be transported up the mountains by ropeway from the villages.

An explosive charge in a road tunnel is about to be detonated and the " Dynamite Gang " run out to safety.

farther than ever; great dams are being built to control floods and use the power of the rivers and tides; and the untapped energy of the atom is being harnessed in the new British nuclear power stations.

On a smaller scale, but no less interesting, is the production of such things as radio and television sets, cars, refrigerators, washing machines, and all the other devices to reduce drudgery and enhance the pleasures of living. All of these depend on the engineer for their design, development, production and maintenance.

Looking farther ahead, if space travel is to become common—and it surely will—it will present engineering with a new challenge. New stresses and strains will be set up; new hazards will have to be foreseen and overcome; new techniques and perhaps new materials will be needed in the design and construction of spacecraft, their motors and their control gear. In America, the National Aeronautics and Space Administration laid down that as a basic requirement astronauts must possess a degree in engineering or science.

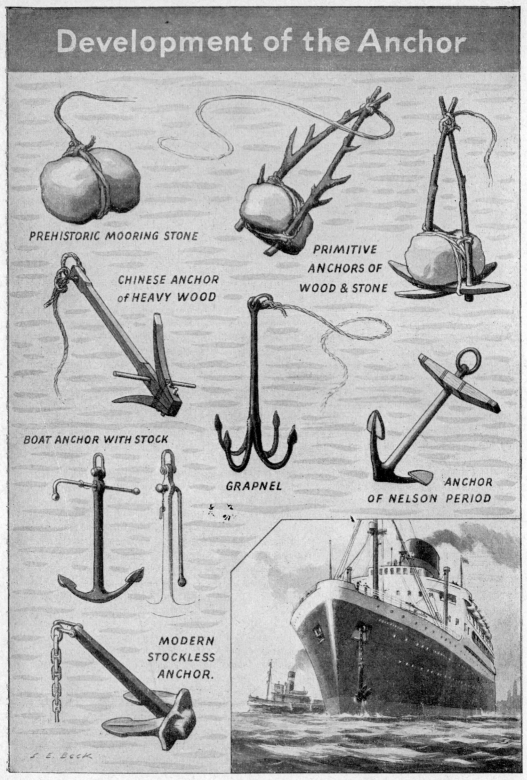

PREHISTORIC MOORING STONE

PRIMITIVE ANCHORS OF WOOD & STONE

CHINESE ANCHOR of HEAVY WOOD

BOAT ANCHOR WITH STOCK

GRAPNEL

ANCHOR OF NELSON PERIOD

MODERN STOCKLESS ANCHOR.

S. E. Beck

ANCHORS

THE anchor, in one form or another, must be almost as old as the boat: the first boat of any kind (if we except the crude raft) was the tree trunk hollowed out by fire and primitive tools, and the men who made such boats must soon have hit upon the idea of using a boulder tied to a rope of thongs in order to keep the craft stationary in a moving current. Other early forms of the anchor were skins filled with sand, and logs of wood loaded with lead.

Crude anchors of this sort were not very effective. The principle upon which they worked relied upon the weight of the boulder or other heavy weight, and its friction on the bed of the river or sea. No one is certain of the date when the anchor with the hook to dig into the bottom was thought of, but it seems certain that it first appeared in the Mediterranean some hundreds of years before the birth of Christ. One classical writer, Pausanias, says that the tooth of the anchor was the invention of Midas, king of Phrygia: another says it was thought of by the Tuscans.

At first, the anchor probably only had one tooth, or fluke as it is properly called, but the second fluke was added by the Greeks and iron began to be used for making anchors, in place of the former wood or stone. This type of anchor, with its two flukes, its shank (shaft) with a ring at the end to which the cable is attached, and its stock which is fitted at right angles to the two flukes, has been in use virtually unchanged in form for two thousand years, and many small craft still use anchors of this type.

The point about the stock being fitted at right angles to the flukes is an important one: it ensures that no matter how the anchor falls on to the sea bed or river bottom, one or other of the flukes will always point downwards to bite into the bottom. Should the anchor fall so that the stock touches the bottom first, the anchor will roll over under the tension of the cable or chain until one of the flukes does bite.

As we have seen, small ships still use this type of anchor, although nowadays the stock is usually detachable so that the anchor does not take up so much room on board the vessel. The largest anchors of this pattern that were ever made were the massive wooden ones carried by three-decker wooden battleships about 150 years ago—in Nelson's time. There are still a few of them to be seen at the National Maritime Museum at Greenwich and even now they look most impressive.

So far as anchors for large ships are concerned, the great change came in the middle of the nineteenth century when the British Admiralty adopted a new design invented by a Frenchman called Martin. On his anchor, the stock was *parallel* to the flukes but the flukes themselves were hinged together so that normally they lay close to the shank but, when they caught on the bottom, they opened away from the shank until they lay at an angle of about 30° from it.

This design was most successful and it had a number of important advantages over the classic pattern: it could be made much lighter because it had such good holding power, and when the flukes had dug into the bottom, there was no upper one to project upwards with the danger of fouling the bottom of the ship at low tide.

Early in this century, it was realised that the stock of Martin's anchor was not really necessary since the hinged flukes would still operate quite efficiently if the stock was removed, and so this was done. To-day all large ships carry anchors of this stockless type.

There is one other type of anchor which is worth noticing—the C.Q.R. type which is used by many small craft instead of the conventional pattern. This anchor does not have flukes at all; instead it is fitted with a blade rather like that of a ploughshare and it is used with a very long cable so that its drag on the sea bed or river bottom is almost horizontal.

Most large ships carry about five anchors. There will be one fitted in the hawse-holes on either hand in the bows with a third in reserve, probably stowed on deck forward. Besides these three bower anchors, there will be a stream anchor which may be lowered from the stern to prevent the ship swinging, and a kedge anchor which can be used to move the ship short distances in harbour, or at sea if the main engines should break down, by winching the ship on to the anchor by means of the anchor engine.

THE ECHO SOUNDER

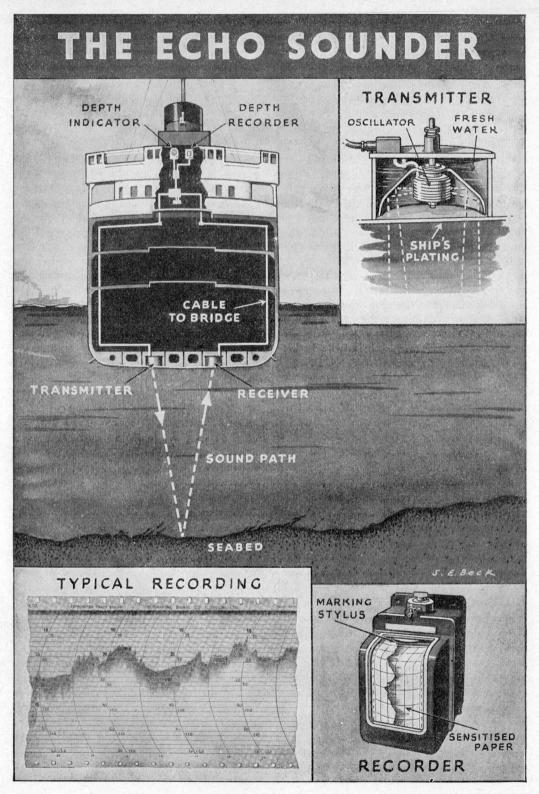

TRANSMITTER

OSCILLATOR   FRESH WATER

SHIP'S PLATING

DEPTH INDICATOR   DEPTH RECORDER

CABLE TO BRIDGE

TRANSMITTER   RECEIVER

SOUND PATH

SEABED

S. E. Beck

TYPICAL RECORDING

MARKING STYLUS

SENSITISED PAPER

RECORDER

THE ECHO SOUNDER

A FEW years ago, if a captain wanted to know the depth of water under his ship, he had to wait while his crew heaved a lead-weighted line over the side to measure the distance to the sea-bed. Nowadays, the lead-line is replaced by sound waves.

The equipment that does the measuring is called an. echo sounder, and its principle is shown in the drawing opposite. It is extremely simple. We know that sound waves travel through water at a speed of 4,800 ft., or 800 fathoms, per second. So, if we send out a single wave or pulse of sound, like the bang of a gun, from a transmitter in the bottom of a ship, and measure the time taken for the echo to bounce back from the sea-bed, we can then calculate very easily the exact depth of the water.

If, for example, the time taken were exactly one second, the sound pulse would have travelled a total there-and-back distance of 800 fathoms, and the water would be 400 fathoms deep.

An echo sounder simply transmits pulses of sound very quickly one after the other, measures the time they take to bounce back to a receiver and records the depth of water on a moving strip of sensitised paper. An interesting point is that, if the sea-bed is covered with mud, some sound waves pass through the mud, producing a second echo which gives also the depth to solid rock.

The brain of the system is the recorder, in which a small arm, like the hand of a clock, rotates continuously at a constant speed, in an anti-clockwise direction. A marking stylus, or pen, ·is fixed to the end of the arm so that it moves in a curved path just clear of the surface of the paper.

Every time the stylus passes a fixed point at the left-hand side of the paper, a pulse of sound is transmitted. By the time an echo is received from the sea-bed, the stylus has moved a certain distance over the paper, and mechanism inside the recorder causes it to mark the paper at that point.

The deeper the water, the longer the echo takes to come back, and the farther the stylus moves. We know that a 400-fathom depth is equal to a time interval of one second. So, if

the paper is divided into 400 divisions and the stylus is made to move over it in exactly one second, each division corresponds to one fathom, and the depth is indicated by the mark of the stylus.

There are many other sound waves in the water, including those caused by the ship's own machinery. Because of this, the sound pulse transmitted is very shrill, and the receiver is so designed that it picks up this sound and ignores the others.

What happens is that, each time the stylus passes the " zero " point on the left of the recording paper, a sudden surge of electrical current is passed into the transmitting oscillator. This converts the current into sound vibrations, which are focused into a beam by the reflector and projected downwards to the sea-bed.

The returning echoes are picked up by the receiving oscillator, which reverses the process, turning the sound waves back into electrical pulses to operate the recorder. Alternatively, if the skipper only wants to see the depth and not record it, he can use a depth indicator, which shows the distance to the bottom on a lighted circular scale.

The speed of the sound waves varies slightly with the temperature, pressure and " saltiness " of the water; but the variation is small enough to ignore when echo sounding is used solely for navigation. At other times—when, for example, it is used to map the sea-bed and approaches to harbours or rivers—the variations can be remedied by calculation or by altering slightly the speed of the motor that drives the stylus arm, so that depths can be measured accurately to within 3 in.

An echo sounder made by the British firm of Kelvin and Hughes, who pioneered the technique, discovered one of the deepest known " valleys " on the ocean floor, 5,700 fathoms (more than $6\frac{1}{2}$ miles) below the surface of the Pacific off the Philippines.

Echo sounding is used a great deal by cable ships. It can also detect wrecks on the sea-bed; and many fishing vessels are fitted with fish-detection echo sounders, by means of which experienced skippers can tell not merely the size and depth of a shoal, but often the kind of fish forming it.

The TONNAGE of SHIPS

THE size of a ship is usually expressed in terms of tonnage, but there are so many different ways in which tonnage is measured that much confusion may be caused.

Merchant ships are usually measured in *gross* and *net* tonnage, but sometimes also in *deadweight*. Naval ships are more often measured by *displacement* tonnage. Yachts are measured by *Thames* or *Yacht Measurement* tonnage.

Gross tonnage is the measurement of all the enclosed space in a vessel, i.e. her total capacity, including holds, engine-room, cabins, chart-room, etc. It is expressed in tons capacity, of which each ton equals 100 cubic feet.

Allied to gross tonnage is under-deck tonnage. This is the total capacity of the ship below the main deck.

Net tonnage is really the earning capacity of a ship. It is the measurement of all space such as cargo holds and passenger cabins, in tons of 100 cubic feet each. Or, put another way, it is the capacity of a ship after deducting from the gross tonnage the size of all un-earning space such as engine-room, chart-room, and crew accommodation.

Thus, in a cargo steamer the gross tonnage may not be very much greater than the net; in a sailing vessel the difference is even less, because there is no engine-room space; but in a tugboat, which is nearly all engine-room and crew space, the net tonnage is reduced to an absurdly small amount.

Displacement tonnage is a measurement of weight, not capacity. It is the weight of the volume of water which the ship displaces in normal trim. It is normally used for warships, because their weight does not alter much when in sea-going trim. They have no cargo to load or discharge.

It is measured by the following formula:

$$\frac{Length \times Breadth \times Depth \times Coefficient\ of\ Fineness}{35}$$

The Coefficient of Fineness is the proportion which the area of the hull at the water-line bears to a rectangle formed by multiplying length by breadth. It is usually a figure between 0·5 and 0·8.

The division by 35 is to convert cubic feet to tons weight. One ton of sea-water measures 35 cubic feet (approximately).

Deadweight tonnage is the weight a ship can carry in cargo, bunkers and stores.

Thames or yacht tonnage is found by the formula:

$$\frac{(Length - Breadth) \times Breadth \times \frac{1}{2}\text{-}Breadth}{94}$$

This is a thoroughly bad form of measurement, because it takes no account of depth. Thus a flat " skimming-dish," like some racing

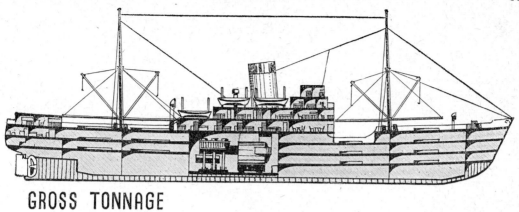

GROSS TONNAGE

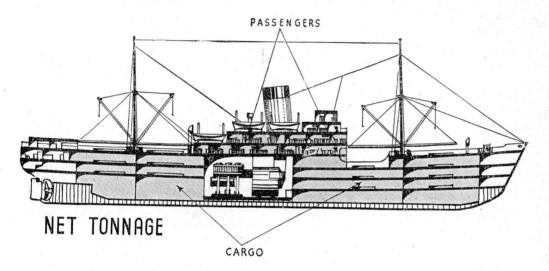

NET TONNAGE

The differences between gross and net tonnage are shown in these two diagrams by the shaded portions. In gross tonnage all the enclosed space (including holds, engine-room, cabins, etc.) is measured and 100 cu. ft. taken to equal one ton; in net tonnage, on the other hand, only the earning capacity of the ship is measured.

hulls, has the same tonnage measurement as a full-bodied cruiser of the same length and breadth.

SHIPS WITH BULGES BELOW THE WATER-LINE

This method of measurement was used for all merchant ships until about the middle of the nineteenth century. It resulted in ships being built with absurd depths and great " bulges " below the water-line, in order to carry the maximum amount of cargo on a small tonnage, since harbour and other dues were calculated and charged on tonnage.

Thus British ships were slow and cumbersome as compared with those of America and other countries which had more sensible methods of measurement. Until the British system was changed and the laws took effect there was very real danger that British merchant shipping would be ruined by the competition of better and faster ships.

The method is, however, still used for almost all British yachts. It gives a very much higher figure in most cases than either the gross or net measurement.

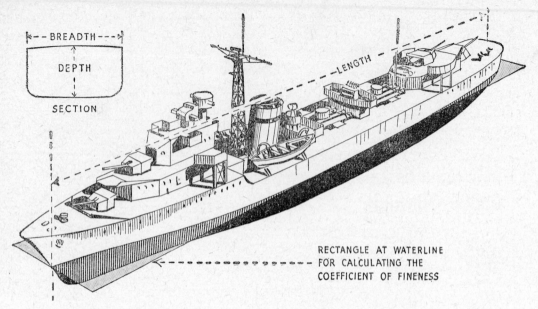

Here is a diagram of a naval ship showing the measurements by which displacement tonnage is calculated. This is a measurement of weight, not capacity.

Many tricks have been adopted from time to time to defeat the tonnage rules and consequently reduce taxes. One was the building of large " open " shelters on the decks of passenger ships, which could not be measured as " enclosed " spaces.

On the other hand, when it was desired to increase the gross tonnage of one big liner so that she could be advertised as " the largest ship in the world," all such shelters were enclosed so that they could be included in the measurement.

There are other special methods of measurement, mainly designed for the calculation of port and other dues. Such are the Panama and Suez Canal tonnages, which are, however, only variations of the standard British gross tonnage.

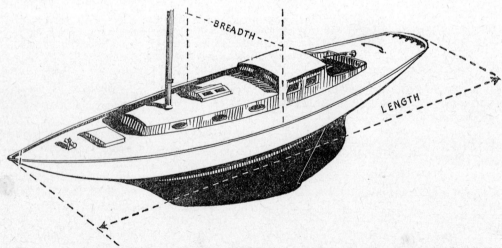

Thames or Yacht measurement, by reason of its unusual formula, often produces the same tonnage measurement as that of a cruiser of the same length and breadth.

A B.B.C. Television Outside Broadcast team may be working at a considerable distance from their base, and sometimes spare parts and replacements have to be flown to them at short notice.

WIRELESS AND TELEVISION
An Explanation of How They Work

IF Julius Cæsar or Sir Walter Raleigh could spend a day or two in our modern world, they would marvel at the sight of people riding around in buses nearly as big as a house, at great man-carrying " birds," filling the sky with the thunder of their jet-engines, and at the way a room can be lighted in an instant by the flick of a switch. But none of these things would astound them so much as the small radio and television sets that stand in the corner of a room in your home.

Most of you will have been listening to the wireless or watching TV for as long as you can remember. You probably take them for granted, as part of your daily life, without ever stopping to think how wonderful it is that we can produce music and moving pictures out of thin air. You know that there is nothing magical about either radio or television; but do you know how they work?

If not, try to remember what happened last time you threw a stone into a river or pond Circular ripples flowed out from where the stone entered the water, growing larger and larger until they either hit the edge of the water or faded away. Sound and light both travel in waves, in the same way as ripples, except that their waves are very much closer together and travel very much faster.

SOUND WAVES

We cannot normally see sound waves, which is just as well because the air is full of them all the time. When you bang a drum, for example, the parchment drumhead vibrates at the rate of a few dozen times a second, creating pressure waves in the surrounding air. These waves travel outwards in all directions, like ripples, and when they reach your ear they stimulate nerves and produce the sensation we call sound.

A human voice sends out similar sound waves, but at a much higher rate—known technically as a " high frequency "—of up to several thousand vibrations a second. As a result its note appears less deep than the banging of the drum; because the higher the frequency of vibration the shriller is the note.

Unfortunately, like ripples, sound waves gradually become weaker and fade away as they get farther and farther from their source. This is why we have difficulty in calling a friend on the far side of a large field and why we use a telephone to talk to somebody even farther away.

THE ROLE OF THE MICROPHONE

The secret of the telephone's efficiency is its microphone, which catches the sound waves, or air vibrations, from your voice as you talk into it, and turns them into an electric current of exactly the same frequency. This varying current can be transmitted over long distances through wires, and will work a telephone receiver, which turns the electrical vibrations back into air vibrations, so that they can be heard by the person at the other end of the line.

Wireless works in much the same way except that, as its name implies, it cuts out the telephone wires and can, therefore, transmit messages to an endless number of receivers all at the same time, even if they are aboard ships at sea or aircraft in the air. It does this by making use of another, different, type of wave called a radio wave.

RADIO WAVES

Like light and heat, radio waves are a form of what is known as radiant energy. They consist of electro-magnetic vibrations of enormous frequency—ranging from hundreds of thousands to many hundreds of millions of vibrations each second—and they travel through the air at a speed of 186,000 miles per second.

The human ear can convert into sound only frequencies between a few dozen and a few thousand vibrations per second: so we cannot hear radio waves. But we can use them to enable us to hear other sounds over vast distances.

What happens is that, at the broadcasting station, alternating electric current of " radio " frequency is generated by means of valves, and is made to flow in the transmitting aerial. This causes radio waves of the same frequency to " ripple out " into space, and they are picked up in the form of a weak high frequency current by the aerial of your home radio.

You never hear these " radio frequency " currents, because the cone of your loudspeaker cannot vibrate quickly enough to turn them into sound. In any case, they would be far beyond the range of your ears. The important thing is that they can be used to carry " sound " through the air from the broadcasting station, at a speed of 186,000 miles per second, instead of at the normal 760 m.p.h. speed of sound, just as an aeroplane can carry a 4 m.p.h. man at 500 m.p.h.

THE AUDIO- AND RADIO-FREQUENCY CURRENTS COMBINED

In the broadcasting studio, the programme is performed in front of a microphone which, as already explained, converts the sound air vibrations into electric currents of the same

Radio-telephone used by a " banksman " in winter to maintain contact with the crane-driver and give him instructions.

frequency. These " audio-frequency " currents are then amplified, or made stronger, by means of valves, and combined with the very fast radio-frequency currents. The result of this is that the strength of the radio waves leaving the transmitting aerial varies continually according to the tone and volume of sound picked up by the microphone. Radio technicians say that the radio waves are modulated at sound frequency; and modulation is a term to remember because it is becoming increasingly important, as you will see later.

Having picked up the rather weak combined sound-frequency and radio-frequency waves with your aerial, the rest is fairly simple. Some valves inside your wireless set amplify them: others separate the sound frequency ripple which you want from the radio-frequency " carrier " which, having done its job by bringing the programme to you at the speed of light, is no longer needed. The sound frequency ripple is amplified even more and passed on to the loudspeaker, which is a kind

of overgrown telephone receiver able to convert the electrical vibrations back into the sound you hear when you switch on your wireless set.

AMPLITUDE MODULATION

The system of broadcast transmission described so far, and which is most widely used for home radio reception all over the world, is known as amplitude modulation (AM). It gets its name from the fact that the signal picked up by your aerial consists of a high frequency radio wave of constant frequency and amplitude, which carries a low frequency sound ripple of varying amplitude.

It is easier to understand what this means if you remember that the frequency of the ripple varies according to whether the sound picked up by the microphone is deep or shrill; and that its amplitude or height corresponds to the loudness of the sound.

ELIMINATION OF INTERFERENCE

The main drawback of AM radio is that

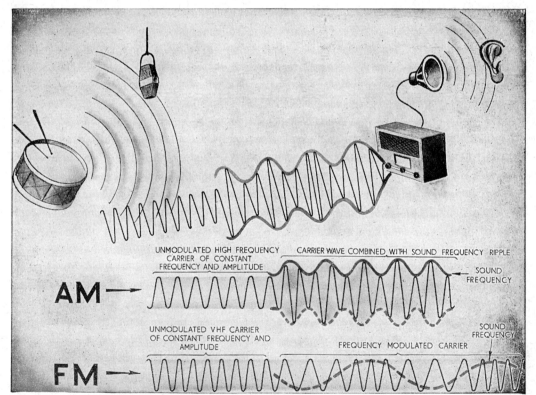

Sound waves picked up by a microphone are turned into an electrical current of sound frequency. The transmitter sends it out by high frequency carrier wave and this is picked up by the radio set and the sound frequency is transformed to the sound vibrations you hear.

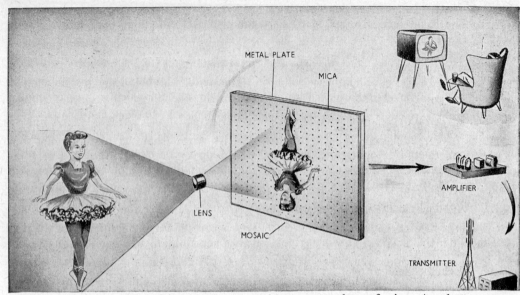

The studio scene is focused by the TV camera lens on to a sheet of mica. An electron gun transforms the picture into electrical impulses and these are transmitted, picked up by your TV set and converted back into a picture by the cathode ray tube.

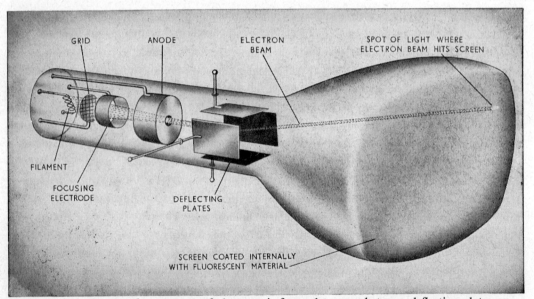

In the cathode ray tube a stream of electrons is focused to pass between deflecting plates or a deflecting coil. By varying continuously the charge in each plate, the direction of the beam can be changed, so that it builds up the picture on the fluorescent screen.

there are so many broadcasting stations throughout the world that it is difficult to separate their programmes. Half-way through your favourite play, the dialogue might suddenly be drowned by a brass band concert from another station in France or Germany.

The frequency on which the "intruder" broadcasts might be so close to that of the B.B.C. station to which you are listening that even the most careful tuning will not get rid entirely of the unwanted noise.

Frequencies are controlled by international

A wide angle view of the Centre Court during Wimbledon 1968 while this great sporting event was being televised in colour by the B.B.C.

agreement to eliminate interference as much as possible: but the band of available AM frequencies is so narrow that some overlapping cannot be avoided. For that reason, the B.B.C. is now transmitting programmes on an entirely new broadcasting system known as frequency modulation (FM), and in due course sufficient new transmitters will be built to cover the whole of Great Britain.

FM transmission cannot be picked up on ordinary AM wireless sets: nor can it usually be received satisfactorily over long distances. But these are small disadvantages compared with the total elimination of interference—even that caused by storms and your neighbour's vacuum cleaner—and the fact that the quality of sound reproduction is very much improved.

HOW THE FREQUENCY MODULATION SYSTEM WORKS

In the FM system, the "carrier" is still a high frequency (actually a very high frequency, VHF) radio wave of constant strength or amplitude. For those who like figures, these VHF waves have a frequency of around one hundred million vibrations per second, compared with about one or two million in an AM system; or wavelengths of only two or three metres, instead of a few hundred metres. But the sound frequency part of the signal is applied not as a ripple which varies the amplitude of the carrier, but as a kind of "shudder" which varies the frequency of the carrier wave. In other words, it causes the carrier frequency to wobble above and below its normal level. The number of wobbles per second varies with the tone of the sound waves picked up by the microphone: the amount of the wobble corresponds with the loudness of the sound.

The main difference inside a receiver designed for FM programmes is that its valves have to get rid of any AM signals picked up by the aerial and convert the incoming FM

Transistors are tiny devices used to replace larger valves in radio and television sets. Twelve of them will fit into a thimble.

signal into an AM one, as well as separating the sound from the carrier frequency.

THE TRANSMISSION OF PICTURES

Now, what about television? You would expect this to be a rather more complicated business than ordinary sound radio, and it is, because the signal sent out by the transmitter has to tell the cathode ray tube in your TV set not only the shape of all the people and objects in the picture, but also their colour in black, white and all the intermediate shades of grey.

It cannot do all this at once, any more than you can read all the words on this page in one glance. Instead it builds up the picture in horizontal lines, from left to right, just as you read these words. The quality of the picture varies according to the number of lines of which it is made up. The more lines, the better the picture. The B.B.C. uses 405 lines and 625 lines, and if you look closely at a large TV screen you can often see them.

In addition, each line is made up of a large number of spots of light known as picture elements and which correspond to the individual letters in a line of type. The light value (degree of darkness) of each of these spots is transmitted at high speed by the cathode ray tube, from left to right and line by line, to build up a picture on your screen at home. Each spot appears on the screen for only a tiny fraction of a second before being replaced by the next one so that, in fact, you never see a complete picture. But as the picture is repeated 25 times a second it gives the effect of a complete continuous picture, just as a cinema film does.

THE TELEVISION CAMERA

The television camera works like a cathode ray tube, in reverse. Instead of the film you use in your camera, it has a sheet of mica coated with a special chemical. When a scene is focused on this sheet by the camera lens, a kind of electrical picture is built up. Those parts corresponding to the lighter parts of the picture carry a large electrical charge: the dark parts carry practically no charge. A device called an electron gun, which is part of the camera, neutralises these charges, spot by spot and line by line. As each is neutralised, a small electric impulse flows from a metal plate at the back of the mica sheet, and this is amplified and used to modulate a radio-wave " carrier," as in sound broadcasting.

It is this signal which is picked up by your TV aerial, separated from the carrier, amplified and passed on to the cathode ray tube, which does the rest.

IMPROVEMENTS MAKE FURTHER ADVANCE POSSIBLE

None of it is quite as simple as it sounds in this very brief description, and new inventions are continually changing and improving both wireless and TV techniques. Tiny devices called transistors, just over half an inch long and a quarter of an inch in diameter, have almost completely replaced the much larger valves. " Printed circuits," consisting of fine metallic lines printed on to plastic sheets, can be used instead of some complicated wire circuits. Both have made possible much smaller, simpler radio and TV sets.

Radio and television are no longer just inventions which bring entertainment into our homes, but the key to efficiency in an endless number of jobs from calling the flying doctor in the Australian " bush " to landing airliners automatically in bad weather and enabling one man to supervise the operation of a dozen machine tools at once from an armchair.

Looking to the future, it may not be many years before TV cameras aboard pilotless space rockets bring us our first exciting close-ups of the distant planets, as they have already of the surface of the Moon.

THE MARVELS OF YOUR BODY

IF SOMEONE threw a handful of sand in your face, you would shut your eyes in an instant to keep it out. You don't have to stop to think. In fact, you can't help closing your eyes. The mere sight of something coming at your face makes you blink automatically. What actually happens is that a danger signal flashes along the optic nerve with which you see, but before that message reaches the part of the brain you see with, it has triggered off a message down other nerves to the muscles that cause a blink. This is known as a nervous reflex.

There are many other reflexes like this. For instance, if you meet a very appetising smell, your mouth waters, and if you could see inside your stomach you would see it become red and secrete gastric juice, in readiness for the coming meal. That is why it is such torment for a hungry person to see or smell good food he can't get. The reflex just makes him hungrier than ever.

The point about reflexes is that they are involuntary. You don't have to think about them, and it wouldn't make any difference if you *did* think about them.

The examples I have just given are born in all of us, but there are other reflexes we acquire by habit or training.

When a baby learns to walk it has to think about it a lot, to put each foot in the right place and try to keep its balance. But once you have learned to walk, it becomes automatic and you can think of other things while you are doing it. It is the same thing learning to ride a bicycle. For a few days it is very difficult, then suddenly the reflex comes, something seems to click, and you ride without any difficulty at all.

The same thing applies with swimming or learning to drive a car or play the piano. When you are learning such things, every movement has to be thought out slowly and separately, but once the proper sequence has been established in your brain it can be repeated indefinitely without giving it any attention at all. In fact, it works much better if it is left alone. Thinking about it and bothering whether you are doing it properly only makes you clumsy. And, of course, it is very difficult if you have learnt a thing badly to unlearn, and learn again the proper way, because you have to get rid of the automatic response you have made before you can start making another.

That is why anyone who teaches you anything at all, from algebra to skating, insists on your learning it a step at a time in the proper way. It seems a great bore at the time, but it pays in the long run.

HOW MANY SENSES HAVE YOU GOT?

In learning things, you use your senses. Many people will tell you there are five of them: sight, hearing, touch, taste and smell, and we often hear of someone who is said to have a " sixth sense," generally because other people can't quite understand how he does things.

The fact is we have a good many more than five. We have a sense of pain which warns us not to burn our fingers or try out our new knife on our own toes. We have a sense of balance that stops us falling over. We have a sense of pressure which tells us if we are walking on grass or on concrete, and if we have packed

John, aged nine months, in a continental play-pen, designed to teach a child to walk.

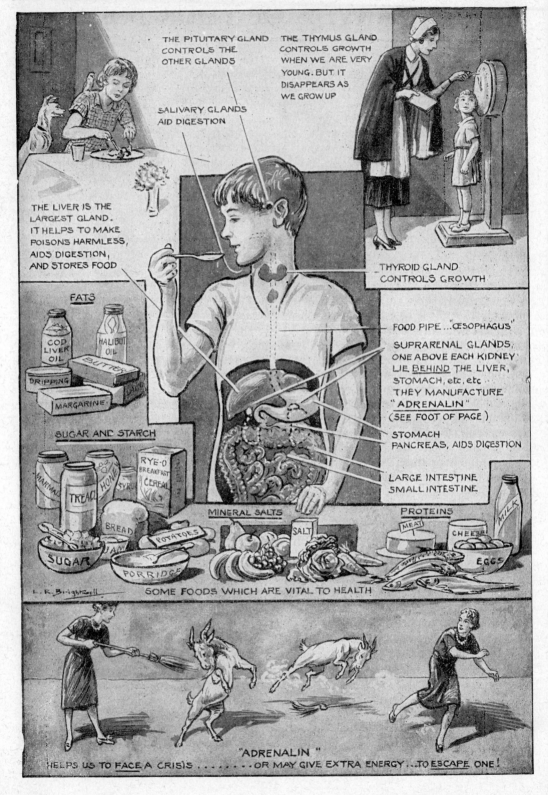

THE PITUITARY GLAND CONTROLS THE OTHER GLANDS

THE THYMUS GLAND CONTROLS GROWTH WHEN WE ARE VERY YOUNG. BUT IT DISAPPEARS AS WE GROW UP

SALIVARY GLANDS AID DIGESTION

THE LIVER IS THE LARGEST GLAND. IT HELPS TO MAKE POISONS HARMLESS, AIDS DIGESTION, AND STORES FOOD

THYROID GLAND CONTROLS GROWTH

FOOD PIPE ..."ŒSOPHAGUS"

SUPRARENAL GLANDS, ONE ABOVE EACH KIDNEY LIE BEHIND THE LIVER, STOMACH, etc., etc. THEY MANUFACTURE "ADRENALIN" (SEE FOOT OF PAGE)

STOMACH PANCREAS, AIDS DIGESTION

LARGE INTESTINE SMALL INTESTINE

FATS

COD LIVER OIL — HALIBUT OIL — BUTTER — DRIPPING — MARGARINE

SUGAR AND STARCH

MARMALADE — TREACLE — HONEY — SYRUP — RYE-O BREAKFAST CEREAL — BREAD — JAM — POTATOES — SUGAR — PORRIDGE

MINERAL SALTS

SALT

PROTEINS

MEAT — CHEESE — MILK — EGGS

L. R. Brightwell

SOME FOODS WHICH ARE VITAL TO HEALTH

"ADRENALIN" HELPS US TO FACE A CRISIS . . . . OR MAY GIVE EXTRA ENERGY . . . TO ESCAPE ONE!

too much in that rucksack. We have senses of heat and of cold, a sense of hunger and a sense of being too full, and many more. The man with the "sixth sense" is just a bit sharper at using his ordinary senses than other people.

All the sensations from our senses are telegraphed along nerves to our brains, and are sorted out there. They are actually conveyed by minute electric currents, and the result on the brain is to form a sort of electric pattern, perhaps rather like an illuminated advertisement sign.

We learn to recognise all these patterns as meaning different things, and unless the patterns just result in a reflex action like blinking, we decide what to do about it. We may do nothing, we may act at once, or we may wait and see. Waiting and seeing involves memory, which means that lots of patterns are stored up for future use. And generally we don't act just on the information received at the moment, but we combine that information with one or more memories before we decide.

For example, you are batting in a cricket match and a fast ball comes towards you. If it has never happened before, your reaction is probably to blink, or to duck. But because you have been taught to play, and have memories of this particular pattern, you bring memory in with what you see, do an action you have made automatic, and hit the ball for six. And all this happens in a fraction of a second.

LINES OF COMMUNICATION

The brain is connected with two sorts of nerves. These are sensory nerves, coming from the eyes, the ears, the skin and so on, which give it information, and motor nerves, going out to all the muscles and joints, telling them to hit a ball, give out a yell, or write out a hundred lines.

But besides this system of nerves we have another quite independent system called the automatic system. It is only loosely connected up with the brain, and its chief centres are called ganglia—one of the biggest, you have probably heard of, called the solar plexus, is situated behind the stomach.

This automatic system is connected up with all the internal organs. It sees that your heart keeps on beating, that you go on breathing, that food gets pushed along your intestines.

We have an automatic system of nerves which, in certain circumstances, produces reflex actions, making our hair stand on end, making us throw up an arm in self-defence, etc.

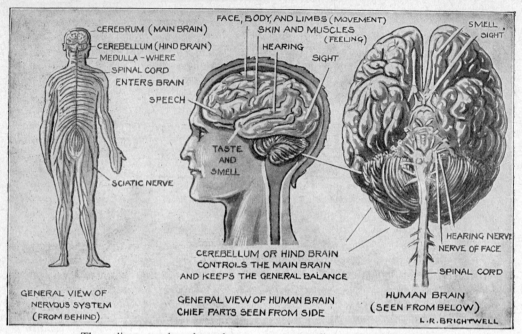

CEREBRUM (MAIN BRAIN)
CEREBELLUM (HIND BRAIN)
MEDULLA – WHERE
SPINAL CORD
ENTERS BRAIN
SPEECH
SCIATIC NERVE

FACE, BODY, AND LIMBS (MOVEMENT)
SKIN AND MUSCLES
(FEELING)
HEARING
SIGHT
TASTE
AND
SMELL

SMELL
SIGHT

HEARING NERVE
NERVE OF FACE
SPINAL CORD

CEREBELLUM OR HIND BRAIN
CONTROLS THE MAIN BRAIN
AND KEEPS THE GENERAL BALANCE

GENERAL VIEW OF
NERVOUS SYSTEM
(FROM BEHIND)

GENERAL VIEW OF HUMAN BRAIN
CHIEF PARTS SEEN FROM SIDE

HUMAN BRAIN
(SEEN FROM BELOW)
L·R·BRIGHTWELL

These diagrams show how the nervous system links up with the brain.

It requires no attention at all, and functions perfectly left alone to do its job. Some of its jobs, like the rate of the heart-beat, you cannot interfere with if you want to, but you can, of course, interfere with the rate of breathing and deliberately hold your breath or breathe faster. But you will find you can only do this for a short time, and then the automatic system takes over again and gets you back on to the right rate.

Although the automatic system is not influenced by deliberate thinking, it is influenced by our emotions. If you are frightened your heart beats faster, your mouth dries up, your stomach " stands still," you take deep breaths. If you are embarrassed you blush perhaps, and your hands sweat. If you are sad you turn pale and weep. The way such things happen is very complicated and wonderful. The centre for emotions is in part of the brain, rather low down and in the middle of your skull, and is connected by nerves with a small object called the pituitary gland, under the brain and just above the back of the nose.

HOW YOUR BODY SENDS URGENT MESSAGES

This gland is a miniature chemical laboratory, turning out about a score of different chemicals, which we call hormones, each with a different job to do. In various parts of the body are other " ductless " glands, as they are called, making more chemical hormones. These hormones are like messengers. If information is wanted very quickly, it goes by the nerves, just as an urgent message goes by telegram or telephone. But if there isn't all that hurry we put a letter in the post, and the body does the same—it pours out a hormone into the blood, and the hormone circulates round till it reaches the place where the message has to be delivered.

There is an important gland in the neck, just below the Adam's Apple, called the thyroid gland. There is another important one just above each kidney, called the suprarenal gland. There are various others, but they are all bossed by the pituitary, which sends along a chemical messenger to tell them how much of their own hormone to make. So, if you are frightened, the pituitary tells the suprarenal to pour out a hormone called adrenalin. Adrenalin makes the heart beat faster, dries up the mouth, makes the stomach stand still, and practically makes your hair stand on end. The purpose of all this is to concentrate all your energies in your muscles and make it easier to dash, either into action or away from it. Which you do, generally depends on training, and is the reason for having discipline in armies.

When you do dash, either away from a bull or towards the end of a hundred yards race, you feel your heart pounding as if it would burst. But of course it never does burst. Its function is to pump the blood round the body, and it does this much more vigorously than you might think. Even when a man is resting in bed, his heart is pumping about a gallon of blood each minute. During strenuous exertion this can go up to ten gallons a minute —the same blood, going round and round, first to the lungs, to collect oxygen from the air, then to the liver to collect food, and on to the brain and the muscles to give them the nourishment they want, and to take away waste as far as the kidneys, which get rid of it, and to take carbon dioxide to the lungs, which breathe it out.

When a man is resting, it takes about fifteen seconds for any drop of blood to go all the way round. During exercise it goes round much more quickly. The heart is, of course, a double pump—two pumps side by side. The one on the right pumps blood to the lungs; the more powerful one on the left pumps it up to the brain, to the finger tips, to the toes.

HOW BLOOD RUNS UPHILL

When the blood reaches its destination it goes through very tiny channels called capillaries, in which most of its speed and pressure

Due to the rarefied atmosphere, oxygen masks are necessary when flying at high altitudes.

are lost. From there it is gathered into veins to take it back to the heart. The original force of the heart-beat has all gone, so what sends it back? From the head it can run back downhill, but from the toes it has a three or four-foot climb. Partly it is sucked up by the movements of the chest in breathing. Partly it is pushed up by the movements of the muscles of the legs in walking and running.

So people who have to stand a long time, like soldiers on parade or shop assistants behind the counter, find their legs aching, because the blood is having a job to do its climb, with no push from below. It helps a lot if they learn to twiddle their toes, to bounce up and down a bit on the balls of their feet, and to contract and relax their leg muscles rhythmically. Occasional spells of deep breathing, by sucking more blood uphill, also relieve the ache.

The blood takes oxygen and food to the muscles, which " burn it up " not exactly like a fire, but on the same principle, creating heat —which is why you get warm when you run —and combining the oxygen and the carbon in the food into carbon dioxide gas. The faster you run, the hotter you get and the more carbon dioxide is formed.

Now there is a small part of the brain called the respiratory centre which controls the rate at which we breathe. Normally this is about fifteen times a minute. But this centre is very sensitive to carbon dioxide. When there is a lot of it in the blood, it stimulates this centre and makes the breathing faster, so as to get rid of this waste product, and you go on puffing and blowing till it is down to a normal amount again. This mechanism works so well that you can get rid of all the waste you form by exercise quite easily.

THE EFFECTS OF LACK OF OXYGEN

It is another matter if you don't get enough oxygen. At the top of Mount Everest, or in a plane in the stratosphere there is very little oxygen to breathe, and if a man was suddenly put there he would breathe more rapidly, but not rapidly enough to get all the oxygen he needed, and would very soon become unconscious. People who go to these heights find breathing very difficult, and usually resort to breathing pure oxygen through a mask. In a stratocruiser the cabin contains air under pressure to make breathing possible. A man who has been made unconscious in this way feels as if he had been knocked out, and when he comes round may look for the person who did it, and quite likely assault the friends who are trying to help him.

Partial lack of oxygen, due to flying too high without using an oxygen mask, has some very curious effects. A pilot may sing and shout, become quarrelsome and rude. He is quite sure he knows what he is doing, but in fact has lost his skill and judgment. The most awful things may happen to the aircraft but he won't worry at all. He has no idea of the flight of time, of the direction he is going, doesn't understand what is said to him on the radio, cannot read anything clearly, and is, of course, very likely to crash. Which is why such very great care is always taken over pilots' oxygen supply.

OUR CENTRAL-HEATING SYSTEM

As the burning-up of food together with the oxygen we breathe in produces heat, it might be expected that we would get hotter and hotter. To some extent, during very violent exertion, this does happen. Athletes after a three-mile race may have a temperature of 103, but they do not feel ill or uncomfortable as an invalid with such a temperature does, and, after resting, their temperatures soon return to normal.

During ordinary life our bodily temperatures are very steady, between ninety-seven and ninety-eight degrees Fahrenheit, usually a little higher in the evenings than in the mornings, and this result is achieved by a very delicate temperature regulating mechanism, rather like a thermostat on a central-heating system. Cold stimulates our muscles to greater heat production. Too much heat is lost by evaporation of perspiration from the skin, by radiation of heat from our bodies, and by the air we breathe out being hotter than the air we breathe in. If we are very hot, we sweat profusely. If we are very cold, we shiver, which puts our muscles into rapid exertion to get our temperatures up again.

This mechanism gets more perfect as we grow up. In very young babies it does not work very well, which is why their mothers have to be rather fussy about the amount of clothes they wear.

THE EYE IS LIKE A TELEVISION CAMERA

There are a good many mechanisms in the body which are very similar to the sort of mechanisms we meet in everyday life. The

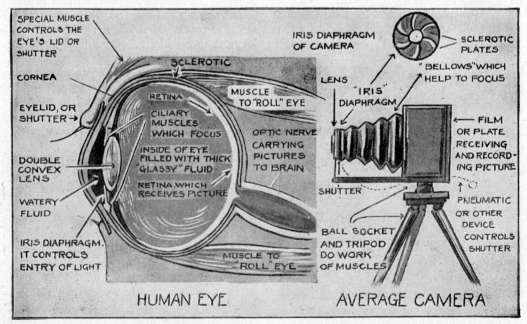

HUMAN EYE   AVERAGE CAMERA

The most wonderful 'camera' of all is the human eye which gives us instant pictures.

eye, for instance, is very like a television camera. There is a lens, to focus the picture, the pupil contracts and dilates according to the amount of light it is desirable to let in, just as the stops on a camera work; and whereas the television camera has an arrangement at the back to turn the picture into electrical impulses, so the eye has a retina, composed of thousands of nerve endings, which send impulses to the brain. On both the back of the TV camera and of the eye the picture is upside down, but this is rectified by the brain as speech or music, in the same way that we interpret the pattern of a number of piano keys being struck and recognise it as a tune.

Just beside this spiral tube in the ear is an organ which has nothing to do with hearing, but controls our balance. It is nothing more or less than three little spirit levels set at right angles to each other, like three sides of a brick meeting at one point. If we get out of the proper upright position in any of the three dimensions, the fluid in these little tubes moves,

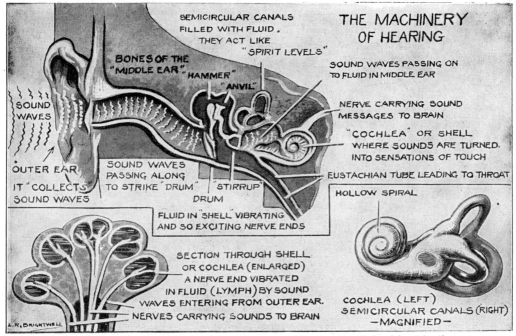

The ear is another miraculous organ, whose workings are explained in this diagram.

in transit. We see the picture on the TV screen right way up, and our brain gives us a similar corrected picture.

A PIANO KEYBOARD IN OUR EARS

Then, again, our ears can be compared to a piano keyboard. The sound waves hitting our eardrums make them vibrate. These vibrations are conveyed to a smaller drum which closes the end of a spiral tube, which gets narrower and narrower. Strung across the tube are fibres, each of which vibrates to a certain note and, when a fibre vibrates, it sends a nerve impulse to the brain. So the total pattern of these impulses is interpreted

sends a nerve impulse to the brain, and this tells our muscles to put us straight again.

When people suffer from giddiness, it is very often because something has gone wrong with this little balancing organ, and seasickness is partly due to our not being able to adjust ourselves quickly enough to the rapid messages of distress coming from it.

EVERY MUSCLE HAS AN OPPOSITE NUMBER

Every movement we make is an example of ordinary mechanical leverage. Our bones are jointed together, and the joints are bridged by muscles. Now a muscle is just a sort of

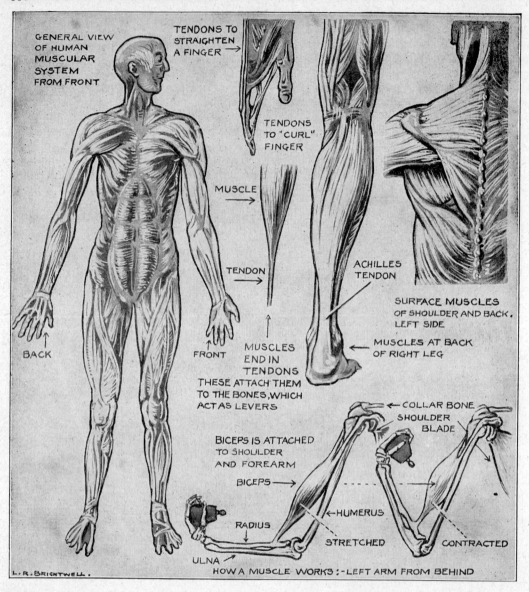

GENERAL VIEW OF HUMAN MUSCULAR SYSTEM FROM FRONT

TENDONS TO STRAIGHTEN A FINGER →

TENDONS TO "CURL" FINGER

MUSCLE →

TENDON →

ACHILLES TENDON

SURFACE MUSCLES OF SHOULDER AND BACK. LEFT SIDE

MUSCLES AT BACK OF RIGHT LEG ←

BACK

FRONT

MUSCLES END IN TENDONS THESE ATTACH THEM TO THE BONES, WHICH ACT AS LEVERS

← COLLAR BONE
SHOULDER BLADE

BICEPS IS ATTACHED TO SHOULDER AND FOREARM

BICEPS →

RADIUS

←HUMERUS

STRETCHED   CONTRACTED

ULNA →

L. R. BRIGHTWELL.   HOW A MUSCLE WORKS :- LEFT ARM FROM BEHIND

tissue which has the property of getting shorter and fatter, or longer and thinner. When it gets shorter and fatter, as you can see by contracting the biceps muscle in your arm, it pulls the two bones to which it is attached, together and, in the case of the biceps, you bend your elbow. Actually the elbow is rather a complicated joint, and you also use your biceps to turn the forearm palm upwards.

Every muscle has to have an opposite muscle to pull the bones back to where they were before, and of course it wouldn't do if both pulled at the same time. So the part of the brain that controls movement has to arrange things so that whenever a muscle contracts, its opposite number relaxes. Sometimes, when we are a bit stiff, or the weather is cold, one muscle starts to contract before the other is ready to relax. Then a muscle gets strained a bit and is very painful for a few days. The pain is mostly due to a little bleeding round the strain, and a little more exercise is the best way to encourage the circulation to get rid of this.

So, if you are stiff after a game of football, go and have another game!

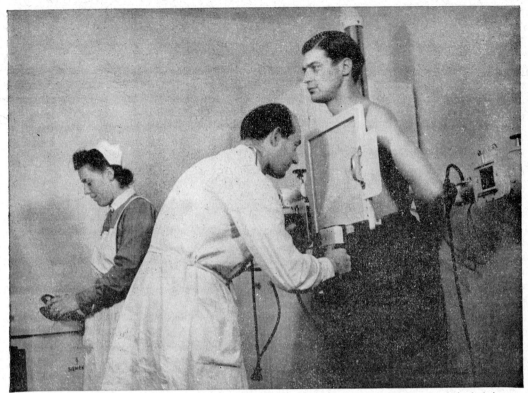

Mass X-ray units, which operate throughout the country, have done sterling work in helping to diagnose tuberculosis. If arrested in its early stages this disease can be completely cured.

RADIOGRAPHY
Diagnosis and Treatment by X-ray

THE diagnostic radiographer is the hand-maiden of the doctor in diagnosis. She takes, develops and prints the X-ray pictures which will help him to determine the nature of an illness or an injury. The therapeutic radiographer is the handmaiden of the doctor in the treatment of certain conditions by deep X-rays and the gamma rays of radium or other radio-active materials. Whilst both careers call for qualities of patience, firmness and kindness in dealing with people who are ill, the former will appeal to the girl who likes to see a quick result of her labours (the X-ray is either a good photograph or she has to take it again); the latter is for the girl who prefers more continuous contact with patients and is prepared to wait months to see the effect of her efforts in the form of improvement in the patient's condition. The radiologist is a qualified doctor who has taken a special course and specialises in the interpretation of X-ray photographs, for which, of course, a full knowledge of medicine is necessary. The radiotherapist is a doctor who similarly special-ises in the treatment of conditions by X-rays.

The radiographer must be interested in things mechanical, because she deals with instruments and their care, and if she is taking the diagnostic side she must be interested in things photographic, because she is producing a photograph of a special kind and about half her time will be spent in the dark room developing prints. But of course radio-graphers are not mechanics merely. The girl who takes up this career must like people and have an even temperament and a reassuring manner, because many patients feel apprehen-sive. She needs to be kind, considerate and businesslike (because she must be able to handle patients, get them to do what she tells them, and administer the department efficiently). She must also be a person who pays great attention to detail, for her own sake and that of her patients.

TRAINING FOR THE DIPLOMA

The course of training for the diploma of the Society of Radiographers in either diagnostic work (M.S.R. (R.)) or therapeutic (M.S.R. (T.)) takes two years. If the student wishes she can take both diplomas over a period of three years, but most prefer to specialise in one field or the other. The examination at the end of the first year is common to both courses, the subjects being general physics, apparatus construction and anatomy and physiology. Thereafter the radiographer has to pass a final examination in radiographic photography and technique and the radiotherapist one in radiation physics and radiotherapy technique. Students have to be at least 18 years of age before they can start their studies and they must be physically fit. A girl who has any form of allergy, such as hay fever, will probably be advised not to take up radiography because her skin is likely to be affected by the photographic chemicals. The minimum educational requirement is the General Certificate of Education with passes in four subjects, including mathematics, English and two science subjects. Training in diagnostic radiography may be taken in a large number of hospitals, where there may be only one or two students or a school. Training in radiotherapy is confined to centres which have the specialised equipment. A therapeutic radiographer, therefore, will probably spend her working life in large towns, whereas a diagnostic radiographer can choose whether she wants to work in a hospital in a country town or a city. Because it is often necessary to take an emergency X-ray in the night, X-ray departments are staffed on a shift basis.

SAFETY MEASURES

Radiographers work only 35 hours a week. This is a safety precaution. Risks from radiation are now negligible, although in the early days of X-rays, before the dangers were known, this was not so. Health control to-day is very strict. The X-ray tubes are encased in lead, to absorb any stray X-rays, continuous exposure to which, as opposed to the momentary exposure which the patient receives, would be dangerous. The radiographer carries in her pocket a film which records any radiation, and this is compared against a standard devised by the National Physical Laboratory, to make sure that the radiation absorbed is within safe limits. Blood counts and hæmoglobin estimates are also routine.

INCREASING USE OF X-RAYS

There is no shortage of posts for the trained radiographer. Increasing use is being made of X-rays in diagnosis, and atomic physics has brought new scope to radiotherapy.

The radiographer has to take X-rays of people who have had accidents—perhaps a road casualty, to see just what is broken; or a child who has swallowed a fishbone or broken a leg. When the orthopædic surgeon is operating, the radiographer goes into the theatre and takes X-rays during the operation. The brain surgeon relies on her to give him a picture which will assist him in operating; the X-ray may reveal a tumour on the brain or perhaps a pressure by a bone on the spinal cord, both of which give rise to neurological symptoms.

X-rays have moved a very long way since Roentgen discovered in 1895 that with his " new ray " he could see the bones beneath the skin. A doctor can inject an opaque dye into a vein which in a moment will reach the kidney. The radiographer then takes a photograph in which that organ is outlined. A " meal " of barium makes the stomach and intestines clearly visible in the same way. Nowadays it is even possible to pass a tiny plastic tube through a vein into the heart itself and by this means X-rays can investigate the auricles and ventricles of the heart. When radium treatment is being given, the paths of the diagnostic radiographer and the therapeutic radiographer come together, for whilst the latter is assisting with the treatment, the former takes X-ray photographs to check the distribution of the radium needles. X-rays have their place, too, in research and in industry.

WHERE RADIOGRAPHERS WORK

The majority of radiographers are employed in hospitals. A small hospital will have only

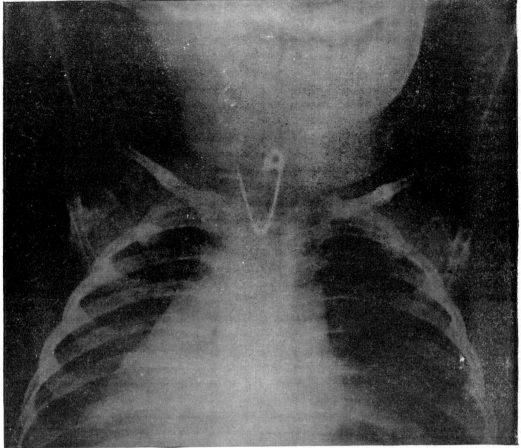

This photograph of an X-ray plate shows an open safety-pin, which a child has swallowed, lodged in his bronchial tube. Fortunately it was possible to remove the safety-pin in hospital.

one or two, a large hospital a number. Radiographers are also employed by local authorities. By means of mass miniature radiography, which can be carried out in factory or town hall, a large number of people can have X-rays taken of their chests cheaply and quickly. Only if the miniature film shows an abnormality is a full plate X-ray taken.

TREATMENT OF DISEASE

Therapeutic radiographers treat disease by the application of X-rays and radiations from radio-active substances such as radium (which was discovered, about the same time as X-rays, by a woman, Mme Curie, and her husband). Most patients are treated as out-patients, attending daily for periods of four or six weeks. During this time the radiographer gets to know them intimately and has to encourage them. The atomic age has brought the Geiger counter into hospital. Radio-active iodine is absorbed by the thyroid and the therapeutic radiographer, using the Geiger counter, can find for the surgeon just what part of the thyroid is not functioning properly. She also operates the powerful X-ray machines which are used in the treatment of deep growths, for instance an apparatus known as a linear accelerator, which produces special, very short X-rays. She puts her patient in position, making sure that he is comfortable, and then operates the machine by remote control, watching her patient through leaded glass windows, rather like a television producer in his control gallery. The products of atomic piles are being used more and more in radio therapy departments.

Radiography offers a satisfying and attractive career for those who like both mechanical things and people.

CABLE LAYING SHIP

LAYING A SUBMARINE CABLE IS A VERY DIFFICULT JOB. SPECIALLY BUILT & EQUIPPED SHIPS ARE EMPLOYED HAVING HUGE CYLINDRICAL TANKS IN WHICH THE CABLE, COILED ON A STEEL CONE, IS KEPT UNDER WATER TO ENSURE AN EVEN TEMPERATURE.

THE CABLE IS 'PAID OUT' FROM THE STORAGE TANKS BY WINCHES AS THE SHIP TRAVELS ASTERN TO AVOID FOULING THE PROPELLERS

CABLE LAYING SHIPS

CABLE laying ships are seldom in the news, because the work they do, although vital to world communications and trade, lacks the glamour of carrying film stars across the Atlantic, or the adventurous appeal of a fighting ship. Yet there is excitement and interest in plenty aboard these vessels.

Their appearance is distinctive, combining the trim smartness of a warship with the graceful lines of a luxury steam yacht. The main clue to their job is given by the row of sheaves at the bows and stern, over which the cable runs. In addition, the vessels operated by the British Post Office fly an unusual flag, consisting of a Blue Ensign bearing a crest which depicts old Father Time regarding with astonishment his hour-glass, which has been shattered by an electric spark. Early proof of this time-shattering ability of the cable service was given at the opening of the Empire Exhibition in 1924, when King George V was handed a telegram that had been sent 31,560 miles around the world in 80 seconds.

Typical of the ships that make this possible is Her Majesty's Telegraph Ship *Monarch*, which made history on 26th September, 1955, by completing the laying of the first telephone cable from the United Kingdom across the Atlantic. Previously, only lighter tele*graph* cables had been laid over such long distances, and transatlantic conversations had to be made by radio-telephone, which is affected by bad weather.

Only the *Monarch* could do the job, as no other ship in the world at that time was able to carry the 1,725 miles of cable which she laid in one length across the deepest part of the Atlantic. Even this 8,056 ton, 480 ft. long vessel had to be modified because, in addition to 5,000 tons of cable, she had to store and lay special repeaters, which were built into the cable at distances of 43 miles. These boost the signals sent through the cable, so that speech can be heard clearly at the far end. They are up to 40ft. long and 2·8 in. in diameter, and contain valves and gold-plated components designed to last 20 years without failure even at depths of $2\frac{1}{2}$ miles, where the water pressure is as much as 3 tons on every square inch.

In the *Monarch*, cables are usually laid over the stern, and the bow sheaves are used for cable repair work. But in other ships the cable is laid over the bows as shown in the drawing opposite. It is coiled in large below-deck tanks, from which it is led over pulleys to the sheaves, with a dynamometer somewhere between the pulleys to measure the strain on the cable. Obviously, this must not be too great, or even the immensely-strong $1\frac{1}{4}$ in. diameter telephone cable might snap.

This is a case where echo-sounding equipment comes in useful, because the ship's master can use it to obtain an accurate picture of the sea-bed as he pays out his cable. In this way, he can avoid strain on the cable by allowing sufficient slack for it to lie on the bottom of the under-water " valleys " and not be suspended from peak to peak.

Not all the problems concern the actual cable-laying. A ship like the *Monarch*, with a crew of 130, might remain at sea for anything up to 100 days without refuelling or entering port. As a result, she has to be fitted to carry large stocks of fuel, stores and fresh water. Then again, she differs from other vessels in that she gradually loses her cargo of 5,000 tons of cable, 2,000 tons of fuel and 1,000 tons of water *en route*: so special arrangements have to be made for her to take on water ballast, or she might become top-heavy.

Nor are such ships concerned only with cable laying. Submarine cables sometimes develop faults and are often damaged in shallow water by shipping. Then the cable ship has to go to the estimated position of the cable and fish for it with grapnels. After it has been hoisted on board, tests are made to discover in which direction the fault lies. Then the cable is cut and one end attached to a buoy. The vessel steams along pulling in the other end until the fault is found. A new piece of cable is then spliced on and the joint thoroughly inspected by X-rays, after which the ship steams back to the good end and joins the two together.

Radar is used to help to locate the buoys, particularly in bad weather, and faults caused by the cable rubbing on a rock or some other obstruction, thousands of feet under the sea, can be speedily found and repaired in the immense, featureless ocean.

A TYPE OF HYDRAULIC HELICOPTER WINCH

RESCUING A MAN FROM THE SEA.
THE HELICOPTER IS FLOWN OVER THE SURVIVOR AND HOVERS AT A HEIGHT OF APPROXIMATELY 25 TO 30 FT. THE CREWMAN LOWERS THE RESCUE STROP WHICH THE MAN IN THE WATER FASTENS ROUND HIS BODY.

THE DOWN-WASH FROM THE ROTOR (WHEN DIRECTLY ABOVE A SURVIVOR FLOATING IN A LIGHT AIRCRAFT DINGHY) MAY BLOW THE DINGHY ABOUT. IT IS ADVISABLE FOR THE MAN TO GET INTO THE WATER WHERE HE CAN MORE EASILY BE PICKED UP.

GROMMET FOR SECURING STROP AND PREVENTING POSSIBILITY OF MAN FALLING OUT.
STROP.

RESCUE DIRECT FROM A WRECK.
WHEN RESCUING MEN DIRECTLY FROM A WRECK IT IS IMPORTANT TO LOWER THE STROP SO IT IS CLEAR OF ENTANGLEMENT AND HOIST THE MEN WITHOUT THE DANGER OF STRIKING ANY OF THE SHIP'S GEAR.

CREWMAN IN THE SEA RESCUING AN UNCONSCIOUS MAN FLOATING ON THE SURFACE.

TELEPHONE WIRE BETWEEN CREWMAN AND PILOT.

HAULING CABLE OPERATED BY PILOT.

AIR-CREWMAN'S WATERTIGHT IMMERSION SUIT.

HOOD.
WATERTIGHT NECK JOINT.
ROLLED WATERTIGHT BODY JOINT.
WRIST WATERTIGHT JOINT.
GLOVE POCKET.
BOOT WATERTIGHT JOINT.
GUM BOOT.

A system of co-operation between the R.N.L.I. and a number of helicopter stations has been arranged in order to facilitate, where possible, rescues from the sea and from shipwrecks. At the helicopter stations shown on the map (top right) there are always rescue crews on watch and ready to answer any emergency call. The crew consists of a pilot and crewman, and the latter wears an immersion suit, rubber-lined and completely water-tight in order that he can, if necessary, be lowered from the

Drawing reproduced by courtesy

SEARCH AND RESCUE HELICOPTERS FREQUENTLY CO-OPERATE WITH LIFEBOAT CREWS IN DIRECTING THE BOAT TO A WRECK THAT MAY BE INVISIBLE TO THE LIFEBOATMEN IN THE MURKY DARKNESS OF A WINTER'S GALE.

HELICOPTER USING HER SIGNAL LAMP.

HELICOPTER SEARCH AND RESCUE STATIONS.

LOSSIEMOUTH
PRESTWICK
EGLINTON
THORNABY
BRAWDY
FORD
GOSPORT
CULDROSE

○ EXISTING HELICOPTER SEARCH AND RESCUE STATIONS.

○ IT IS SUGGESTED NEW STATIONS SHOULD BE ESTABLISHED ROUND OUR COASTS AT FAIRLY REGULAR INTERVALS.

WRECKAGE RECOVERY.
IT IS FREQUENTLY NECESSARY TO RECOVER WRECKAGE FOR IDENTIFICATION PURPOSES.

IF A SHIP IS ASHORE ON A ROCKY COAST, AND IF THE USE OF THE USUAL ROCKET APPARATUS IS IMPRACTICABLE OR THE HELICOPTER FINDS ITS HOIST MAY FOUL RIGGING AND SO PREVENT PICKING UP SURVIVORS DIRECT FROM THE SHIP, THEN THE HELICOPTER MIGHT BE USED TO CARRY A LIGHT LINE ASHORE SO THAT THE HEAVIER BREECHES BUOY CAN BE HAULED OUT TO THE WRECK.

HELICOPTER PAYING OUT A LIGHT LINE FROM SHIP TO SHORE.

THE FORD STRETCHER.
STRETCHER STOWED WITH SIDES LOWERED.
TUBE FRAME.
STRETCHER IN USE.

THE NEW TYPE RESCUE "SCOOP" ABOUT TO PICK UP A MAN, FLOATING ON THE SURFACE.

ROYAL NAVY

HELICOPTER LIFTING AN URGENT SURGICAL CASE FROM A DESTROYER BY MEANS OF THE FORD STRETCHER.

6 FT. DROGUE LINE.
FRAME.
NET.
DROGUE
FRAME.
WIDTH OF MOUTH OF NET 9 FT.

helicopter into the water to assist the man being rescued. When the wreck, or survivor, is sighted the helicopter is flown directly overhead and the rescue strop is lowered. The man to be rescued fits it over his body and is hauled up into the helicopter. The Royal Navy has also developed a scoop for rescue from the sea and a stretcher with high canvas sides for urgent surgical cases being removed from a ship. More helicopter stations are needed to ensure speed of rescue for these craft are slow-movers.

The U.S.S. *Nautilus*, the first submarine to be powered by an atomic power plant. She also has diesel engines and batteries for use in emergencies.

THE ATOMIC SUBMARINE

The Marine Engine of the Future

WHEN the keel of the world's first atomic submarine, the U.S.S. *Nautilus*, was laid in the Groton, Connecticut, yard of the Electric Boat Division of General Dynamics Corporation on 14th June, 1952, President Truman declared: "This vessel is the forerunner of atomic-powered merchant ships and aeroplanes, of atomic power-plants producing electricity for factories, farms and houses. The day that the propellers of this new submarine first bite into the water and drive her forward will be the most momentous in the field of atomic science since that first flash of light down in the desert seven years ago."

At the time, there were many experts who doubted whether an atomic power-plant, with all the necessary shielding to protect the crew from radioactivity, could be packed into the limited space inside even a very large submarine. The *Nautilus* removed all those doubts.

She was launched on 21st January, 1954, by Mrs. Eisenhower, wife of Mr. Truman's successor as President of the United States. Just under one year later, on 17th January, 1955, the historic message "Under way on nuclear power" was flashed ashore by her radio.

In the twelve months that followed, the *Nautilus* made 365 dives and travelled more than 26,000 nautical miles during 75 cruises, without refuelling. Over half of that distance was sailed underwater and, on one occasion, she went for 3 days, 12 hours, without coming to the surface, averaging around $18\frac{1}{2}$ knots during that time. This speed was faster than any other submarine had averaged on a *surface* voyage of similar length and exceeded any underwater speed ever recorded for even one hour.

Before she was refuelled with a new core of enriched uranium in the spring of 1957, she had sailed more than 60,000 miles without refuelling. Such a performance has opened up entirely new possibilities for submarine warfare. In World War II, many submarine commanders were unable to press home an attack on a target because they lacked the speed or endurance to do so. Often, they had to lie quiet and still on the sea-bed, lest the noise of their engines gave away their position to enemy anti-submarine forces on the surface. And, all

The second atomic submarine to be built was the *Sea Wolf*, seen here during the commissioning ceremonies at Groton, Connecticut. The large size of the vessel can be appreciated.

the time, they were faced with the necessity of surfacing regularly to renew their air supply and to recharge the batteries that supplied power for underwater sailing.

THE ADVANTAGES OF
THE " NAUTILUS "

The commander of the *Nautilus* has fewer problems. His ship is fast enough to engage almost any surface craft and there is no fear of running out of fuel. It cannot evade Asdic, which detects the presence of a submarine by producing " echoes " off the metal hull; but the quietness of its engines and its ability to dive to at least 700 feet make it elusive and it does not need to surface frequently in dangerous waters.

Apparently, also, its atomic power-plant takes up much less room than many people expected. A U.S. senator who made a voyage in the submarine has said that he walked from one end to the other of its 300 feet length, which means that there is room for passages around or above the shielding. Yet it even has diesel engines and batteries of the type that form the main propulsion machinery on conventional submarines, for use in emergencies or if the crew want to shut down the nuclear reactor for maintenance.

THE ATOMIC POWER-PLANT

Little has been published about the atomic power-plant, which was supplied by the Atomic Energy Commission. But it is known that the heat generated in the reactor by controlled nuclear fission of uranium 235 is carried off by the heavy water that is used to cool the reactor. The heavy water is then pumped into a heat exchanger (or boiler) where its heat is used to turn large quantities of distilled water into steam.

This steam is led off through pipes to drive

This cut-away diagram of the *Nautilus* shows the lay-out of the submarine. The atomic power plant shown just aft of the submarine's conning tower, is heavily shielded to protect the crew from radio-activity, which makes for weight and bulk, but the core of uranium 235, which is the fuel, is it-self very small. On one supply of this fuel *Nautilus* was able to sail more than 60,000 miles.

1. The atomic or nuclear reactor which contains tubes of uranium 235. This is fuel which generates enormous heat.

2. The return pipe from the condensers for distilled water. The distilled water is immediatley turned into steam by the heat carried by the heavy water.

3. Heat exchanger.

4. Steam supply to turbines.

5. Diesel exhaust and muffler.

6. After access hatch.

7. Condensers, where exhaust steam is condensed back into distilled water, and the distilled water is then pumped back to the heat exchanger.

8. After escape hatch.

9. After crew's quarters.

10. Rudder.

the main propulsion turbines, which are geared to the propeller shafts in the normal way; after which the steam is turned back into water in condensers and led back to the heat exchanger to start the whole process over again.

CONDITIONS ON BOARD

In most other respects the *Nautilus* is like any modern submarine, with the usual " Snort " fresh air intake and exhaust, so that she can renew her air supply whilst cruising just below the surface, air-conditioning equipment, escape hatches and radar control-room in which targets can be detected while the vessel is submerged to periscope depth.

With a weight of 3,180 tons she is, however, extremely large for a submarine and heavier than even the great " Daring " class destroyers of the Royal Navy. This is just as well, because when a crew has to remain underwater for days on end, seeing and hearing nothing of the outside world, and with only entries in the ship's log to show if there is solid pack-ice or a tropical sun overhead, life can become very irksome in cramped quarters.

Even in the *Nautilus*, the crew of 101 officers and men must live, eat and sleep with machinery, armament, hustle and bustle all around them. But there is room for tables for games that do not require too much space, a library, small film projector and gramophones

Although this is a warship, designed and constructed as such, it can be regarded as the forerunner of things to come, for it has already been suggested that by the year 2000 the Merchant Navy might consist almost solely of under-surface craft, able to produce speeds of up to 50 or 60 knots, and perhaps even directed by a single shore-based operator, who would control their crewless journeys.

11. Stern diving plane.
12. Rudder.
13. Propeller.
14. Snort fresh air intake and exhaust.
15. Radar and radio aerials.
16. Twin periscopes.
17. Surface navigating bridge.
18. Main ballast tanks and periscope well.

19. Captain's stateroom.
20. Batteries.
21. Forward access hatch.
22. Officers' wardroom.
23. Crew's mess and galley.
24. Stores.
25. Torpedoes.
26. Torpedo tubes.

with a large stock of the latest records. And the food is unusually good, even though the meat is pre-cut, the eggs frozen or powdered and the milk canned to save precious space.

THE ROLE OF ATOMIC SUBMARINES

The *Nautilus* was the forerunner of a great fleet of atomic submarines for the U.S. Navy. Basically similar to the *Nautilus*, these submarines incorporate a 130-ft. long box-like armament compartment aft of the conning-tower, or "sail" as it is known on these new sea giants. The first five of these submarines belong to the *George Washington* class, and are about 390 ft. long and have a surface displacement of about 5,400 tons. The second

batch, incorporating improvements, are of the *Ethan Allen* class, which are 410 ft. long and displace 6,900 tons. The latest submarines, incorporating further improvements, belong to the *Lafayette* class. Biggest of all, these are about 425 ft. long and displace over 7,000 tons.

All three classes are driven by steam turbines powered by water-cooled nuclear reactors. Each submarine has a 300-ton or greater, capacity, an air conditioning plant, and is also equipped with air scrubbers and precipitators to remove irritants from the air and maintain the proper balance of oxygen, nitrogen and other atmospheric elements. Electrolytic generators permit the submarines to manufacture their own oxygen from sea-water.

All these operational atomic submarines are armed with sixteen deadly Polaris missiles, each carrying a nuclear warhead with a destructive power equal to 500,000 tons of conventional high explosives. When it is realised that the atomic bombs which devastated the Japanese cities of Hiroshima and Nagasaki had a power equal to 20,000 tons, the tremendous power of these atomic submarines can be appreciated.

The first of these FBM—Fleet Ballistic Missile—submarines to deploy on operational patrol was the U.S.S. *George Washington*. She left Charleston, South Carolina, with a full load of 16 missiles on 15th November, 1960.

ROCKETS FROM THE SEA

What makes these submarines even more deadly is that they can fire their rockets, which have a range of up to 3,000 miles, while they are submerged. Nearly three-quarters of the surface of the earth is covered with water and any part of this immense area is a potential hiding-place for one of the submarines. When a submarine is out on patrol, each of its missiles is assigned to a particular target and its built-in guidance system "tuned" accordingly. As the submarine travels, information regarding its changes of position is fed into the guidance system automatically by the submarine's SINS—Ship's Inertial Navigation System—installation, so that the missile remains continually aimed at its specific target. Because of the vital importance of knowing the exact position of a submarine at all times, each ship has three SINS, each checking on the other.

America plans to build about forty of these missile-carrying atomic-powered submarines,

U.S.S. nuclear-powered submarine *Lafayette*. The hatches for the sixteen deadly Polaris missiles can be seen in the flat decking aft of the "sail".

and a number are being built for the Royal Navy. These, like their U.S. counterparts, will also be armed with 16 missiles.

DEVELOPMENTS

Although America has concentrated on military submarines so far, some American experts consider that there may be a big future for atomic-powered underwater merchant craft. The merchant marine of the year 2000 could be under-surface craft with speeds of 50 or 60 knots. An entire fleet of ships could be directed at sea by a single operator in a radio control tower ashore.

President Truman's historic forecast of peaceful developments has, in fact, already come true up to a point. Russia has had at least one atomic-powered ice-breaking craft in service for some time, and America herself built the world's first nuclear-powered cargo-passenger ship. This is the 22,000-ton N.S. (Nuclear Ship) *Savannah*, which is leading the way for other nuclear merchant vessels which will prove to be economically competitive with those powered by conventional means.

The N.S. *Savannah*, the world's first nuclear-powered merchant vessel, passing under the Verrazano-Narrows Bridge, New York.

SUPER VC 10. This superb British airliner can carry up to 180 passengers. The mounting of the engines at the rear of the fuselage results in an exceptionally quiet cabin.

Conquest of the Air

WINGS TO LIFT A WORLD

The dream of the Wright Brothers was to build a power-driven aeroplane, and to fly it successfully. From that dream have come wings to lift a world. . . .

OVER two hundred million passengers go by air each year. Some of them are travelling on business, but the great majority are ordinary people travelling for speed or pleasure. To understand this remarkable growth of civil aviation we must return to the war period when enemy U-boats at sea and the presence of enemy troops on land menaced established lines of communication. Alternative routes were essential, and to sustain the Allied fighting forces, new air links were forged across the centre of Africa, across the 3,000-mile gap between Australia and Ceylon and across great expanses of the broad Pacific. Atlantic flying, an exciting event before the war, became regular and commonplace.

Over these routes and many others flew Dakotas, Skymasters and Constellations designed originally as airliners, but developed as troop transports. Of importance in our story of the post-war expansion of civil aviation is the fact that before the war nearly all airports were grass-surfaced and seldom exceeded 3,000 ft. in length. But to enable these wartime troop transports and the even heavier bombers to operate effectively against the enemy, a world-wide network of vast airfields with concrete runways was built. The cost of these would have been regarded as prohibitive in peace-time and their existence at the end of the war had a marked influence on the development of air travel.

First, they virtually sealed the fate of flying-boats in spite of the fact that before the war this type of aircraft had given Britain an outstanding lead in air travel. Britain's national overseas airline, B.O.A.C., could not afford to maintain marine bases throughout the world, used only by themselves, while their competitors paid relatively small fees at the heavily-subsidised land airports. Flying-boats may become popular again when atomic engines suitable for powering aircraft become available, but America and Russia are the only countries that have continued active development of water-based aircraft since the end of the war, and these have all been for military duties.

Secondly, the existence of the war-time airfields, combined with the fact that the Dakotas, Skymasters and "Connies" were easily convertible for passenger and freight carrying, led to a boom in civil aviation—a boom which within fifteen years saw over *one hundred million* people a year using aircraft as a speedy and comfortable means of going about their business and pleasure.

On the long-range trunk routes of the world, the Americans had it all their own way with most of the passengers being carried in Constellations and Skymasters. One of the most comfortable long-range airliners was the rather dumpy-looking 340-m.p.h. Stratocruiser. This American supremacy in big airliners was due in part to a war-time agreement under which

the United States built all the transport aircraft needed by the Allies, leaving Britain free to concentrate on fighters and bombers.

At the end of the war Britain produced the Avro Tudor and Handley Page Hermes, but it soon became evident that the American lead in piston-engined aircraft was too great for effective competition in this field.

Accordingly, Britain put her faith in the jet-engine experience she had gained during the war, and in 1948 produced the medium-range turbo-prop Vickers Viscount, followed in 1949 by the even more revolutionary de Havilland Comet, first jet airliner in the world, with a cruising speed of 450 m.p.h.

Air travellers quickly appreciated the smooth flying which these aircraft introduced, and also the welcome reduction in journey times. The Viscount turned out to be a best-seller, and over 430 were sold to capture for Britain some of the best air routes all over the world. Particularly important was the big order for 60 aircraft by an American airline—this was the first time a British airliner had been used in the United States.

Britain followed up the Viscount with the Britannia, and later the Vanguard, but these

TRIDENT. First of the second generation of jet airliners, the Hawker Siddeley 121 can carry 100 passengers economically over short ranges. It is designed, ultimately, to be able to make fully-automatic landings.

BOEING 707 PROTOTYPE. From this prototype has evolved the fine 707 Stratoliner airliners now flying on the air routes of the world.

came too late to compete against the pure-jet airliners of the type pioneered by the historic Comet I.

From this early version has developed the much improved Comet 4, more than 70 of which are in service all over the world. This beautiful airliner is powered by four Rolls-Royce Avon turbo-jets, and can carry nearly 100 passengers at 500 m.p.h. for 3,000 miles. The Comet 4 inaugurated the first Trans-atlantic air service in 1958, but unfortunately its range is not sufficient to enable it to fly from Britain to New York against the strong head-winds experienced during the winter months.

Thus, the bigger, longer range American Boeing 707 and Douglas DC-8s took over on this route. Several variants of the Boeing 707 are produced and those used over the Atlantic, known as Intercontinentals, can carry up to 189 passengers. The 707 has proved itself one of the world's great aeroplanes and Britain can be proud of the fact that some operators

CHANNEL CAR FERRY SERVICE. Whilst waiting for your aircraft you can have a drink in the sun and watch cars being loaded and unloaded from the Bristol Freighters.

which started the current fashion of mounting the engines at the rear of the fuselage. This makes the cabin quieter and leaves the wing free and uncluttered to do its primary job of producing lift. The Caravelle has been followed into service by the British Hawker Siddeley Trident and the BAC One-Eleven and their American rivals, the Boeing 727 and Douglas DC-9. The Trident and Boeing 727 are three-engined airliners, the third engine being mounted in the tail of the fuselage and fed with air from a large intake built into the base of the fin. The BAC One-Eleven and DC-9 are twin-engined airliners, able to accommodate up to 79 and 83 passengers respectively.

Rapid strides in the development of air travel have also been made in Russia, which now has a range of modern aircraft suitable for almost any job. The biggest airliner in the world is the 397,000 lb. 167 ft.-span Tu 114. Powered by four 12,000 h.p. turbo-prop engines driving contra-rotating airscrews, this huge airliner can carry up to 220 passengers depending upon the range. It is being supplemented by the jet Ilyushin IL 62 which, like the VC-10, has its four engines mounted at the rear of the fuselage.

specified Rolls-Royce engines for their fleets of this American aircraft. The DC-8 is the latest of the long line of famous Douglas transport aircraft and is very popular with passengers. The DC-8 is also produced in a variety of versions, some of which are powered by Rolls-Royce engines.

In 1965 these fleets of American aircraft were joined by Britain's superb Super VC-10. This "second generation" jet airliner takes full advantage of the technical experience gained with the earlier jets, the major difference being the mounting of the engines at the rear of the fuselage, instead of in or under the wings. This arrangement produces a remarkably quiet cabin. It is spacious, tastefully decorated, has a very efficient air conditioning system and comfortable seats. The Super VC-10 is powered by four Rolls-Royce Conway turbo-jets, each producing 22,500 lb. thrust. Up to 180 economy-class passengers can be carried.

As more experience is gained and jet engines become more efficient, so the advantage of quick and smooth jet travel is being brought to the short-haul routes. First of these short-haul airliners was the Sud Aviation Caravelle,

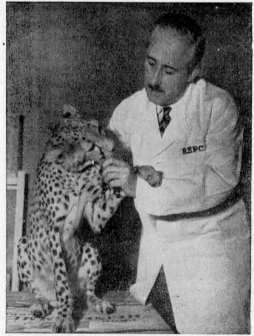

A cheetah "passenger", en route from Nairobi to New York, at London Airport.

Oil-well drilling equipment being carried by a Blackburn "Universal" freighter, 22 ft. long by 7 ft. wide. The load weighed 12 tons.

So much for the passenger side of air travel since the war. On the freight side, equally big expansion has taken place. Often, expensive as air freight is, other considerations enable its users actually to *save* money.

For example, occasionally a ship breaks down in a foreign port. Every day it remains in harbour costs its owner hundreds or even thousands of pounds in wages and insurance. At one time the best an owner could do was to send out a replacement part by the fastest ship available. To-day, they telephone the nearest airline and the spare part is winging its way to the crippled ship in a matter of hours. Some of the parts are surprisingly big. An average cargo ship's propeller shaft weighs anything from four to seven tons. A propeller flown to Bermuda for the S.S. *Leondras* weighed 1,550 lb. The main engine-turning wheel, air-lifted to a tanker, was 8 ft. 3 in. in diameter—so big that it could only be squeezed in the aircraft's hold diagonally. Some parts, indeed, have been *bigger* than the fuselage of the aircraft carrying them. Pan American have flown spare four-bladed propellers, with the ends of two of the long blades poking through the sides of the cabin. Some 6½-ton steel shafts were too big even for this, and were carried to their destination slung from specially constructed beams *beneath* the fuselage of the aircraft concerned.

In the more remote parts of the world aircraft play as important a part in the life of the community as do cars and trains in Britain. Australia has her famous Flying Doctor Service. This enables individual farmsteads often separated from each other by scores of miles, and hundreds of miles from the nearest doctor, to call for and receive the help of a skilled doctor in a matter of hours.

Hitherto unexplored areas of countries such as Borneo are being opened up by air operations similar to the one flown by the Shell Company in Ecuador, when an 11,000-lb. mud pump was lifted to a new oil well which was completely inaccessible in any other way.

Perhaps the most interesting class of air freight carried these days is animals. The practice of carrying animals in aeroplanes has expanded to such an extent over the years that every fifth "passenger" carried by B.O.A.C. is four-legged, one with two legs or no legs! Home pets, such as dogs, cats and canaries are commonplace but, in their turn, almost all animals have been carried by air. Lions, tigers, panthers, monkeys by the thousand, even elephants, have temporarily sprouted wings. In fact, about the only animal that has not flown is the poor giraffe. His long neck has kept him firmly on the ground so far!

As can be imagined, special care has to be taken when some animals are carried. A heavy cage with iron bars is usually reserved for lions and tigers. Cages have to be specially designed

SIKORSKY S61-N, 25-seat, twin-turbine helicopter in service with B.E.A. on the Land's End-Scilly Isles route.

AIR FREIGHT. Grand Prix racing cars about to be loaded aboard a BOAC Canadair CL 44 freight aircraft. The entire tail of the fuselage swings to one side to facilitate loading.

so as to be nose- and paw-proof, particularly where bears are concerned. Squirrels, porcupines and rats travel in metal-lined boxes, otherwise they would quickly gnaw their way to freedom. Monkeys like to travel with other monkeys, and have to be given a blanket to wrap themselves up in during the journey. Zebras and deer are incredible fidgets and require boxes padded to at least 12 inches to prevent them hurting themselves. Partridges and pheasants develop the awkward habit of jumping up and down whilst airborne and require a piece of canvas stretched across their cage, about two inches below the roof, to form a "crash barrier."

Some animals normally considered dangerous make good passengers. Crocodiles, for instance, require no food and are quite happy as long as they are squirted with water now and again. Frogs and toads do not drink, but must be kept damp otherwise they cannot breathe through their skins, and dry up and die.

One of the strangest tips learnt regarding the carriage of animals by air concerns elephants. It used to be difficult to keep these huge beasts content during a flight and the picture of an elephant going berserk in an aircraft is not a pretty one. Then, one day, a passenger list included an elephant and a small white chicken.

During that trip the elephant became so interested in the chicken that he seemed to forget he was flying. The next elephant was given a chicken to keep it company and again it seemed remarkably contented. As a result, when elephants travel by air they are always accompanied by a white chicken and everyone seems happy.

But the best animal story of all concerns a cargo-handler at New York's La Guardia airport who thought he would do his good deed for the day by offering to exercise a big husky-like dog that had arrived some time previously. On the way he gave the animal a drink of water, which it proceeded to drink with great thirsty sips. Another cargo-man, who had been raised on a farm, noticed this and remarked that dogs and other animals *lap* water with their tongues; the only "sippers" that he had ever heard of were—*wolves*. Back into his crate went Brother Wolf in double quick time and the cargo staff still wonder if the owner really knew what he was sending home!

People being flown over the oceans; cars across the Channel; medical supplies over the desert; mining equipment over jungles and animals by the hundred thousand. More and more, aviation is now affecting the lives of every one of us.

One of the strangest shapes ever to fly, the Bell X-22A, experimental V/STOL aircraft.

Conquest of the Air

STRANGE SHAPES IN THE SKY

OF the many aeronautical developments of the 1939-45 war, none changed the concept of air power more than the new-found power of jet propulsion.

It provided the aircraft designer with just what he wanted at the right time. For perhaps the first time a power plant provided him with all the power he needed and more. In the early days designers tended to use conventional layouts, merely replacing the piston engines with turbo-jets, as on the Gloster Meteor fighter. But it soon became apparent that to get the best out of their new engines, new shapes of aeroplanes would be required. For the first time the airframe structure, not the engine, was limiting performance.

Good streamlining became of more important than ever. The new breed of jet aircraft was, perhaps, epitomised by the Hawker Sea Hawk. One of the first jets produced for operations from carriers, this aircraft was a picture of sleek speed from nose to tail. Its fine lines were preserved by fitting the engine air intakes and jet exhausts in the wing roots. "Splitting" the exhaust pipe detracted little from the efficiency of the engine and had the advantage of providing more space than usual in the fuselage for fuel tanks. With no propeller clearance to worry about the under-carriage was strangely short and the pilot, placed right up near the nose of the finely streamlined fuselage, had a first-class field of view—a feature which was becoming sadly neglected on some of the last piston-engined fighters.

REDUCING DRAG

As speeds increased, the need to reduce drag assumed paramount importance. Ever thinner wings became the order of the day. Wind tunnel tests in Germany during the war had indicated that wings sliced through the air more easily if they were "bent" or swept backwards in the same way that a knife cuts more easily if it is tilted.

The first post-war jet to take advantage of this German research and to have swept wings was the North American F.86 Sabre, which captured the World Air Speed Record with a speed of 670 m.p.h.

In the quest for ever higher speeds, the wings of fighters have been swept back more and more until, in the case of the BAC Lightning supersonic fighter, the ailerons had to be positioned on the tips rather than the trailing edge of the wing. Wings with this degree of sweep are but a short step from the now familiar delta configuration. By filling in the triangular space between the trailing edge of the wing and the fuselage, a strong, efficient wing is created, capable of housing a good proportion of the numerous gadgets and some of the fuel required in modern aircraft.

Although the delta-wing is basically a simple shape, the quest for higher speeds soon resulted in some strange delta-winged aircraft. Of these the strangest, surely, was the XB-70.

This was a big six-engined aircraft designed as a strategic bomber to replace the B-52 Stratofortress in service with the U.S. Air Force by the mid-1960s. Unlike most supersonic bombers, which cruise below the speed of sound for a proportion of each flight, the B-70 was designed to travel the entire distance to the target and back—a total distance of up to 7,600 miles—at 2,000 m.p.h., i.e., at three times the speed of sound.

The slender nose of the B-70 projected some 60 feet ahead of the wing and this, coupled with its unusual shape, made the aircraft resemble a huge insect from some angles. In flight two small wings, or foreplanes, projecting from the fuselage just aft of the cockpit, added to the bizarre shape of the aircraft.

At times people watching a B-70 flying could be excused for beginning to wonder if their eyes were playing tricks. The reason for this was the wing-tips, which folded down as much

HAWKER SEA HAWK. This sleek, finely streamlined naval fighter epitomised the new breed of jet aircraft.

SUPER SABRE. Although they are now commonplace the sharply swept wings were a strange shape in the sky when this aircraft went into service in the early 1950s.

BAC LIGHTNING. The wings of this British 1,500 m.p.h. fighter are swept so sharply that the ailerons had to be positioned on the tips of the wings.

DELTA DART. Strange shapes have evolved from the basic simplicity of the triangular delta-wing.

B-70A VALKYRIE. The tips of the wings folded down at high speed making the shape of this 2,000 m.p.h. research aircraft even stranger.

as 65° to improve manœuvrability and stability while crusing at 2,000 m.p.h.

Changing operational requirements resulted in the abandonment of the B-70 as a bomber, but two were built for aerodynamic research. In May, 1966, the second of these flew at 2,000 m.p.h. for the then unprecedented time of 32 minutes. Shortly afterwards this aircraft was lost in a tragic accident when a "chase" aircraft collided with it at the end of a long flight. The remaining aircraft is now in a museum.

Another strange delta-winged aircraft is the Viggen. This formidable Swedish multi-mission combat aircraft gains its strange shape from its massive delta foreplane, mounted ahead of the main wing. From a distance and at certain angles the machine gives the impression of being two aircraft flying in close formation.

The purpose of the foreplane is to improve the take-off and landing performance. On some aircraft the nose is lifted for take-off by generating a down-load on the tailplane, this down-load tends to act against the lift being generated by the wing. On the Viggen the foreplane is used to lift the nose; this force thus adds to the lift developed by the wing.

DROOPING NOSES

Yet another crop of strange shapes will be with us soon when supersonic airliners enter service. In level flight these sleek aircraft present a finely streamlined appearance, but during take-off and landing they resemble weird insects.

The reason for this is that a delta-wing develops its maximum lift at a much greater angle of attack than an ordinary wing, the angle being about 40° compared with the normal 15°. This means that when taking off and landing—when maximum lift is required—the nose of the aircraft points high in the sky, obscuring the view of the pilot. Designers have overcome this by arranging for the nose of the aircraft to hinge down, or drop, enabling the

X-24A. Lifting-body research aircraft, designed to help the development of manned spacecraft able to perform in orbit, and also to fly in the atmosphere like aircraft and land at airports.

XC-142 VTOL aircraft tilts its entire wing, complete with engines, for vertical flight. For normal level flight the wing and engines are tilted down to the conventional position.

VIGGEN. Swedish multi-mission combat aeroplane, carrying two air-to-surface missiles beneath the main delta-wings.

pilot to see ahead in the normal manner.

With their drooped noses, the Russian supersonic airliner, the TU-144, and the Anglo-French Concorde, assume an insect-like appearance. On the Concorde this effect is amplified by the curved shape of the delta-wing and its turned-up wing-tips.

FLYING CRANES

Some of the strangest shapes in the sky are presented by aircraft designed to land and take off vertically. The best known of this type of machine is the helicopter. The need for a tail rotor and the absence of a conventional wing gives all helicopters a unique and distinctive look, but two in particular are without doubt strange shapes in the sky.

One is the U.S. Sikorsky Skycrane. As its name implies, this is a flying crane, designed specifically to lift heavy and bulky loads. The fuselage is little more than a tubular beam carrying the tail rotor at one end and the crew cabin at the other, with the two massive engines and complicated rotor hub assembly on top in the middle. The payload, which can be anything from a box-like pod to a bulldozer, is just hooked on to the beam.

The second strange-looking helicopter is the Russian Mil.10. This is also a flying crane. It has a conventional fuselage, but a massive four leg landing gear, designed to straddle its bulky payloads, gives it a uniquely odd appearance, both in the air and on the ground.

Although helicopters can rise vertically, in level flight they are inferior in performance to conventional aircraft with fixed wings.

Attempts to produce aircraft that can take off and land vertically and yet have a level flight performance comparable to that of conventional aircraft have resulted in some of the strangest shapes yet in the sky.

TILTING WINGS

Some designers think that tilting wings are the answer. On these aircraft the wing, with the engines, tilts up 90° so that the aircraft can take off like a helicopter. In the air the wing is rotated back to its normal position, when the machine flies like a conventional aeroplane. When in hovering flight these machines present a bizarre appearance.

Few VTO aircraft, however, are more ungainly than the Bell X-22A. Described by one expert as "a collection of outsize beer barrels draped over a discarded box-car" this aircraft is lifted vertically by four propellers mounted in barrel-like ducts located one at each corner of the fuselage. For level, forward flight, the huge barrels, with their propellers, are rotated to the horizontal position.

The drooped nose on the Anglo-French Concorde gives the supersonic airliner a strange bat-like appearance.

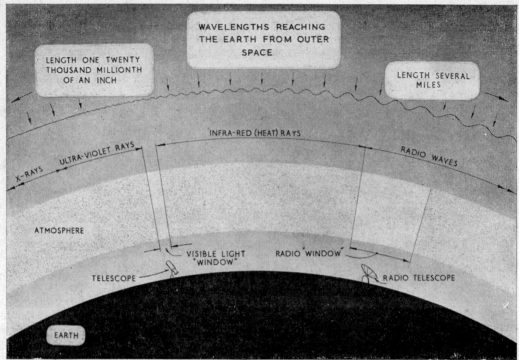

Fig. 1. The Earth's atmosphere blocks all waves from outer space, except those with lengths in the optical "window," (passing visible light) and the radio "window." The relatively wide view of the radio "window" is readily apparent.

RADIO ASTRONOMY
A Young Science

So called empty space is full of several forms of energy. This is transmitted by electro-magnetic vibrations of greatly varying wavelengths. The wavelengths range from the minute fraction of an inch of the gamma and cosmic rays to long radio-waves of several miles wavelength. Most of them are absorbed by the atmosphere, and therefore do not reach the surface of the Earth.

Near the middle of the complete range of wavelengths—known as the electro-magnetic spectrum—is a narrow group of great importance. For, not only do the waves in this group penetrate the atmosphere, but the human eye is sensitive to light in the wavelength range and can " pick them up." If this were not so, we would be completely blind, which would not be a pleasant prospect!

Until recently our knowledge of the Sun, the stars and the great outer galaxies had been gained solely from the study of these visible light waves coming through the optical " window " in the atmosphere (Fig. 1). Even if the human eye could pick up a wider range of wavelengths, this would not help us much, because of the blocking effect of the atmosphere.

In addition to the visible light " window " in the atmosphere, however, there is another, more extensive one, which lets through a proportion of the longer waves reaching the earth. These are called radio waves, because they are of the type used for ordinary radio transmissions. The existence of this " window " was first discovered by an American engineer, Jansky, in 1931, and other crude experiments were made in 1939.

RADIO TELESCOPES

The great advances made in radio and radar techniques during the 1939–45 war gave the astronomer a really effective tool with which he could study the waves coming in through this radio window—the radio telescope. For, just as a " visual " telescope can collect visible light, a " radio " telescope can be made to collect radio waves.

Because of the relatively long wavelengths of radio waves, however, a radio telescope looks quite different from an ordinary telescope. The waves are collected by a circular aerial, often little more than wire netting spread on a light framework (the counterpart of the mirror in a visual telescope), and then fed into a receiver similar to a television set. Finally, there is some device for measuring the signals, such as a pen recorder giving a trace on a paper chart representing the strength of the incoming signals. Such a trace is shown on Fig. 2.

The first post-war observations of radio waves, with the improved equipment, confirmed preliminary pre-war experiments that there appeared to be *no connection* between the radio signals and the astronomical bodies such as stars and galaxies with which astronomers had been familiar. On the other hand, the signals appeared to emanate from definite

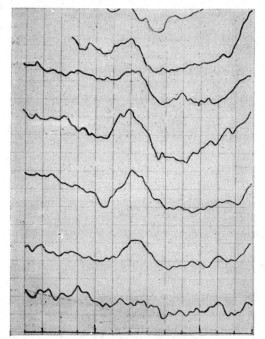

Fig. 2. How Andromeda appears to radio astronomers. Each line corresponds to the output of a radio telescope as it swept through different parts of the nebula.

points in space. Astronomers in Sydney, Australia, picked up a particularly powerful source in the constellation of Cygnus; others at Cambridge, England, an even stronger one in Cassiopeia. If these signals had coincided with visual stars, the discoveries would have caused little surprise. But, search as they might, astronomers could find no visual stars to which the signals could be attributed.

UNIVERSE OF DARK STARS

Soon many other, less intense, radio stars were discovered and, with one exception, none could be tied up with an existing visual star. The radio stars and visual stars are thus quite different " objects." At the time there was interesting speculation that, lying around and between the stars we could see, were large numbers of " invisible " radio stars whose existence we did not suspect until radio astronomy came along.

The exception to the " invisibility " of radio stars referred to previously is the Crab Nebula, an enormous mass of glowing gas forming the remains of a supernova explosion, observed by the Chinese in A.D.1054. But such explosions are comparatively rare and it was not thought that these were the answer to all the radio stars plotted.

And so an intensive search for the sources of the most powerful radio stars was made with the big 200-inch telescope on Palomar Mountain. The result was what appears to be gaseous clouds in collision. They are extremely faint and difficult to see, even after long photographic exposures, but the signals seemed to be concentrated on the clouds.

More recently, other signals have been traced to distant galaxies in collision. Although a galaxy contains many millions of stars, they are so far apart that the stars themselves rarely collide. The tenuous gas existing between the stars, however, inter-collides and appears to produce intense radio waves.

Thus, although one or two mysteries surrounding radio waves appear to have been partially solved, much remains to be learnt of the great masses of dark or faintly luminous objects which emit radio waves.

Nearer the Earth, radio astronomy has enabled us to find out more about the solar system. Although it is a poor reflector, radar echoes have been " bounced " from the

Moon, the results indicating that its surface is covered with a thin layer of dust less than an inch deep. Before these experiments some astronomers had suggested that the surface was covered by dust to a depth of hundreds of feet, or even miles. If this were so a spaceship making a landing would have probably sunk deep down into this dust surface without trace. Now, whatever else may be found up there, we can at least be sure that this hazard will not be present.

RADIO WAVES FROM THE SUN

The atmosphere of the Sun has been found to emit radio waves and the study of these emissions is throwing new light on the conditions in the solar atmosphere. The longer the wavelength on which we observe the radio " light," the larger the Sun appears to be. On a wavelength of five metres it is almost twice as large as the visible Sun, whilst at very long wavelengths it is nearly as large as the orbit of Mercury!

When the Sun's surface is disturbed by sunspots the radio emission received on earth is many thousands of times more intense, and it has been possible to show that the increased radiation comes from small areas very near the dark patches of the sunspots themselves. The solar flares which occasionally occur in the region of sunspot groups are accompanied by even more intense bursts of radio energy, and the sources of these enormous signals move outwards through the solar atmosphere at speeds of millions of miles an hour.

In order to learn more about the Moon, Sun and the distant " dark stars " bigger and better radio telescopes are required. For the same reason that ordinary astronomers have wanted bigger optical telescopes to collect more light, so radio astronomers want bigger radio telescopes to give more resolution and to pick up signals from even greater distances.

The resolution of a telescope depends on the diameter of the instrument compared with the wavelength. The radio waves have a wavelength over a million times longer than that of visible light, and to equal the resolution of the 100-inch telescope on Mount Wilson a radio telescope would have to be something like 10,000 miles in diameter! This is, of course, quite impossible, so radio astronomers do the best they can with more reasonably-sized telescopes, but this is the reason why, whilst the size of optical telescopes is measured in inches, we have to think in terms of feet and yards for radio telescopes.

RADIO INTERFEROMETERS

One way of overcoming the size problem on radio telescopes is to use *two* aerials spaced several hundreds of yards apart. The signals from the two aerials are connected to a common input radio receiver. As the Earth rotates the stars appear to move across the sky, revolving around the North Celestial Pole, which is close to the Pole Star. As a radio star transits (passes over the aerials) the receiver connected to it records a signal which pulses up and down. These interferometers, as they are called, can measure the size and position of a radio star to within about a thousandth of a degree.

But they are not so sensitive to faint signals as telescopes using bowl-shaped aerials, and, of course, they can only examine those areas of the sky at which they are pointed by the natural rotation of the earth.

WORLD'S BIGGEST RADIO TELESCOPE

At Jodrell Bank, Cheshire, is the world's biggest steerable radio telescope. Known as the Mk. 1, it is operated by the University of Manchester. The bowl-shaped aerial is 250 feet in diameter and is pivoted at two points so that it can rotate at the push of a button. The towers supporting the bowl move on bogies on a circular railway track over three hundred feet in diameter. Altogether, the complete telescope weighs over 1,500 tons, yet so accurately is it made it can be controlled to within an accuracy of nearly a hundredth of a degree.

This very remarkable telescope which has been used to track many satellites has enabled Britain to maintain a pioneering lead in this new astronomical science.

RADAR OBSERVATION OF METEORS

Because of the ability of radio waves to penetrate cloud, radio astronomy has increased our knowledge of meteors since the war. A meteor is a tiny particle from space, varying in size from about that of a pea down to tiny particles smaller than grains of sand, which enter the Earth's atmosphere at speeds much greater than a rifle bullet. Fortunately for us,

The world's biggest steerable radio telescope at Jodrell Bank, Cheshire. It consists basically of a 250 ft. diameter copper mesh bowl weighing 30 tons, supported by two 180 ft. towers.

they get very hot by friction in the highest layers of the atmosphere and evaporate, leaving a trail several miles long. Occasionally a particle is big enough to survive its passage through the atmosphere and so reach the Earth's surface. It is then known as a *meteorite*.

Meteors burning up are, of course, the cause of the common "shooting star" trails visible on any clear night. Visual and photographic study of these trails used to be the only way to obtain information about them. Even so, we knew that about 100 *million* meteorites entered the Earth's atmosphere *every* day. We also knew that occasionally the Earth rushed through an extra thick concentration of meteors, producing what is known as a "meteor shower." But we did not know where this vast number of meteors came from.

When a meteor burns away it leaves behind it for a short time a dense trail of electrons, as well as the light by which we see it. This electron trail enables us to detect the meteor by radio. Basically, the process is very simple.

A radio wave sets the electrons in the trail into vibration, so that they then reflect the radio wave back towards the Earth. By measuring the time the wave takes to travel to and from the trail, the exact height, speed and direction of the meteor can be determined. The height is measured by timing the delay between the transmission of a radio wave and its reception after being reflected by the disturbed electrons in the meteor's trail. The speed of radio waves is 186,000 miles a second, so the delay in time enables us to calculate how far a wave had to travel before being reflected, and hence we can find the meteor's altitude. We now know that even more meteors strike the Earth on the sunlit side than on the "outer" side. We also think that virtually all meteors originate within the solar system.

Radio astronomy is a young science and we may rest assured that there is much more it will teach us—and that it will uncover many new exciting mysteries to puzzle us!

THE HIGH-TEST PEROXIDE SYSTEM OF PROPULSION

The high-test peroxide system, known as H.T.P., is shown here being used in a submarine to produce greater underwater speed than any attained previously. The diagrammatic drawing on the right shows how the engine works. There is no necessity to use a " snort " breathing tube and the engine generates sufficient power to give an underwater speed of over 20 knots, compared

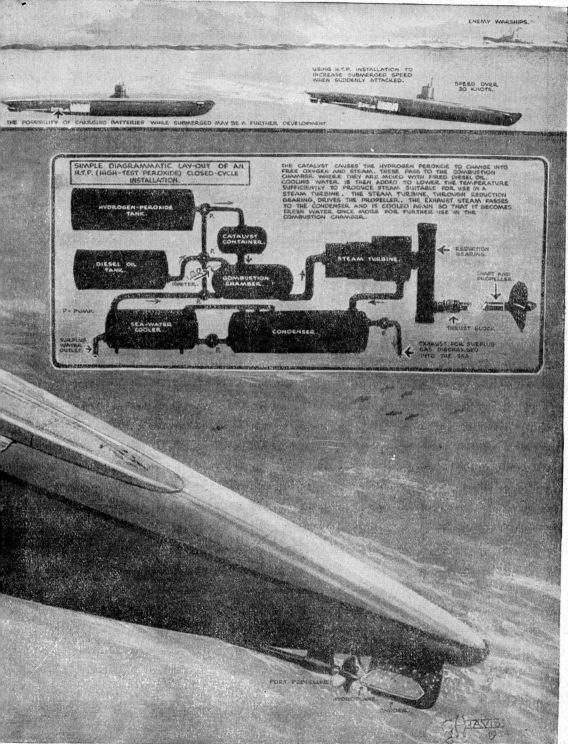

SIMPLE DIAGRAMMATIC LAY-OUT OF AN H.T.P. (HIGH-TEST PEROXIDE) CLOSED-CYCLE INSTALLATION.

THE CATALYST CAUSES THE HYDROGEN PEROXIDE TO CHANGE INTO FREE OXYGEN AND STEAM. THESE PASS TO THE COMBUSTION CHAMBER WHERE THEY ARE MIXED WITH FIRED DIESEL OIL. COOLING WATER IS THEN ADDED TO LOWER THE TEMPERATURE SUFFICIENTLY TO PRODUCE STEAM SUITABLE FOR USE IN A STEAM TURBINE. THE STEAM TURBINE, THROUGH REDUCTION GEARING, DRIVES THE PROPELLER. THE EXHAUST STEAM PASSES TO THE CONDENSER, AND IS COOLED AGAIN SO THAT IT BECOMES FRESH WATER ONCE MORE FOR FURTHER USE IN THE COMBUSTION CHAMBER.

with the 8-10 knots achieved by submarines conventionally powered by electric motors. First used in connection with the V2 rockets fired by the Germans against this country in World War II, it was later used experimentally in U-boats, though too late to be used against the Allies.

Drawing reproduced by courtesy of ILLUSTRATED LONDON NEWS

Sir Adrian Boult rehearsing the Vaughan Williams Sea Symphony with the London Philharmonic Orchestra prior to a recording being made.

HOW GRAMOPHONE RECORDS ARE MADE

WHEN you make any sort of noise, you cause a disturbance in the air around you. The air is first pushed up together, then stretched out—compression and rarefication, we call it—and this disturbance is passed on so that waves are produced in the air sufficient to act upon the ear-drums of any person who is, as we say, "within hearing."

If you make a high-pitched noise like a shrill whistle, the waves are very small, so that the air is compressed and rarefied probably thousands of times in one second. If the noise is a low bass note, there are fewer vibrations in one second. The number of vibrations per second which any one note sets up is the frequency of that note, and this frequency is measured in cycles per second.

If you have a piano, go and play the A above middle C. This will cause sound waves in the air at the rate of 439 per second. If you play the A an octave higher, the frequency of that note is 878 cycles per second, while the frequency of A an octave lower is 219.5 cycles per second.

No voice or musical instrument produces one simple series of sound waves. Whenever one note is sung or played, other notes at various distances above it are mixed in with it. Of course, we don't hear these other notes separately, but it is mainly these harmonics, as they are called—the number, strength, and spacing of them—which give to instruments their different, distinctive tone colours.

It is obvious then that if we record an instrument or a whole orchestra, we want it to sound just like the real thing when the record is played. We must, therefore, have machines sensitive enough to deal with those high notes which we cannot hear separately, but which give the instruments their particular tone. We must be able to record and reproduce a wide range of frequencies—as much as from 40 cycles per second to 15,000 or more.

THE VIBRATING DIAPHRAGM

The compression and rarefication of the air caused by sounds were first recorded in 1857. A sensitive piece of material called a diaphragm will react to sound waves just like a human ear-drum. If you stretch a piece of greaseproof paper tightly over one end of an open cylinder you will have made a diaphragm. If you join two such tins with a length of thread running through the diaphragm on each and knot it to keep it in place, then get a friend to hold the other tin so that the thread is taut, you can talk to each other as if you were using a telephone.

By causing a diaphragm, to which a lever was attached, to vibrate, the inventor, in 1857, made the lever vibrate as well, and caused it to make marks in some soot spread over a piece of paper. But this record, of course, could not be played back, because another lever could not be made to follow the tracks in the soot so as to make the diaphragm vibrate again—the process backwards.

EDISON'S FIRST RECORD

Edison, in 1876, was the first man who made a record which could be played back. He cut a spiral groove in a brass tube, and so arranged a diaphragm on the end of a short brass cylinder that a cutting needle attached to it would follow the track of this spiral. He then covered the brass tube with tin-foil, and spoke into the cylinder while turning the tube round. As his talking made the diaphragm move, his needle pressed the tin-foil down into the spiral groove to varying depths. He could then make a needle follow these dents in the tin-foil, causing the diaphragm to vibrate

Not the controls of a spaceship, but the console used by engineers in a recording studio.

again, and thus recreate the same sound waves in the air that his voice had created in the first place.

Edison, and also Graham Bell and C. S. Tainter, later replaced the cylinder covered with tin-foil by a wax cylinder on which the cutting needle moved not up and down, but sideways. This instrument was called the phonograph. In 1887, Emil Berliner produced an instrument which he called the gramophone.

This caused the removal of lamp-black from paper, and the record was then copied in stronger material. In Berliner's second model a flat disc covered with a semi-liquid coating, such as ink or paint, was used instead of the cylinder. Then, in 1888, he used a wax-coated metal or glass disc which, after the recording, was placed in an acid-bath. Where the wax had been cut away by the recording needle, the acid ate into the base, and the recording was thus etched in a fairly permanent way.

HOW EARLY RECORDINGS WERE MADE

After another ten years, the manufacture of disc records could be regarded as a successful proposition. Players or singers were gathered before one or more horns, which protruded from a screen on the other side of which was the recording machine. The horns were used to concentrate the sound on to the recording diaphragm. There were many complications; it was very uncomfortable if more than a few people were being recorded; also the recording machine could not handle loud notes so that the musicians had to keep swaying away from the horn.

In 1904 all records were still originals and not copies. Peter Dawson recalls that he used to record in front of a battery of twelve horns, making twelve separate original records, singing the same song six hours a day, five days a week until the required number of records had been made. Later on, however, metal master records were " grown " by an electro-plating process from the original wax recording, and the records were pressed from these masters.

The clockwork motor was introduced at the end of the nineteenth century, and by 1905 the sound-box was evolved. This consisted of a mica diaphragm held lightly at its edges, and with a lever balanced on a knife-edge running from the centre of the diaphragm to the needle point; the movement of this lever was controlled by delicate springs. The sound was " amplified " by the horn, mounted directly on the sound-box, but in the effort to amplify, the horns increased in size till they became too heavy and had to be connected with the sound-box by a piece of tubing called the " tone-arm." This tone-arm was made into a tapering continuation of the horn, which itself later disappeared into a cabinet.

THE MICROPHONE AND ELECTRICAL RECORDING

Meanwhile, new wonders of science— microphones and amplifiers—had been developed. These were now applied to the gramophone industry, and by 1929 recordings could be made with the performers standing as they would be at an ordinary public concert. They sang or played into microphones now; the sound waves they created still caused the diaphragm to move, but instead of mechanically moving the cutting head, this movement now was changed into an electric current which was passed through amplifiers to make it stronger, and was then changed back into a mechanical force to move the V-shaped cutting tool operating upon a blank wax disc which was carried on a turntable driven by weights.

The turntable also moved horizontally along a threaded spindle so that the cutting tool traced a spiral of about 100 turns to the inch. The disc was then dusted with graphite and a negative disc grown from it. A wax impression was then taken from this copper negative, and the discs from which the records were to be pressed (known as matrices) prepared from this wax. If new matrices were later needed, it was then possible to go back to the first copper negative.

The materials used for records at this stage, and still used for some types, were resins and gums (mainly shellac), and various mineral fillers. Now that it was possible to record electrically instead of mechanically it was also, of course, possible to have electrical reproducers. Not only did these have electrical motors, but they also repeated the process of electrical recording in reverse.

The next step was the announcement in 1945 by the Decca Company of full frequency

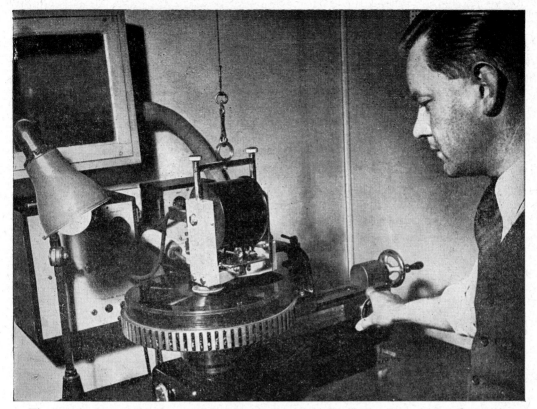

First step in the making of a record is to cut the " original disc." The magnetism on the tape is changed back into electrical impulses which move the cutting point on the disc.

range recording. For the first time it was possible to record nearly all the frequencies audible to the majority of people, and to manufacture gramophones capable of reproducing everything that was on the record.

LONG PLAYING RECORDS

It was not long after the last war that long playing records were successfully introduced in America, and in 1950 they were introduced into this country. They were an immediate success with record collectors.

The long playing record is made of a plastic material which not only renders it flexible, but overcomes the problem of surface noise. It also makes possible more realistic reproduction of music than even the best shellac record can give, while the advantages of not having to change the record every four or five minutes are obvious. The long playing time of this new type of record is obtained by winding the spiral groove about two-and-a-half times as closely as on the old type, and by having

the record turn at only $33\frac{1}{3}$ revolutions per minute instead of at 78.

This means that the marks which the cutting needle makes, and which the playing needle has to follow on the long playing record are much smaller. Therefore a much smaller playing needle or stylus, as it is called, must be used; also this stylus must be made from a sapphire or diamond—the steel or fibre needle will not play long playing records. Again, at $33\frac{1}{3}$ r.p.m., the slightest variation in speed will be heard, so that a reliable motor must be used.

MAKING A RECORD TO-DAY

When we make a record to-day, we can record the music at a public performance or in theatres, concert-halls, or special studios. The recording engineer and his staff must first decide where the microphones are to be placed.

For an orchestral session three microphones are usually employed, and if there is a soloist,

The original disc is cleaned and then coated with a silver solution. This picture shows the disc in the automatic silvering unit, with the cover raised.

he or she has a fourth one. When the conductor or soloist has rehearsed the music, a trial recording of that part is made. In a public performance, it is possible for a performer to make a tiny mistake which might not be noticed. A record, however, is going to be played over and over again, so everything must be perfect.

When a recording is being made, the sound waves created by the performers are picked up by the microphones and changed into electric impulses. These are fed through controls in the recording room. Having been monitored in the recording room, the electric impulses are then fed to the tape room. The tape is wound on spools on the tape machine, and as it runs across the recording head it is magnetised by these electric impulses. At the same time, the music is played back, so that the engineer can tell immediately if a fault occurs.

As soon as the recording is finished, the music has to be taken from the tapes and put on to a disc. The magnetism on the tape

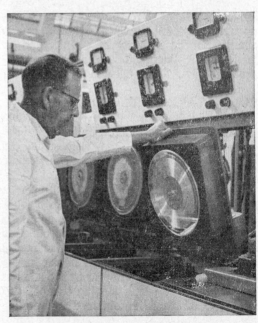

The silvered disc is then nickel-plated and copper-plated, to make the master.

A 7-inch record press about to be closed. The stampers, or matrices, labels and pre-heated rolled biscuit are in position.

While all this processing is going on, the mothers and stampers have to be constantly washed and polished, for the slightest particle of dust caught in a groove would have a serious effect on the finished record. The stamper is still not strong enough to withstand the tremendous pressure of the machines which press records. Therefore, with the music face carefully protected, a strong copper backing is welded on, and it is at this stage also that the hole is punched in the centre. The music face must also now be strengthened, and so a thin layer of chrome is plated on to it. After more cleaning, the stamper is ready to go into the record press, and the first test pressing is made. Only now can any fault which might have occurred since the cutting of the original disc be discovered. If the test pressing is approved, the factory will go on to press finished records.

For long-playing records the material used is a plastic of the polyvynyl-chloride group. The raw material is issued to the record press in the form of thin rectangles called biscuits, and a number of these are kept on a hot-plate to make them soft and pliable. The record press has one matrix on the top and one

is changed back into the electric impulses, which can be used to move a cutting point on a disc just as the force of sound waves themselves moved the cutting points of the earliest record-making machines.

Once one of these discs has been played, it is of no more use to the record factory, so that if anything goes wrong during the cutting of a disc it cannot be discovered until many stages later in the manufacturing processes. At the record factory a thin film of silver is thrown down on to the disc from a silver-nitrate solution. It is then possible to electroplate this silvered surface with nickel and afterwards with copper. Now the nickel and copper must be separated from the silver-plated disc, giving an original and a negative impression of it—that is to say on the negative the grooves are now bumps. This negative is called the master.

The next step is to go through the same process twice more producing a positive (called the mother) from the master, and another negative (called the matrix or stamper) from the mother. From now on, the disc and the master are filed, in case of accident with the mothers.

The pressed record. The surplus material round the edge is automatically trimmed off.

The records are finally inspected visually and then placed in their sleeves ready for boxing.

on the bottom. The press man rolls up one of the biscuits, places the labels in the press, followed by the biscuit. He then pulls up the glass panel in front of the press which closes and squeezes out the biscuit with high pressure combined with heat into all the tiny grooves on the two matrices. The matrices are then cooled before the press opens, and the press man removes the finished record. Samples are taken from each batch of records and tested to reveal any production faults using special test consoles and headphones. All records are finally inspected visually and then sleeved ready for distribution.

TAPE RECORDING

Tape recording has been known since about 1898, but only since the last war has it been regularly used for commercial recordings.

The principle is that variations in the current passed through an electro-magnet, called the recording head, cause corresponding magnetisation of the tape as it travels across the head.

The advantages of recording on tape are obvious. Tape recording equipment and tapes are easy to move about; much more than four or five minutes of music can be recorded without a break; or on the other hand, should a mistake be made in the performance, it may be possible to rectify this by re-recording a small section of the music, and inserting this section in the tape instead of re-recording the whole of one disc; if an unsatisfactory recording has been taken, this can be erased, and the tape used again, whereas once cut, a disc is useless.

WHEN CARUSO AND MELBA MADE RECORDINGS

When Edison and Berliner first invented their recording machines, they thought of them as little more than amusing toys. Music-lovers were slow to realise their possibilities, but when such great musicians as Caruso and Melba consented to have their voices recorded (in 1902 and 1905 for the first time respectively), it was obvious that the gramophone record was to achieve a permanent place in musical life, and the technical excellence of present-day recordings has ensured its popularity.

STEREO RECORDS

The latest development in the record world is that of stereophonic reproduction, and this is used by many record enthusiasts. The principle is this. When you listen to music, or any other sounds, you do so with both ears. It is this which gives the effect of space and direction. Mono or non-stereo recordings are made with one microphone or group of microphones all connected to one recording head. When you play such a record, all the sound comes from one source. The effect of this is similar to the effect in the realm of sight if you cover one eye: you can still see, but you lose all sense of depth except that provided by your memory. In other words, if you did not know that various objects were different distances away from you, using only one eye they would all appear to be the same distance.

TWO SIMULTANEOUS RECORDINGS

To produce from records a similar sense of perspective, as we call it, in the realm of hearing, you have to use " two ears " throughout the whole process. Thus two microphones (or two sets of microphones) must be used to make two recordings at the same time. When these two recordings are played back at the same time, using two amplifiers and two speakers placed at the right distance from each other, they are heard by your two ears and give the effect of having an orchestra, or whatever it may be, spread out in front of you as it would be in the concert hall.

To have these simultaneous recordings on the two tracks of one tape both reproduced at the same time is obviously the simplest method of achieving stereophonic reproduction.

STEREOPHONIC DISCS

To the vast majority of people the normal record is still a disc, not a tape. As early as 1930, demonstrations of stereophonic discs were given by A. D. Blumlein, whose valuable research into stereophony is acknowledged by all. Not until much greater advances had been made in electronics, was it possible to continue Blumlein's work.

There are three ways of achieving the necessary simultaneous reproduction of two recordings from a disc. The first is called the carrier system and involves having the two recordings mixed in a simple cut on the disc and separated electronically in reproduction. This has been discarded for commercial purposes because, excellent as is the resulting quality, the method is far too expensive. The second is to have twin tracks as on the tape recording which we have described. This also obviously halves the playing time of the record. The other is to combine in one groove the hill-and-dale method of recording described in the first paragraph of the section on Edison's first record with the lateral method normally used to-day.

All British record manufacturers have now elected to standardise this last method of the complex cut. But instead of being simply vertical and horizontal, each cut is made at an angle of 45° to the surface of the record. Record enthusiasts who want to buy stereophonic records will have to make sure that they have the right equipment on which to play them. They will *not* play like ordinary long playing records if used on ordinary equipment. The equipment for playing them will, however, also play ordinary long playing records, and the special stereo pick-up head will give improved reproduction of ordinary LP's.

Special equipment was at first expected to be very expensive in view of the duplication required. It is not, however, as costly to build a stereo amplifier as it is to build two complete single amplifiers, and an extensive range of moderately priced reproducers has been developed for domestic use. These have brought the tremendous benefits of stereo recording within the reach of most people. An important part of any stereo system is the speakers and a wide range to suit all pockets is available. Modern speaker and cabinet techniques have enabled the development of small speakers having very good sound reproducing qualities. The benefits of stereo are the sense of spaciousness and perspective which it gives; the clarity which results from this; and the greater illusion of reality in such things as opera recordings where it is possible to imagine the performers moving about on the stage (from the direction from which their voices are heard to come) just as voices can be heard coming from different directions in modern cinemas showing films with stereophonic sound-tracks.

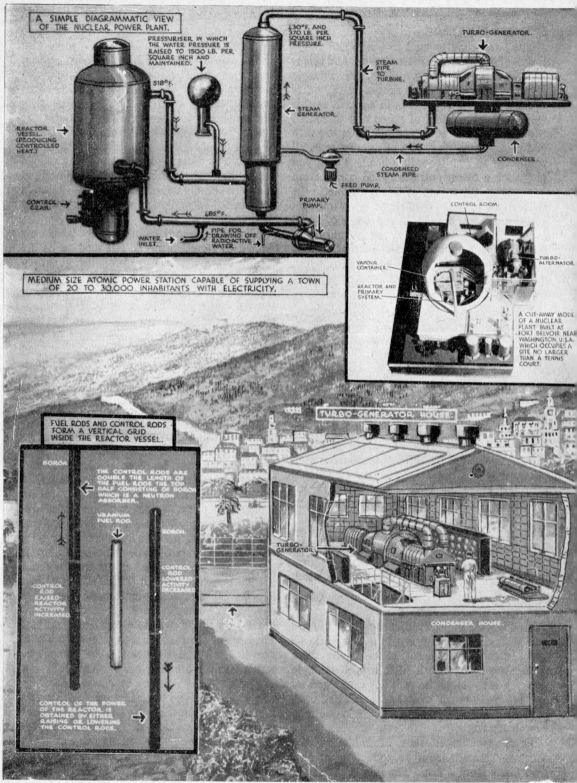

A SIMPLE DIAGRAMMATIC VIEW OF THE NUCLEAR POWER PLANT.

PRESSURISER IN WHICH THE WATER PRESSURE IS RAISED TO 1500 LB. PER SQUARE INCH AND MAINTAINED.

130°F. AND 370 LB. PER SQUARE INCH PRESSURE.

TURBO-GENERATOR.

518°F.

STEAM PIPE TO TURBINE.

STEAM GENERATOR.

REACTOR VESSEL (PRODUCING CONTROLLED HEAT.)

CONDENSER.

CONTROL GEAR.

CONDENSED STEAM PIPE.

FEED PUMP.

PRIMARY PUMP.

WATER INLET.

PIPE FOR DRAWING OFF RADIOACTIVE WATER

485°F.

CONTROL ROOM.

VAPOUR CONTAINER

TURBO-ALTERNATOR.

REACTOR AND PRIMARY SYSTEM.

A CUT-AWAY MODE OF A NUCLEAR PLANT BUILT AT FORT BELVOIR NEAR WASHINGTON, U.S.A. WHICH OCCUPIES A SITE NO LARGER THAN A TENNIS COURT.

MEDIUM SIZE ATOMIC POWER STATION CAPABLE OF SUPPLYING A TOWN OF 20 TO 30,000 INHABITANTS WITH ELECTRICITY.

FUEL RODS AND CONTROL RODS FORM A VERTICAL GRID INSIDE THE REACTOR VESSEL.

BORON

THE CONTROL RODS ARE DOUBLE THE LENGTH OF THE FUEL RODS THE TOP HALF CONSISTING OF BORON WHICH IS A NEUTRON ABSORBER.

URANIUM FUEL ROD.

BORON.

CONTROL ROD RAISED REACTOR ACTIVITY INCREASED.

CONTROL ROD LOWERED ACTIVITY DECREASED

CONTROL OF THE POWER OF THE REACTOR IS OBTAINED BY EITHER RAISING OR LOWERING THE CONTROL RODS.

TURBO-GENERATOR HOUSE.

TURBO-GENERATOR

CONDENSER HOUSE.

Small atomic power units, based on that used so successfully in U.S.S. *Nautilus* (*see* "*The Atomic Submarine*" *pages* 118-22) are being constructed in different sizes producing 2, 5, 10, and 25 megawatts, and they can be built on a space the size of a tennis court, hence their name. These units produce electricity or heat, and for a town of 10,000-20,000 inhabitants a ten megawatt unit could be built at a cost of £2,000,000. They are particulary useful for remote and underdeveloped areas and the completion time for building and the ultimate

SMALL TOWNS OR DRIVE CARGO SHIPS

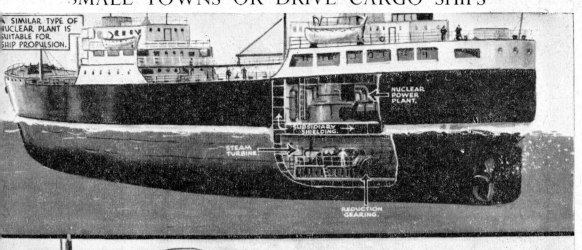

A SIMILAR TYPE OF NUCLEAR PLANT IS SUITABLE FOR SHIP PROPULSION.

NUCLEAR POWER PLANT.

SUBSIDIARY SHIELDING.

STEAM TURBINE.

REDUCTION GEARING.

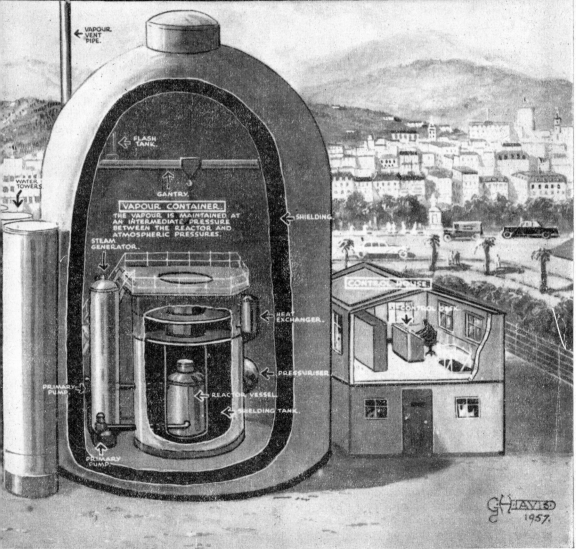

VAPOUR VENT PIPE.

FLASH TANK.

WATER TOWERS.

GANTRY.

VAPOUR CONTAINER.
THE VAPOUR IS MAINTAINED AT AN INTERMEDIATE PRESSURE BETWEEN THE REACTOR AND ATMOSPHERIC PRESSURES.

STEAM GENERATOR.

SHIELDING.

CONTROL HOUSE.

CONTROL DESK.

HEAT EXCHANGER.

PRESSURISER.

PRIMARY PUMP.

REACTOR VESSEL.

SHIELDING TANK.

PRIMARY PUMP.

G H DAVIS 1957.

cost to the consumer would be much the same as for conventional generators. These small atomic power units can also be adapted for use in cargo ships and, as forecast in the article quoted opposite, it may not be long before merchant ships are using this new means of propulsion in preference to the older methods. The uranium "fuel" which is used has a long life and, in the case of ships, it would only be necessary to refuel once in every eighteen months or two years.

Drawing reproduced by courtesy of ILLUSTRATED LONDON NEWS

GETTING AWAY FROM THE EARTH

Before a space-ship can go to the Moon it will first have to " escape from the Earth." What this
means, and why it is so, is simply explained here in an exciting way.

BEFORE a rocket can journey to the Moon, Mars or any other planet for that matter, it must first get away from the Earth. That may seem rather obvious, but the main problem holding up the early exploration of outer space is not so much the provision of air or food, heating or cooling, or navigation and control, but simply the initial " escape " from the Earth. That is the reason why, whenever the subject of space travel is being discussed, you usually hear the phrases " escaping from the Earth " and " escape velocity." They are important to a basic understanding of space travel, so let us find out what they mean.

You know that anything you have projected into the air has always come down. No matter how high you have jumped you very soon find yourself back on the Earth again! Similarly, no matter how hard you have thrown a stone or cricket ball up into the air, it has always come back.

THE PULL OF GRAVITY

The reason for this, of course, is the gravitational pull of the Earth. Now gravity is one of those things that we are so used to that we tend to take it for granted. Normally we do not realise that it is acting on us all the time. We usually only notice it—or rather its results—when we fall over, jump off a wall, or sit on a chair that isn't there. But there is nothing that you or anyone else can do about gravity; it acts on everybody and everything all the time.

Gravity may be defined as the *tendency of a body to attract, and to be attracted by, another body.* The actual force of any gravitational pull depends on the weight, or mass as it should be called, of the body concerned and the distance you are from its centre.

The gravitational attraction of the Earth is sufficient to give any unsupported object an acceleration towards the ground of 32 ft. per second. This means that an object starting from rest would, if there were no air to slow it down, cover 16 ft. in the first second, 48 ft.

in the second second, 80 ft. in the third and so on. That is, it would be travelling at 22 m.p.h. at the end of the first second, 44 m.p.h. at the end of the second, and 66 m.p.h. at the end of the third. It is the gravitational pull of the Earth which gives us our apparent weight and is known as " g." Thus, when you read about a space-ship accelerating at 2g, it means that the acceleration is making everything on board appear twice as heavy as it usually is. 3g would indicate three times its normal weight.

On the surface of the Earth the gravitational force is almost constant at 1g, but other planets have different gravitational pulls because of their different structure and size. For example, the gravitational pull of the Moon is only one-sixth that of the Earth. This means that on the Moon you would weigh one-sixth what you do on Earth. Your muscles would remain as strong as they are now, however, and so you would be able to run, taking tremendous strides, or jump heights that would make any Olympic athlete green with envy. You would also be able to carry a much heavier load than you can on Earth. This was an important factor when men landed on the Moon, for it made the very cumbersome space suits that were necessary a little more bearable to wear, and eased the manhandling of several heavy items of scientific equipment that were taken along.

Like the Moon, most of the other bodies of the Solar System have gravities considerably less than that of the Earth. On some tiny " planetoids " gravity is so small that it would take several minutes for an object to fall a couple of yards.

An exception is the giant planet Jupiter, the gravitational pull at the surface of which is more than double that of Earth. So that even if we do ever manage to go to Jupiter we may never land on her surface (assuming she has one to land on, for all we can see through telescopes is the top of an immensely deep and turbulent atmosphere, and it may be that she has no real solid core) for our twice

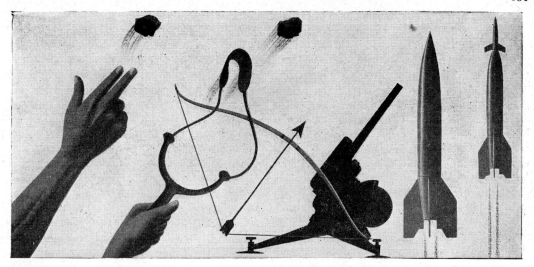

The faster an object is thrown into the air the higher it will go.

normal weight would make it painful to breathe and difficult to move. But even Jupiter is insignificant compared with the Sun, the pull of which is twenty-eight " g," whilst that of some distant stars is a hundred times greater again.

But back to Earth. When you throw a stone up into the **air** gravity begins to slow it down from the moment it leaves your hand, gradually brings it to rest, and then starts to pull it down again. The same thing happens to an anti-aircraft shell or small rocket. Gravity drags them back so that, ignoring the effect of air resistance, they strike the Earth at the same speed at which they started upwards.

But you will know that the harder you throw a stone the higher it will go. The powerful charge of an anti-aircraft gun is sufficient to send up the shell many miles, and rockets have struggled up hundreds of miles before being dragged to rest. In other words, the faster a thing starts off, the higher it will go. This being so, it seems logical to assume that if we could impart a sufficiently high speed to a stone, shell or rocket, it would go up and not return. This, in fact, is just what happens when the speed exceeds 25,000 miles an hour.

ESCAPE VELOCITY

This speed of 25,000 m.p.h. is known as the " escape velocity "; that is, it is the velocity we have to reach if we are to get away from the

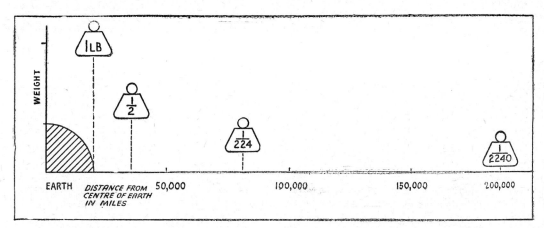

Although the influence of gravity extends to infinity, this diagram shows how it is reduced at varying distances from the Earth. 200,000 miles away a ton weighs about a pound.

Earth with the minimum expenditure of power. This speed would *not* take a space-ship "beyond the reach of gravity," as you sometimes read in magazines, because the gravitational field actually reaches out to infinity. However, because its strength becomes weaker the farther you go from the Earth, it becomes negligible after a few hundred thousand miles or so. The strength of gravity becomes weaker in strict proportion to the square of the distance from the Earth, or any other body. To help you to understand this, it can be compared with the light of a candle, which decreases at the same rate.

At a distance of one foot a candle lights up a square foot of white card with a certain brightness. At a distance of two feet the same

never dies completely. It might dwindle to a millionth part of its original strength—but it can always dwindle some more.

Now imagine you are on a bicycle and approaching a steep hill. You know that if you try and cycle up it at normal speed you will gradually slow down until you have to get off and walk. So what do you do? You put all you've got into a flying start. You pedal furiously and rush at the hill. You reach the bottom and start to climb. At once gravity gets to work on you and you begin to slow down gradually. But if you start with sufficient speed your impetus will carry you to the top. This speed for the hill can be likened to the speed which is required to climb the hill of space.

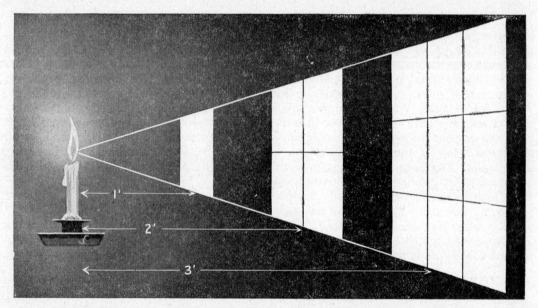

Like the light from a candle, gravity spreads out with distance and becomes weaker in proportion to the square of the distance.

amount of light is spread over 4 square feet. Therefore, the light is only *one-quarter* as bright as it was one foot away. Three feet away the light is spread over nine square feet and is only one-ninth as bright. The area illuminated increases, and the brightness of the light decreases in proportion to the square of the distance from the light. 1,630 miles above the Earth gravity is only half as strong as it is at the surface.

So you can see that gravity continues to spread and weaken with distance, but that it

Like you and your bike—if a space-ship took off with a speed of 25,000 m.p.h. it would be slowed down by gravity the moment the motors were switched off. But the speed is sufficiently high to ensure that at any particular distance from the Earth the space-ship's speed is just greater than the opposing gravitational force.

On the 240,000-mile journey to the Moon a ship will travel slower and slower until its speed has dropped to a few hundred miles an hour. Ever more slowly it will approach the neutral point where the gravitational pull of

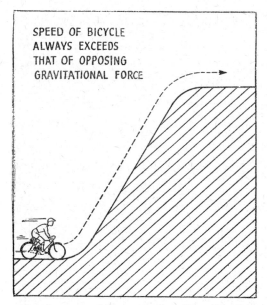

Coasting up a hill on Earth is like climbing the hill of space.

the Earth equals that of the Moon. It will edge past the point and begin to " fall " towards the Moon. If it were not slowed down it would crash into the surface at about 5,000 m.p.h., this being the " escape velocity " of the Moon.

WHY HIGH SPEED IS ESSENTIAL

You may wonder why a space-ship must get up to 25,000 m.p.h. in order to reach the Moon.

After all, a jet airliner travelling at 500 m.p.h. would take less than three weeks to cover the distance. This is quite true, but there are several reasons why it is considered essential to have high speeds for space travel.

A low speed, for example, would mean increased exposure to cosmic radiation and would increase the risk of colliding with a meteor. Also, although three weeks might be acceptable for a trip to the Moon, a journey to Mars would take nearly 11 *years* at 500 m.p.h. Thus for effective space travel we must have high speeds—and they must be reached as quickly as possible. In fact, the higher the speeds and the quicker they are attained the more economical it will be. The reason for this is all bound up with the all-important fuel requirements.

A space-ship could be designed, on paper, to travel to the Moon at a leisurely 500 m.p.h. The amount of fuel required to lift the weight of the ship when empty and the weight of the crew, supplies and instruments could be calculated. This fuel itself would have to be lifted and the lifting of fuel continuously against gravity requires more fuel, and the carrying of this extra fuel in turn calls for yet more fuel. It is a vicious circle and ultimately our space-ship works out as a monster weighing hundreds of thousands, if not millions, of tons. Such a vessel would be fantastically expensive and difficult, if not impossible, to build. We must, therefore, try to make the period of firing as

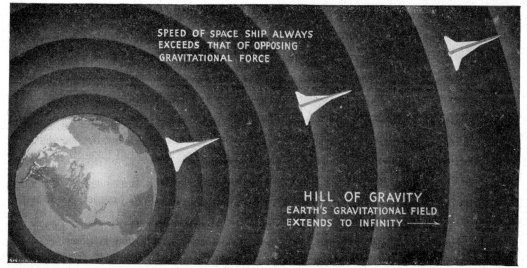

When coasting, a space-ship's speed must always be greater than the opposing gravitational force.

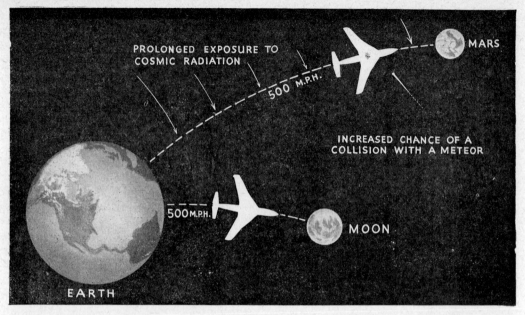

PROLONGED EXPOSURE TO
COSMIC RADIATION

500 M.P.H.

MARS

INCREASED CHANCE OF A
COLLISION WITH A METEOR

500 M.P.H.

MOON

EARTH

Using much fuel and flying at 500 m.p.h. a space-ship could reach the Moon, but there would be increased danger from exposure to cosmic radiation and from collisions with meteors.

Jules Verne's space gun is fired. Any crew would have been killed instantly.

brief as possible for the sooner the fuel is consumed and its energy given to the space-ship the more economic it will be. Ideally, a space-ship ought to use all its fuel instantaneously at take-off, so that none of it would have to be lifted against gravity at all.

This is what happens to a shell when a gun is fired—the charge explodes and in an instant the shell has accelerated to maximum speed and is out of the barrel. It was this fact that led Jules Verne to put forward his solution to space travel in his famous story *From the Earth to the Moon*. He proposed a gigantic gun, 900 ft. long, cast as a well in the ground, The space-ship was the projectile and was about 9 ft. in diameter. Jules Verne probably believed that his space-gun would really work; but we know now that not only would the projectile have been melted by air resistance before it left the barrel, but the violent impact of the tremendous initial take-off would have killed the crew instantly.

A compromise is thus needed. Something between the prohibitive expense of a low-speed rocket and the violent concussion of Jules Verne's space-gun. The type of motor with which this was achieved is described in the article entitled "Ways and Means" which follows.

WAYS and MEANS

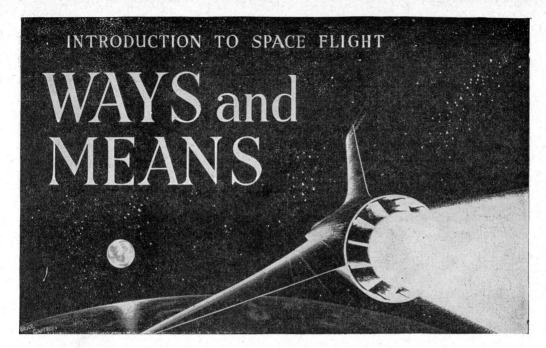

Rocket motors of the kind that can take us to Mars are already in existence! But, for economical space travel, we might have to wait for atomic propulsion. This article describes some of the other kinds of motors that one day might be used for interplanetary flight.

WE do not know how we are going to get to Mars. This may surprise you. After all, over the last few years large numbers of books on space travel have been published, many of them by eminent scientists and engineers. This is quite true, but the mere existence of such a large number of books and magazine articles, often containing graphic descriptions of widely differing space-ships, driven by wonderful engines, indicates that we do not know *exactly* how interplanetary-travel will be achieved. About the only thing really certain is that, one day, we *will* get to the planet.

All we can do at the moment is to work out how we might be able to make the journey in the light of present-day knowledge, perhaps taking into account improvements that can reasonably be expected to be made. But no one can look very far into the future, or predict the very wonderful and far-reaching scientific advances that will almost certainly be made.

We must never forget that what appears quite impossible now might be in everyday use tomorrow. The past is full of examples of things which were " proved " impossible by experts living at the time. For example, one hundred-and-fifty years ago many important mathe-

maticians were busy " proving " that the new-fangled steamships could never cross the Atlantic, as their coal consumption would be too great. More recently, barely 10 years before the Wright brothers made their first historic flight at Kitty Hawk on 17th December, 1903, the famous American astronomer, Simon Newcomb had written: " The demonstration that no possible combination of known substances, known forms of machinery and known forms of force can be united in a practicable machine by which men shall fly long distances through the air, seems to the writer as complete as it is possible for the demonstration of any physical fact to be."

Bearing in mind such past experiences, and with several atomic-submarines actually built and with atomic-powered aircraft under development, it is easy to understand why many scientists consider that it will be an atomic-powered space-ship that will make the first journey to Mars.

THE ATOMIC SPACE-SHIP

At the moment we have only the vaguest ideas of how atomic energy might be used to propel space-ships. So far, the main purpose

155

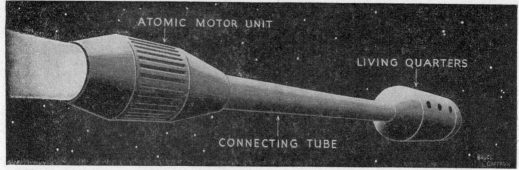

The " Dumb-bell " atomic space-ship places the greatest possible distance between the pile and the crew's quarters.

of atomic motors is to provide heat. They are merely glorified furnaces.

The simplest way of designing an atomic propulsion unit is to arrange for a propellant to be pumped right through the middle of the pile. The idea is that the pile would heat and expand the propellant to form a propulsive jet. The interesting feature about this suggestion is that as the heat is being provided by the atomic pile, almost any liquid would be suitable as the propellant. Hydrogen, ammonia and methane

are three good ones. The last two are particularly interesting, as atmospheres of these gases exist around several plants scattered through the Solar System. So there may be natural refuelling stations strung out across space ready for us to use one day!

It has been suggested that a dumb-bell shape might be suitable for an atomic space-ship, as it would put the biggest possible distance between the pile and the living quarters. The front sphere would contain the control cabin

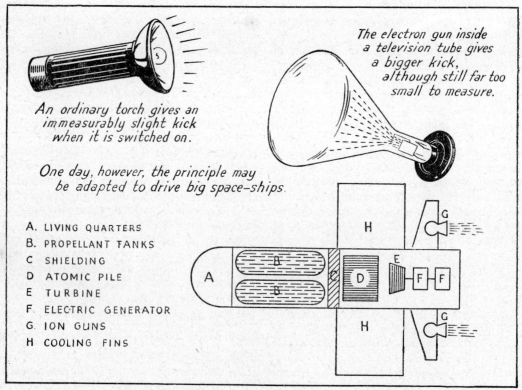

An ordinary torch gives an immeasurably slight kick when it is switched on.

One day, however, the principle may be adapted to drive big space-ships.

The electron gun inside a television tube gives a bigger kick, although still far too small to measure.

A. LIVING QUARTERS
B. PROPELLANT TANKS
C SHIELDING
D ATOMIC PILE
E TURBINE
F. ELECTRIC GENERATOR
G. ION GUNS
H COOLING FINS

The ion-electric rocket with its relatively small amount of thrust will be assembled in space.

and crew's quarters, and the aft one would house the propellant tanks, pile and jet chamber. In order to provide sufficient thrust the propellant will have to be heated up enormously. This means, of course, that the pile will have to be very hot. This is fairly easy to achieve, the difficult part will be in transferring this heat to the propellant. If it cannot be transferred quickly enough the pile will just melt. This is a problem which has yet to be solved, so let us look at another possible power unit for space-ships, early versions of which are running to-day. This is the ion-electric rocket.

THE ION-ELECTRIC ROCKET

The principle of the ion-electric rocket is inherent in the electron gun used in the cathode ray tubes of a television set. These guns shoot a beam of electrons on to the rear of the screen, and so build up the picture you see. In a television set the recoil is negligible, but in an enlarged and improved " gun " appropriate electric and magnetic fields can be made to accelerate charged particles to speeds near that of light to form a usable propulsive jet. The

Testing an ion-electric rocket, designed to propel space-craft at speeds of 100,000 m.p.h.

amount of thrust produced by this method is very small, so small in fact that a space-ship fitted with such an engine would not be able to rise from the Earth's surface. Ion-electric rockets will thus only be used once a space-ship is already in space, their attraction being that they can run for very long periods compared

" Flying Saucers " could be powered by electro-magnetic-drive motors.

with present-day chemical rockets. Although the thrust is very small, the long running time means that, ultimately, very high speeds can be reached.

SPACE-DRIVES

Perhaps, one day, when we have learned a good deal more about the mysteries of gravitation and space, we may be able to produce one of the miraculous " space-drives " often envisaged in science-fiction magazines. The big advantage of such a motor would be that accelerations of any magnitude could be produced without strain on the ship or the crew. It is not speed itself which is dangerous—as you read this you are spinning round the Sun at something like 55,000 m.p.h.—it is the rate at which the speed is increased that normally imposes the strain. Even if the ship was increasing speed at 1,000 gravities, the occupants would still feel quite weightless. The reason for this is the force generated by such a device would act uniformly on every atom of the spaceship and crew. At the moment, of course, we have not the slightest idea of how to start designing such a motor, but the suggestion is by no means as absurd as it may at first appear. The gravitational fields of planets—the Earth included—produce just such an effect! If you were falling freely towards the Earth you would, of course, be accelerating at one gravity as you neared the surface, and yet you would feel quite weightless.

Again, the various forms of electro-magnetic drive motors suggested as being the power units of " Flying Saucers " offer other tantalising possibilities. We really know so little about electricity and magnetism that few scientists will declare outright that such motors are not possible, or that we will *never* be able to make one.

So far, we have been investigating some of the exciting motors that may be used to take us through space in the distant future. But what about to-day? Is there a form of motor available that can take us to the Moon now? There is—it is the rocket.

You may wonder why the sort of jet engines used in the Concorde airliner or the Vulcan bomber could not be adapted for use in a spaceship? The answer is that almost all the engines used in aircraft—piston, turbo-jet, turbo-prop, diesel, ram-jet or athodyd—need *air* before they can work. Each of the tre-

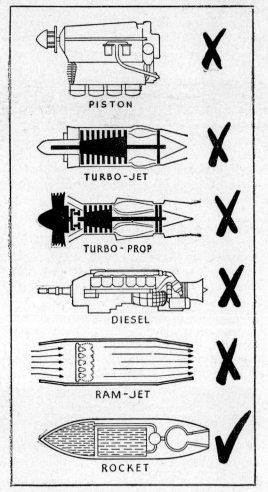

Of all existing motors, only the rocket can work in the vacuum of space.

mendously powerful Olympus engines of the Vulcan, for example, give the aircraft an eight-ton push near the ground, but in the thinner air at around 60,000 ft. this power drops to about *half a ton* and would decrease to *nothing* farther up. The Vulcan, or any other jet aircraft for that matter, cannot climb indefinitely, because sooner or later the height is reached where the air is too thin either to support the aircraft, or to enable its engines to develop the power to push it along. Where there is no air, the piston and jet engines stop. And, of course, there is no air in the vacuum of space.

HOW A ROCKET WORKS

Now, how is it a rocket will work in a vacuum? Imagine a metal cylinder, closed at each end, poised in space as shown in Fig. 1a. Now imagine an explosion inside the container. The force of the expanding gases tries to burst the container, but it is too strong. So what happens? Nothing! Inside there is a force pushing against end A, but this is balanced by an equal force acting against end B and so it does not move sideways. The forces acting against the top of the cylinder trying to push it upwards is balanced by equal forces acting downwards and so it does not move in that direction either (Fig. 1b).

But now imagine that the cylinder is un-blocked at end B (Fig. 1c). The tube will still not move up or down as these forces still cancel each other out. The force formerly acting on end B, however, now has nothing to push against and so rushes out of the end of the tube unhindered. This leaves the force acting on end A which, having nothing to balance it, pushes the container to the left. The same sort of thing happens in a rocket, except that instead of one bang there is a continual series of explosions.

The important fact to grasp is that it is *not* the gases that fly to the right out of the cylinder that do the work. It is the gases bottled up trying to move to the left. This being so, it is easy to understand that the presence of air actually lowers the power of a rocket. Not only does air provide resistance to the nose of the rocket but it tends to obstruct the free flow of the exhaust rushing out. So, not only will a rocket *work* in a vacuum, it works *best* in one.

The principle of the rocket, whether it is atomic, electric, or the type you fire off on Guy Fawkes' day, is tied up by the third of Sir Isaac Newton's famous Laws of Motion, " To every action there is an equal and opposite re-action." In simpler words, this means that a force in one direction creates an equal force in the opposite direction. The force of the gas rushing out of the rear of a rocket is accom-panied by an equal force acting in the opposite direction inside the combustion chamber and this drives the rocket forward.

A simple experiment will illustrate the principle. Imagine yourself standing on a small wheeled trolley weighing as much as you do. Place your feet against one edge and jump off. Common sense and Newton's Law tells us that whatever speed you jump off at will be exactly equal to the speed with which the

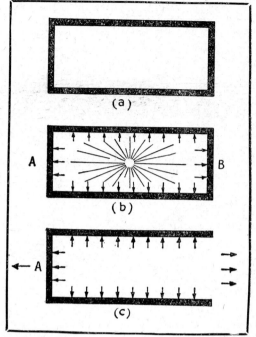

This shows how a gas reacts when one end of the tube is opened.

trolley rolls in the opposite direction. If the trolley weighed twice as much as you, then its speed would be half yours; if it were half your weight it would roll away twice as fast. The Law of Reaction is as simple as that.

And, if you have never jumped off a trolley, you will, I am quite sure, have noticed how a boat tends to move away from the bank as you step ashore from it. It is no good trying to jump off quickly because the greater effort will make the boat move even farther away from the bank. Remember, every force is accom-panied by an equal force acting in the opposite direction.

Another familiar example occurs when a gun is fired. The bullet shoots forwards and the gun " kicks " backwards. Of course there is a big difference between the weight of the two, but the law of reaction still holds.

CHEMICAL ROCKETS

All the rocket motors being used to-day to launch satellites and space-ships are of the chemical " firework " type. That is, they rely upon the combustion of chemicals to expel exhaust material, and so produce the reaction to force the motor along.

EXAMPLES OF
ACTION and REACTION

ACTION

REACTION

ACTION

REACTION

ACTION

REACTION

RECOIL (REACTION!) CHAMBER

The famous Law of Motion, " To every force there is an equal force in the opposite direction,"
is illustrated in the everyday happenings shown above.

All the conventional rocket motors use two chemicals, known as the fuel and the oxidant. The oxidant, as its name implies, provides the oxygen to support combustion in the vacuum of space, and the fuel provides the energy.

In the simplest rockets the two chemicals are mixed together to form a putty-like substance; this type is known as a solid-propellant rocket.

The most powerful motors, however, use liquid propellants, and are thus known as liquid-propellant rockets. Most of these are bi-propellant; that is, they use two separate liquids—a liquid fuel and a liquid oxidant. A common oxidant often used in to-day's rockets is liquid oxygen. This boils at *minus* 183°C., and it is this extreme coldness that is responsible for the coating of ice that forms around the middle of most rockets before they take off. The two propellants are normally stored in separate tanks, and are only mixed upon injection into the combustion chamber.

The propellants are forced into the combustion chamber either by pumps, or by pressure in the tanks. In the latter case, gas is stored at high pressure and, by means of valves, is allowed to enter the propellant tanks, where it literally blows the propellant into the combustion chamber.

A big rocket motor burns propellant at a prodigious rate. In an Atlas or Titan missile the propellant is forced into the combustion chamber at the rate of hundreds of gallons every second. On such rockets the propellant is normally pumped into the combustion chamber. These pumps often need engines of several thousand horse power to drive them. The pump on the giant one-and-a-half-million-pound-thrust F-1 motors of Saturn 5 developed in the United States needs 60,000 h.p., and forces over three tons of propellant into the combustion chamber *every second*. This is the kind of motor which was used to launch the *Apollo 11* spacecraft on its journey to the Moon in July, 1969.

This four-chamber Gamma rocket motor powers Britain's Black Knight research rocket. It has proved extremely reliable.

More than one-and-a-half million pounds of thrust streams from a giant U.S. F-1 Moon-rocket motor during a night test.

B.S.   F

STEPS TO THE STARS

Man has used steps since the beginning of time, and will need their help to reach the planets.

IN order to overcome the Earth's gravity a certain speed has to be attained. This speed, 25,000 m.p.h., is known as the escape velocity, or as in Russia, as the "second cosmic" speed.

For practical reasons it is desirable to attain this speed as rapidly as possible. In theory one could, of course, leave the Earth at a more leisurely pace, say at a steady 1,000 m.p.h. But, with present-day rockets and technology this is not possible, as it would require a prodigious amount of fuel. This is because the motor of a rocket rising from the surface of the Earth is not only lifting the weight of the structure, equipment and, in the case of manned spacecraft, the crew, but the weight of the unburnt fuel. It is also working against gravity. The more rapidly the escape velocity can be attained, the shorter is the fight against gravity; the time any unburnt fuel is being lifted is shorter, and the less fuel is used.

Once escape velocity is attained the motor can be stopped and the rocket will continue to coast away from the Earth. Gravity will slow it down, but never sufficiently to bring it to rest, so that the rocket will always continue to draw away from the Earth.

In practice the speed at which a rocket accelerates is determined partly by the maximum "g" forces the crew can withstand, and partly by the maximum aerodynamic loads imposed as the rocket rises through the dense lower layers of the atmosphere.

How is the enormous speed, 25,000 m.p.h., needed to escape from the Earth, attained?

It can be shown mathematically that the speed of a rocket depends on the speed of its exhaust. The faster the jet rushes out, the bigger the reaction inside the rocket and the faster it is thrust on its way. If the exhaust speed is doubled, the speed of the rocket will be doubled.

HIGH RATIO NEEDED FOR SPEED

It can also be shown that in order to reach the speed of its own exhaust a rocket must carry 1·72 times its empty weight as fuel. In other words, the ratio between the weight of the fuel and the weight of the rest of the rocket must be 1·72 to 1. Thus, a rocket weighing 3 tons empty, would have to carry just over 5 tons of fuel if it were to reach the speed of its jet.

It is easy to design a rocket that achieves this ratio. The German V-2 war-rocket did better and the American Viking high-altitude research rocket achieved the creditable ratio of 4 to 1. This means that for every pound of structure, control equipment, pumps and motor, there were four pounds of fuel.

Much better ratios have been achieved by refined design in later rockets such as the Atlas, Titan, Blue Streak and Saturn. In these there are no separate fuel tanks; the outer skin of the rocket itself is used as the tank wall.

DESIGNING A SMALL SPACESHIP

Let us imagine that we are designing a small spaceship and that we want it to fly at about 5,000 m.p.h.—the speed of its exhaust. The weight of the structure, skinning, cabin, instruments, motors, provisions and crew of three might be about 6 tons. Now we know that if a rocket is to fly at the speed of its exhaust it must carry 1·72 times its empty weight as fuel. Thus, our spaceship must carry 1·72 × 6 = 10½ tons of fuel. The total weight would be 16½ tons.

The speed can be increased by cramming in more fuel, that is, by increasing the mass ratio. A ratio of 6·4 to 1 would enable a speed double that of the exhaust to be reached. A ratio of 6·4 to 1 would mean carrying 6·4 × 6 = 38 tons of fuel.

Our spaceship could now reach a speed of 10,000 m.p.h., but this is still 15,000 m.p.h. below the desired escape velocity.

Let us cram in even more fuel. 114 tons of fuel would give a speed of 15,000 m.p.h., whilst 330 tons would raise it to 20,000 m.p.h. In theory, 1,086 tons of fuel—that is, a mass ratio of 181 to 1—would enable a spaceship to reach the desired speed of 25,000 m.p.h.

In practice there are several factors which would make even more fuel necessary. One

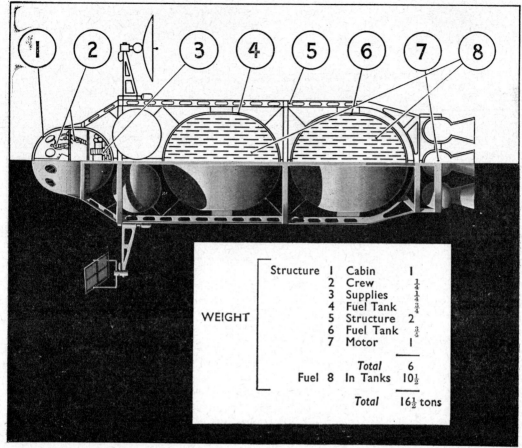

This diagram shows how the total weight of a spaceship is made up. By carrying fuel weighing 1.72 times it own weight, it can reach the speed of its exhaust.

WEIGHT	Structure	1	Cabin	1
		2	Crew	$\frac{1}{4}$
		3	Supplies	$\frac{1}{4}$
		4	Fuel Tank	$\frac{3}{4}$
		5	Structure	2
		6	Fuel Tank	$\frac{3}{4}$
		7	Motor	1
			Total	6
	Fuel	8	In Tanks	$10\frac{1}{2}$
			Total	$16\frac{1}{2}$ tons

is the friction of the air, which would slow our spaceship down as it climbed up through the atmosphere. Of much greater importance would be the effect of gravity, which would be continuously pulling the spaceship back and reducing its speed by 20 m.p.h. for every second it climbed. When these factors are taken into account the actual mass ratio required works out at nearer 1,000 to 1. Using existing fuels this would, in theory, give a speed of 25,000 m.p.h.

AN IMPOSSIBLE FUEL WEIGHT

Of course, 6,006 tons would be a big rocket, but not impossibly big; the Saturn 5 used to launch the Apollo spacecraft to the Moon weighs 3,000 tons, and much heavier ships have been built to sail the seas. Even so we could not build our spaceship. Have you guessed why? Let us examine the weight distribution a little more closely. A mass ratio of 1,000 to 1 means a thousand tons of fuel to be carried for every ton of the spaceship itself, This is, of course, the snag. It cannot be done. Nobody could design a fuel tank weighing 6 tons to hold 6,000 tons of fuel, let alone a tank *and* motors, cabin, provisions and crew. Likewise, it would be quite impossible to carry 1,086 tons, 330 tons, or even 114 tons of fuel in a 6-ton spaceship. However it might be possible to put 38 tons in, that is, achieve a ratio of 6·4 to 1. We have not yet managed to build such a spaceship—remember, the 6 tons would have to cover the weight of the structure, skinning, controls, motor, provisions, crew *and* fuel tanks. It will not be easy but may be practicable.

This means that the best we can hope for,

Historic occasion. One of the first applications of the step-principle was the American Bumper-Wac research rocket. In 1949, one of these set up a then world altitude record of 242 miles.

using present-day fuels, is a speed equal to twice that of the exhaust, or about 10,000 m.p.h. To go faster we must either develop more powerful fuels or think up some new methods of construction.

Many people are hard at work in secret laboratories and workshops all over the world doing just this. There is, however, a definite limit to the power we can expect from the use of fuels. This theoretical limit seems to be about double the best achieved to-day so that the very highest speed we can ever hope to achieve with our spaceship is only 20,000 m.p.h.—5,000 short of the target figure.

OVERCOMING THE IMPOSSIBLE

At this point readers might well begin to wonder how it is that men have gone to the Moon, and that unmanned craft have managed to overcome gravity in order to reach out to the planets Mars and Venus.

The answer is that a technical "trick" is used to enable rockets to reach the velocity of escape. This trick is the step-rocket.

THE STEP-ROCKET

As the name implies, a step-rocket is a big rocket consisting of several smaller ones perched one on top of the other. The idea is that if a rocket, which can reach a certain speed, is made the payload of a bigger rocket which can reach the same speed, then the smaller one will be able to go twice as fast as either rocket could itself.

The step idea is not new. The principle was used often in the early history of polar exploration, and during the first exciting conquest of Mount Everest. When climbing a mountain one man, by himself, can carry only enough provisions to enable him to climb so far. He can climb higher if he starts out with a larger number of men who turn back at some point, after handing on their surplus stores. Many hundreds of porters started out on the lower slopes of Everest, but most of them turned back at various camps after handing on their surplus stores to smaller groups. This procedure was repeated until, finally, the last party handed on their stores

Step-rockets are assisting the conquest of space in the same way that "steps" of porters assist the conquest of mountains. The principle was also used in early polar exploration.

to two men, Sir Edmund Hillary and Tiger Tensing—who then reached the summit.

MULTI-STEP-ROCKETS

As far as rockets are concerned there is no need to stop at four steps. Any number of steps may be used and if we build a rocket with a sufficient number any speed you want may be obtained—in theory.

The snag is that as the number of steps is increased the weight goes up alarmingly. The payload of a high-performance rocket is likely to be only about one-twentieth of its total weight. Each step will thus weigh twenty times the weight of the steps above. For a one-ton payload, the weight would go up like this. Single-step, 20 tons; two-step, 400 tons; three-step, 8,000 tons; and so on. Practical considerations indicate that three or four steps are as many as we can cope with.

An interesting multi-step-rocket was the German Rheinbote, used to bombard Antwerp during the closing stages of the last war. Some 37 feet long, this missile included no fewer than four steps The launching weight was 3,780 lb. whilst the warhead was only 88 lb.; the relative smallness of the latter compared with the

original weight indicates well the disadvantage of carrying the step principle too far.

Let us consider three steps for our 6-ton spaceship. Each step would contribute one-third of the desired escape velocity, or 8,333 m.p.h. When allowances have been made for air friction and gravitational retardation the mass ratio works out at 10 to 1. The total weight of the three steps would then be about 24,000 tons of which nearly 23,000 tons would be fuel.

This tremendous weight could be reduced by about half if the rocket, instead of struggling up vertically, turned parallel to the earth when sufficient height had been gained.

To-day the step-principle is firmly established

The Rheinbote, a four-step German rocket used to bombard Antwerp during World War II. Weighing 3,780 lb., its warhead weighed only 88 lb.

and, in fact, all the satellites and spaceships launched so far have been boosted aloft by step-rockets.

Unless some new form of propulsive power is developed the principle is also likely to be used to launch the big spaceships of the future.

AMERICA'S SATURN 5

The most impressive step-rocket of which details are readily available is America's *Saturn 5*, used to launch the Apollo spacecraft to the Moon.

Saturn 5 is a three-stage rocket, weighing about 3,000 tons when fully fuelled and standing 280 feet tall. The giant vehicle is capable of boosting a payload of 285,000 lb. into a low Earth orbit or sending 100,000 lb. to the Moon.

The first stage, 138 feet long by 33 feet in diameter, is powered by five Rocketdyne F-1 engines, each of which develops a thrust of 1·5 million lb., nearly 750 tons. Known as the S1-C, the stage is built by Boeing in New Orleans.

The second stage, the S-11, is over 81 feet long by 33 feet in diameter. Made by North American Rockwell in California, it is powered by five J-2 engines each developing a thrust of 200,000 lb.

The third stage, the S-IVB, built by McDonnell Douglas in California, is 58 feet long and

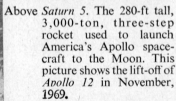

Above *Saturn 5*. The 280-ft tall, 3,000-ton, three-step rocket used to launch America's Apollo spacecraft to the Moon. This picture shows the lift-off of *Apollo 12* in November, 1969.

Left Expended S-IVB third stage of the *Apollo 7* test mission, shown orbiting over the Florida peninsula. The round white disc inside the panels is a simulated docking target similar to that used on the Lunar Module for docking during lunar missions.

22 feet in diameter. It is powered by a single J-2 engine of the type used in the second stage.

At lift-off from Cape Kennedy, the five engines of the first-stage burn simultaneously, gulping kerosene fuel and liquid oxygen at the incredible rate of 28,000 lb. a *second*. Initially the rate of climb is incredibly slow; in fact it takes about 8 seconds for the rocket to clear the launching tower. Speed builds up rapidly and 2 minutes 31 seconds later, with its fuel almost exhausted, the first stage has lifted the spacecraft to a height of about 40 miles and boosted its speed to 6,000 m.p.h. It is then jettisoned, to splash down harmlessly in the South Atlantic, its brief, but important, task completed. Separation is assisted by eight 88,000 lb.-thrust solid propellant retro-rockets pointing forward, which fire for half a second to brake the giant stage.

A few seconds later the five engines of the S-11 second stage ignite and begin to build up thrust. The engines burn for over six minutes and boost the speed of the rocket to 15,000 m.p.h. and the altitude to 100 miles. Then it too is jettisoned, at a point some 800 miles down range from the launching pad. As in the case of the first stage, solid propellant retro-rockets are used to back the second stage away at separation.

The third stage also carries two solid propellant rockets—pointing rearwards. These are used to help move the third stage forward and away from the second stage at separation, and also to settle the liquid propellants in the bottoms of the tanks in preparation for the ignition of the single J-2 engine.

For normal lunar missions the engine of the S-IVB third stage fires twice. The first burn lasts for about $2\frac{1}{2}$ minutes and increases the speed to a little over 17,000 m.p.h. and places the Apollo spacecraft in a 100-mile high Earth parking orbit. The craft is then thoroughly checked and if all is well the engine is restarted and burns for over 5 minutes to give the craft escape velocity and place it in a trajectory that will take it to the Moon.

Once coasting safely to the Moon the Command Module, with the Service Module attached, separates from the third stage and carries out what is known as the transposition and docking manœuvre. The Command Module turns round and then noses back to the third stage and connects with the Lunar Module which lies cradled in the nose of the stage up to this moment. When the two craft are securely docked the Command Module gently withdraws the Lunar Module. Then, with the spidery-looking craft perched on its nose, the Command Module turns round and continues its coasting flight to the Moon.

The S-IVB stage, its task done, drifts on in space, also towards the Moon, and spends its life either looping round the Moon and Earth, or it enters a planetary orbit and begins to circle the Sun. Sometimes the stage is deliberately guided to crash into the Moon. This was done on the ill-fated *Apollo 13* mission when the stage was crashed into the Moon to create a shock wave for the Moonquake instruments left behind by the astronauts of *Apollo 12*.

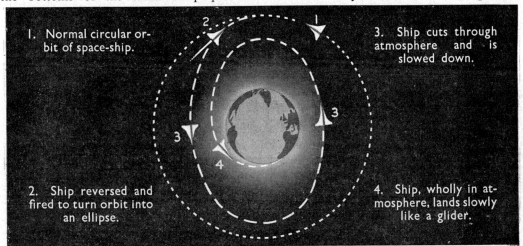

1. Normal circular orbit of space-ship.

3. Ship cuts through atmosphere and is slowed down.

2. Ship reversed and fired to turn orbit into an ellipse.

4. Ship, wholly in atmosphere, lands slowly like a glider.

Aerodynamic-braking. How the friction of the atmosphere is used to slow down spaceships and so save the heavy and expensive fuel that would otherwise be required.

American space laboratory based on the S-IVB third stage of the *Saturn 5* launching rocket. It is designed for periods of duty lasting up to 56 days.

Introduction to Space Flight

LABORATORIES IN SPACE

The establishment of space stations will be a major step towards the conquest of space.

EVEN before *Sputnik I* was launched in 1957, scientists, engineers—and military staffs—looked forward to the day when space stations would be orbiting the Earth.

Such stations—or laboratories—will have many unique advantages over their counterparts on the surface of the Earth.

For example, in Earth laboratories the creation of even a partial vacuum for research purposes is an expensive and time-consuming process, and the best vacuum that can be produced is not as good as that which exists naturally in space. An orbiting laboratory will thus be ideal for experiments requiring a vacuum.

On the surface of the Earth it is almost impossible to create conditions of weightlessness. A laboratory in orbit will be falling freely and all objects within it will appear weightless. A laboratory in orbit will thus be ideal for experiments requiring an absence of gravity.

An obvious advantage of a laboratory in Earth orbit is that of an observation platform. Astronomers will be able to study the stars unhampered by the distortion caused by the atmosphere. Geologists, using extremely sensitive detecting devices now under development, will be able to survey the crust of the Earth and assist the location of new reserves of oil and minerals.

Visual observations from such stations in space will supplement the meteorological data being gathered by America's Tiros and Nimbus, and Russia's Meteor, weather satellites. The military data being gathered by the reconnaissance satellites of Russia and America will also be supplemented.

Laboratories in space will have many more uses, ranging from those associated with the field of medicine to helping determine the human tolerance to long-term operations in the alien environment of space.

Looking ahead several years, journeys to the Moon and the planets will also be easier and less costly if they could begin and end at a station in space instead of on the surface of the Earth.

In view of the foregoing it is not surprising that both the United States and Russia have ambitious plans for constructing space stations at the earliest opportunity.

Few details of Russia's long-term plans are available, but official announcements over a number of years hint that she may be devoting more money and energy to this aspect of the conquest of space than to the exploration of the Moon.

Russia has already conducted several important experiments closely connected with the development of space stations. Two such experiments were the automatic rendezvous and docking missions of *Cosmos 186* and *188* in 1967, and *Cosmos 212* and *213* in 1968.

SOYUZ SPACE STATION

These two unmanned trials were later followed in January, 1969, by the launching of the two manned spacecraft *Soyuz 4* and *5*. In space these two craft rendezvoused and docked to form what the Russians called the world's first spacestation. Each Soyuz spacecraft comprises three sections: a Service Module,

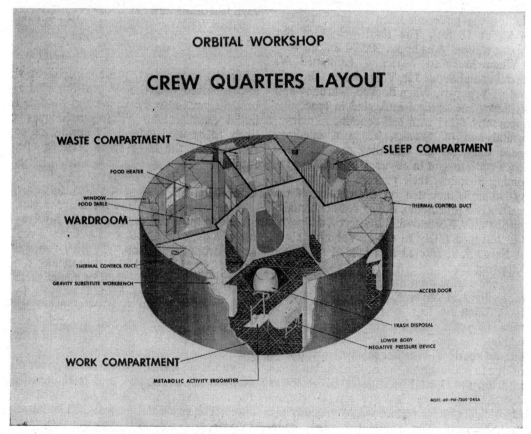

SKYLAB LIVING QUARTERS SECTION. Astronauts will go to bed in the sleep compartment in bags hanging up on the wall. With no "up" or "down", this has advantages over sleeping horizontally.

a Command Module and an Orbital Module.

The Service Module contains the main power supply and a large restartable engine, and supports two large wing-like solar cell panels. The Command Module is located immediately forward of the Service Module and contains couches for three cosmonauts. As the title implies, this is the nerve centre of the craft and contains all the main instrumentation and navigational equipment, and embodies the blunt heat shield needed for re-entry. The Orbital Module, forward of the Command Module, is slightly bigger and roughly spherical in shape and is used for rest and work purposes. The interior volume of the Command Module is about 140 cubic feet and that of the work/rest module about 175 cubic feet. For a comparison, the internal volume of an average family four-seater car is about 150 cubic feet.

When joined to form a "space station" the two Soyuz craft had an overall length of more than 50 feet and a maximum diameter, excluding the girder-mounted tracking aerials, of about 12 feet. The total weight of the "space station" was about 30,000 lb.

When launched *Soyuz 4* contained V. Shatalov and *Soyuz 5* B. Volynov, Y. Khrunov and A. Yeliseyev. When docked, Khrunov and Yeliseyev left *Soyuz 5* and, clad in spacesuits apparently fitted with self-contained environmental control systems, began a one-hour space walk. At the end they re-entered the space station—not in *Soyuz 5*, but in *Soyuz 4*, joining Shatalov, their passage being assisted by handrails mounted on the outside of the craft. After four hours, *Soyuz 4*, now containing Shatalov, Khrunov and Yeliseyev, undocked and returned safely to earth. Volynov, alone in *Soyuz 5*, re-entered and landed safely the following day.

In some ways even more impressive was the triple flight of *Soyuz 6, 7* and *8* in October, 1969, when no less than seven cosmonauts were in space simultaneously. During this mission the three craft rendezvoused in orbit, but did not dock. Whether this was intentional, or due to malfunction, is not known, but while in orbit, the Orbital Module of *Soyuz 6* was de-pressurized and used for several welding experiments under conditions of vacuum and weightlessness. The equipment used, code-named *Vulcan*, was operated by remote control.

SKYLAB PANTRY. An engineer checks out the removal of a food canister from its stowage in the wardroom.

After the experiment, the compartment was re-pressurized and the samples retrieved and brought back into the Command Module for initial examination. Welding techniques are likely to be used extensively during the construction of the large space stations of the future.

U.S. SKYLAB

America's initial plans for a space station are along quite different lines, and involve the use of a huge S-IVB stage of a *Saturn 5* rocket as an orbital workshop. The S-IVB measures some 58 feet long and 22 feet in diameter, and it is planned to use the shell of one of these as the basis of a space station manned by a crew of three. It will have a useful volume of about 10,000 cubic feet and will weigh about 130,000 lb. It is thus much bigger and heavier than the Soyuz space station.

The stage will be stripped of its power plant and normal equipment, and re-equipped and furnished as a space station. An air-lock will be fitted. The space station will then be launched into orbit. A second launch will then take up the crew who, in an Apollo Command Module-type of craft, will rendezvous and dock with the space station.

The space station, or Skylab as it is referred to unofficially, will provide working and living conditions for the crew for 28 days, after which they will return to Earth in the Apollo Command Module "ferry" craft. A second crew will then occupy the space station for up to 56 days. Later crews may stay up even longer.

In view of the importance of astronomical observations from space, the Americans have plans for attaching a large telescope to the space station. Rather ingeniously the mounting for the telescope is based on the ascent stage of the Apollo Lunar Module, which contains the elaborate, but well-proved, probe and drogue docking collar and other equipment necessary for this tricky manœuvre. The telescope is about 150 in. long by 80 in. in diameter, and will be mounted on a rack embodying controls for alignment.

The main body of the Skylab is divided into three broad areas; one for research, one for power and air generating equipment, and one for living in.

The research section, as its name implies, is to be used for conducting the various experiments and observations. About 50 experiments are being planned. These are divided into five groups covering scientific, technological, applications, operational and medical matters.

The power section houses the elaborate equipment and systems needed to keep the station operating both as a laboratory and a home.

The living section, known officially as the "habitability support system", is, perhaps, the most interesting section of all. This is the section in which the astronauts will eat, sleep and

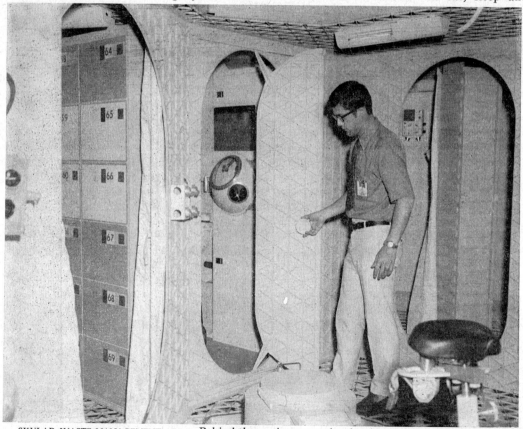

SKYLAB WASTE MANAGEMENT AREA. Behind the engineer are the sleeping quarters. The bulbous fixture visible through the open door is a zero-*g* hand-washing device for the astronauts. The bicycle seat in the lower right corner is part of an exerciser that generates electrical power as an astronaut pedals.

Early prophetic design for a four-man space station, based on the *Atlas* booster rocket. The principle has been adopted for the U.S. space station now under construction, which is based on the third stage of the *Saturn 5* booster.

be comfortable during their off-duty periods.

ASTRONAUTS' QUARTERS

The astronauts' quarters are divided into sleep compartments, a personal hygiene area and a wardroom.

The sleeping compartments are little bigger than a cupboard, as the astronauts will sleep vertically, "hanging on the wall" in sleeping bags. The possibility of horizontal sleeping arrangements was studied, but the vertical position was considered the best of all the positions considered. This decision may seem strange to us on Earth, but in a condition of weightlessness, as the Skylab will be when it is in orbit, it will not matter, for there will be no up or down.

This was dramatically demonstrated during the flight of the *Apollo 13* spacecraft after its Service Module had been crippled by an explosion on the way to the Moon. During the exciting and dangerous journey back to Earth, Fred Haise, the Lunar Module pilot slept "upside down" in the narrow tunnel linking the LM to the Command Module, with his head projecting into the LM and resting on the cover of the ascent engine.

On the Skylab, although the sleeping compartments are small, each has a privacy partition, storage lockers, tissue dispensers and a waste-paper container.

In the hygiene area is a "flushing toilet", a vacuum cleaner, a washing bowl and storage compartments for toothbrushes, razors and other personal items.

One amenity the astronauts will not have is a shower or bath. Designers have given this problem serious attention, but at the present state of development it is not practical to provide these. Instead, the astronauts will take sponge baths.

The wardroom is a general purpose compartment, serving as a galley, dining-room and study. Kitchen equipment includes refrigerators, food storage cabinets, a table and restraint harness that will be worn while food is being prepared, a water chiller, drinking water dispensers and three ovens. Each astronaut will have his own separate supply of drinking water to minimise the risk of infection.

For the longer duration missions, the Skylab will need almost a ton of food. This will include 250 lb. of dehydrated food, 400 lb. of intermediate moisture and wet pack food, 250 lb. of frozen food and 50 lb. of fresh food. Complete meals will be packaged for each member of the crew.

The wardroom embodies a large observation window in spite of the extra weight and slight increase in danger this entails. The window will help to minimise the closed-in feeling some people experience, even on islands. Astronauts feel that they will be able to make valuable scientific contributions by just gazing out of the window and recording their observations.

AIR AND WATER

A major problem in the development of space stations is the supply of oxygen and water. In the Russian Soyuz station and the U.S. Saturn S-IVB stage station these are provided from storage vessels, as they are on a submarine. The Soyuz craft was only in orbit for a short while and thus presented no problems; on the S-IVB station the storage vessels will have to be recharged at regular intervals. For long duration missions in orbiting space stations, i.e. for missions extending over three months, a regenerative life support system is the answer. That is, a system that can provide a breathable atmosphere and fresh water without re-supply by continuously reclaiming carbon dioxide and body waste water for re-use.

A series of tests to evaluate such a regenerative system and to develop the technology and procedures for long duration missions was conducted in the U.S. during 1970. Four volunteers occupied a space station simulator for varying periods of time, during which they had to monitor the performance of the equipment in the simulator, maintain it and attempt repairs—just as astronauts would if they were in orbit.

ARTIFICIAL GRAVITY

From the Soyuz and U.S. Skylab space stations will evolve the bigger stations of tomorrow, although it will be a long time before the hotel-cum-research laboratories often depicted in glossy magazines become a reality.

A space station, as previously mentioned, will be in a condition popularly known as "free-fall" or zero "g". Occupants will have no apparent weight, because gravity will be unopposed as the station falls freely as it circles the Earth.

Although superb fitness and intensive training has enabled astronauts to cope with this condition much more readily than was at one time expected, and some astronauts definitely enjoy being weightless and able to float about effortlessly, it presents problems and could well constitute a hazard to health if experienced for a period of weeks or months.

Because of this, considerable thought has been given to the possibility of introducing an artificial gravity and, fortunately, there is a relatively simple method by which this can be achieved. It involves the use of centrifugal force. If a space station is spun on its axis, like a top, then the crew will be pressed against the outside wall in the same way as we are attracted to the surface of the Earth.

To the crews, the outside wall will be "down", and they will be able to walk about on it without bouncing and floating about. If the rate of rotation is correctly chosen, they could experience normal weight and would be unable to distinguish between artificial gravity and the real thing.

Although basically simple, the spinning method does present problems. One is that unless the diameter is very great, gyroscopic forces become acute, and could disturb the delicate ear mechanisms which balance us.

Experiments indicate that if normal gravity is required, a minimum diameter of two miles is necessary. Obviously it is impractical to build a station this size but the effect could be achieved by attaching two space stations to a length of cable and then spinning the pair like a South American bolas.

The final solution will probably be a compromise between zero "g" and normal gravity. Even a slight spinning action would ensure that there was a "down", so that if something was dropped, it would fall to the floor and not float away. Even a slight gravity would ease the problems of eating—and make it possible to install a bath.

A MODERN RUNWAY
AND AN AIR

LATEST TYPE JET FIGHTER AIRCRAFT (LENGTH ABOUT 40-45 FT.)
WITH FULL LOAD.
TAKE-OFF RUN 1500-3000 FT.

0   1000 (LENGTHS IN FEET)   2000   3000   4000

THROUGH THE MAIN RUNWAYS AT LONDON AIRPORT ARE OVER 9000 FT. LONG IT IS POSSIBLE THEY WILL NOT BE LENGTHY ENOUGH FOR AIRCRAFT OF THE FUTURE.

SOME IDEAS RECENTLY TESTED TO SOLVE THE PROBLEM OF VERTICAL TAKE-OFF OR OF SHORTENING THE RUN REQUIRED.

TAKE-

TERMINAL BUILDINGS

SCALE 1000 YARDS.

TURNING.

IN NORMAL FLIGHT.

RISING VERTICALLY.

ON THE GROUND.

EXPERIMENTS ARE BEING MADE USING A MOBILE RAMP.

TAKE-OFF ROCKETS.

COMPARED WITH THE LONG RUNS REQUIRED BY AIRCRAFT TO TAKE-OFF AND LAND BIRDS ARE AIRBORNE AFTER A FEW STEPS AND A JUMP.

NAVY

JETTISONABLE ROCKETS ARE NOW IN USE TO ASSIST IN TAKE-OFF.

ROCKETS JETTISONED.

TAKE-OFF A BY BLOW-D FLAPS.

THE CONVAIR XFY-1 AN AMERICAN DESIGN FOR VERTICAL TAKE-OFF.

A SUGGESTED DESIGN FOR A SUPERSONIC AIRCRAFT WITH VERTICAL THRUST MO FOR TAKE-OFF OR LANDING. AS THESE MOTORS WOULD ONLY BE IN ACTION FOR 8 OR 10 MINUTES AT A TIME THEY WOULD HAVE A VERY HIGH POWER-TO-WEIGHT AND BE SIMPLE IN CONSTRUCTION.

PROPULSION MOTOR.

PROPULSION MOTOR.

THE ROLLS-ROYCE "SOAR" TURBO-JET WHICH MAY BE TH FORERUNNER OF THE VERTICAL-LIFT ENGINES OF TOMOR

DIAMETER 16 IN.
WEIGHT 275 LB.
THRUST 1,810 LB.

To solve the problems of the take-off and landing of the heavier and ever-faster aircraft of to-day and to-morrow, scientists and aircraft designers have tried out many ingenious ideas for assisted take-off and slower, safer landing. Our artist has explained pictorially some of the American and British experiments in vertical take-off and landing which have the greatest possibilities for future development. It should be possible in

Drawings reproduced by courtesy

A LARGE LINER (LENGTH ABOUT 60-90 FT.)
WITH FULL LOAD.
TAKE-OFF RUN 7000-8000 FT.

5000   6000   7000   8000   9000

NDING.

TESTS HAVE PROVED
THAT THIS SYSTEM
REDUCED THE LANDING
RUN BY 35 PER CENT.

SUCTION SLOT.

BLOWER.

SUCTION SLOT.

DOWN THE
ARD

SOME WAY HAS TO BE FOUND TO SOLVE THE PROBLEM OF LENGTHY
TAKE-OFFS AND LANDINGS. THIS HAS LED TO THE ROLLS-ROYCE EXPERIMENTS
WITH THE "FLYING BEDSTEAD".

A SLIGHT INCLINATION
CAUSES FORWARD
FLIGHT.

FORWARD
CONTROL JET.

AFTER
CONTROL JET.

JET.

TO REDUCE THE LANDING SPEED
OF FAST FIGHTERS PARACHUTE
BRAKES HAVE BEEN USED.

GRUMMAN "TIGER"
ITS AIR-BRAKES
IN USE.

REVERSE
JET PIPE.

THE FAIREY "ROTODYNE", NOW BUILDING, WILL USE A POWERED ROTOR FOR
VERTICAL TAKE-OFF AND LANDING AND STANDARD PROPELLERS FOR FORWARD
FLIGHT, WHEN THE POWER-JETS OF THE ROTOR WILL BE SHUT OFF.

ST
SAL.

BY-PASS
DUCT.

TAIL
PIPE.

STANDARD
JET MOTOR.

REVERSE
JET PIPE.

ALTERING THE FLOW OF THE EXHAUST GASES TO ACT AS A BRAKE.

HE FUTURE IT MAY EVEN BE POSSIBLE TO USE THE MAIN
PULSION ENGINES WITH PART OF THEIR POWER DEFLECTED
IVE CONTINUOUS VERTICAL LIFT, SO THAT WINGS WILL NO
GER BE REQUIRED—THUS ANTICIPATING THE MYSTERIOUS
"FLYING-SAUCER".

MAIN ENGINES PORT AND STARBOARD
OF ENGINE ROOM.

VERTICAL
LIFT
JETS.

WITH THE
COMING OF
VERTICAL LIFT
HEAVY COMPLICATED
UNDER-CARRIAGES
WILL BE NO
LONGER REQUIRED

G H DAVIS
1955

the foreseeable future to design a wingless machine which would use the main motors to
provide continuous lift by directing part of the jet stream vertically downwards under
the centre of gravity in addition to providing sufficient thrust for forward propulsion. By
cutting the forward thrust a machine of this type could safely be landed vertically. This
would avoid lengthy runways and comparatively risky landings and take-offs at high speeds.

Refuelling-in-flight enabled the Boeing B-50 *Lucky Lady* to fly round the world without landing. Refuelling-in-space will hasten the day of manned flights to the planets.

Introduction to Space Flight

REFUELLING IN SPACE

Many suggestions have been put forward for achieving travel in space, but rocket scientists realised that they were all a long way short of the complete answer. Then, in 1949, an idea appeared which overnight promised to make inter-planetary travel a reality within our lifetime.

IN the article entitled " Steps to the Stars " which appears on pages 162-67, we learned how the technique of the pick-a-back rocket is going to help us to achieve the all-important speed necessary for economical flight in space. The article also explained how, even using step-rockets, as they are called, if the journey to the Moon is to be made in one go, then the Moon-ship at take-off will be a colossal structure weighing many thousands of tons.

It would not be *impossible* to build such a ship from the engineering point of view. But it would obviously be exceedingly difficult and it would also be extremely expensive—much more so than it need be.

By using a simple trick, the weight of a Moon-ship can be reduced to a matter of tons and the cost to but a fraction of what it would be otherwise. The trick is to refuel the space-ship on the way.

The principle of " refuelling " is common enough. *You* use it every day. If you have ever been camping it is most unlikely that you set out with all the supplies—food, water and fuel —required for the complete holiday. You bought food and obtained fuel. You " re-fuelled " on the way. The same principle applies when you go off on holiday in the family car. Just because it cannot do more than 150 miles on a tankful of petrol, this does not prevent you reaching your destination— you just fill up on the way.

In the world of aeroplanes, refuelling in flight has enabled fuel-thirsty jet fighters to cross the Atlantic non-stop, and bombers to fly around the world without landing.

In aviation, in fact, one does not expect an airliner to fly between distant terminals without stopping to refuel. We know it is quite unnecessary for an aeroplane to carry all the fuel needed for both the outward and the return flight. Yet, when we came to consider the possibility of journeys to the planets, the nearest of which is nearly a quarter of a million miles away, this is precisely what was envisaged. No wonder the space-ships began to resemble structures the size of the ocean liner *Queen Elizabeth* and the whole idea seemed pretty hopeless.

The idea of refuelling in space changed the picture completely and it is cause for satisfaction that members of Britain's Interplanetary Society were among the first who suggested this for the purpose of space-travel. The difference between what had been considered up till 1949 and the new suggestion is rather like the difference between crossing a river in one mighty jump and getting across by means of stepping-stones.

It can be argued that there are no filling stations in space. This is true at the moment, but within the next quarter-century engineering developments will take place which will make such stations quite practicable.

Winged ferry-ships may be used to carry up the pre-fabricated parts of manned space stations in the not-too-distant future. Forming the top stage of a big three-step rocket weighing 7,000 tons at take-off, this will be loaded with supplies, or pieces of a space station to be assembled in space, and then fired. At the desired height it will go into an orbit, unload its cargo and then return for another load. On the way back the ferry-ship will lose speed by using the friction of the air as a brake and finally land, lightly loaded, as a glider, at a speed lower than that of many present-day air liners.

A similar ferry-ship could be used to refuel space-ships in space. This is how a typical refuelling flight might be made. We will assume that the actual Moon-ship has already been assembled in space, 700 miles above the surface of the Earth. Finished, meticulously checked, but empty, it is circling the world effortlessly, its centrifugal force tending to make it fly off into space, exactly balanced by gravity tending to pull it back to Earth.

The tanker-ship will be fully refuelled and then launched. Climbing rapidly it will soon reach the same height as the circling Moon-ship, when it will level out at a speed of about

REFUELLING-IN-SPACE. The high speed of the orbiting vehicles will not be apparent, and in some respects the procedure will be simpler than refuelling aeroplanes in flight—there will be no slipstream to worry about!

The experience gained with equipment such as this Flight Refuelling package unit will prove useful when space-ships are refuelled.

rocket-pistols, propel themselves over to the Moon-ship. Alighting on the hull with their magnetically-soled shoes they quickly connect the pipe to a cock projecting from the side of the hull.

Then, under the action of powerful pumps in the tanker the precious fuel is transferred from the tanker to the Moon-ship. After half an hour the operation is complete and the pipeline is disconnected and withdrawn into the tanker, which then descends to Earth for another load.

Instead of using pipe-lines to transfer the propellant, an alternative scheme would be to carry it into the orbit in pressurised containers. These could then be fixed in position on outrigger girders forming part of the space-ship. This would result in a structure of the lightest possible construction. It would look most ungainly—but then streamlining is not necessary in the vacuum of space.

16,000 m.p.h. and manoeuvre into an orbit matching that of the Moon-ship. Intricate guidance and control equipment will take the tanker closer and closer to the Moon-ship. At the correct distance all power will be shut off and the two craft will then whizz round together without any further expenditure of power.

A hatch in the hull of the tanker opens and two space-suited figures emerge dragging a flexible pipe behind them. One of them attaches the pipe to his suit, and the two engineers then jump off the tanker and, using small hand

The idea of transferring fuel from tanker to Moon-ship, at a speed of 16,000 m.p.h. sounds exceedingly dangerous. But, in fact, the speed will not come into the operations, and to each other the two ships will appear motionless. If you find this difficult to understand—well, did you have any trouble when you " passed the sugar " at breakfast this morning? Of course not, even though you and the person concerned

An alternative method of refuelling in space to that shown on page 177, will be to launch the fuel in containers and then attach these to the waiting space-ship.

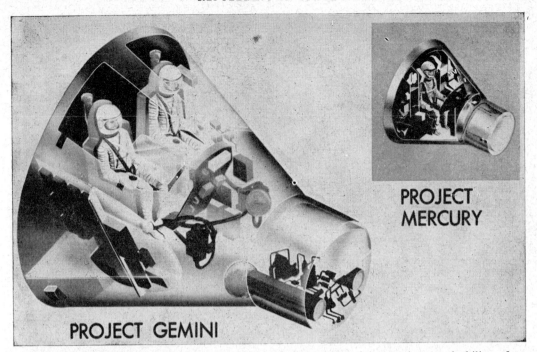

PROJECT MERCURY

PROJECT GEMINI

American Gemini two-man space-ship designed for initial trials on the practicability of rendezvousing in space. *Inset:* Mercury space-ship used for the first American space flights.

were travelling at about 55,000 *m.p.h.*—due to the rotation of the Earth round the Sun! In some ways refuelling in space will be simpler than refuelling in the air, because there will be no slipstream to worry about.

After several trips of the tanker, the Moon-ship will be fully fuelled, ready for the long 240,000-mile journey to the Moon. This seems a long way compared with the mere 700 miles the Moon-ship is above the surface of the Earth, but in terms of fuel and speed it is well over half-way to the Moon.

To make the journey as cheaply as possible the Moon-ship will accelerate rapidly to the escape velocity and then, switching off its rocket motors, will coast for the remainder of the journey. As the Moon-ship is already circling the earth at 16,000 m.p.h. it has only to increase its speed by 9,000 m.p.h. to reach escape velocity of 25,000 m.p.h. and overcome the pull of gravity and complete the journey to the Moon.

In addition to the two methods of refuelling in space already described, it would be possible to achieve the desired result by launching the space-ship in two sections, and then joining them together in orbit.

Experiments connected with refuelling in space have already started. The first test was made by the American astronaut Scott Carpenter during his exciting three-orbit flight around the Earth in the Mercury space-ship *Aurora* 7. During the flight he released a small balloon and a quantity of plastic discs. The balloon was painted in various colours and as it drifted away the astronaut noted which colour was the easiest to see. He also reported for how long he could see the plastic discs. The purpose of these tests was to see how well humans can use their eyes in the strange conditions in space. The experiments helped to show how accurately a space pilot could rendezvous with another space-ship in orbit.

Further tests were carried out with the Gemini two-man space-ship. This enlarged successor to the Mercury was developed specially for experiments on manned rendezvous techniques. During the tests the rendezvous target was an Agena satellite launched into orbit. In August, 1962, two Russian astronauts, sent up on an identical orbit, were in visual and radio contact during their flights.

Experiments such as these hasten the day of frequent long-distance space journeys.

MOMENT IN HISTORY. 12th April, 1961. A young Russian Air Force pilot, named Yuri Gagarin, turns at the top of the stairs and waves to his colleagues. A few hours later he became the first human to orbit the Earth, in the spacecraft *Vostok 1*.

MAN IN SPACE

Man was not intended for ever to remain in the cradle of the Earth.

THE following announcement over Moscow Radio marked one of the great days in the history of the world:

"The World's first satellite spaceship, the Vostok, *with a man on board, has been put into orbit round the Earth by the Soviet Union on 12th April, 1961. The pilot space-navigator of the satellite spaceship* Vostok *is a citizen of the U.S.S.R., Flight Major Yuri Alexeyevitch Gagarin."*

Ever since the first artificial satellite had whirled aloft in 1957, scientists had known that it was only a matter of time before a man went into space, but the knowledge of this fact did not detract from the excitement the announcement caused. Man had, for the first time, overcome the forces which throughout all previous ages had bound him firmly to Earth. Just as in the past the first experiments in boat-building

Space Pilot No. 1, the late Yuri Gagarin, the first man to orbit the Earth.

180

John Glenn, America's first astronaut, squeezes himself into the Mercury spacecraft *Friendship 7* during the last part of the countdown before his exciting spaceflight on 20th February, 1962. The Mercury spacecraft was shaped like an enlarged television tube, and the astronaut lay with his back towards the blunt end.

had opened the way to the exploration of oceans and continents, and the Wright brothers *Flyer* of 1903 had marked the dawn of the conquest of the air, so Yuri Gagarin's spaceflight ushered in a new era of exploration which eventually will take Man to whole new worlds.

THE EARTH FROM SPACE

The first historic flight of man in space was not a long one; it lasted 108 minutes. In fact Gagarin completed only one orbit before re-entering the atmosphere and landing safely by parachute near a village called Smelovaka, some six miles from the planned landing area.

After his successful return to Earth, Gagarin described some of the things he saw:—

"The sunlit side of the Earth is very clearly visible and one can easily distinguish the shores of the continents, islands, great rivers, large bodies of water and folds in the terrain.

"The picture of the horizon is a most strange one and is very beautiful. You can see a most impressive transition from the bright surface of the Earth to the completely black sky in which you can see the stars.

"This range of transition is a very thin one —a kind of film, a narrow belt girdling the globe. It is of a soft light blue colour and the entire transition from blue to black is very smooth and beautiful."

In August Major Titov went into orbit in *Vostok 2* and circled the Earth 17 times to become the first man to spend a whole day in space.

AMERICAN LAUNCHING BROADCAST

It is rather sad that these historic launchings were conducted in conditions of great secrecy, so that the world at large knew nothing of the missions until the cosmonauts were actually in orbit. Several years passed before the Russians released the details of Gagarin's lift-off.

Things were quite different when, the following year, the Americans were ready to attempt to put their first manned spaceship into orbit, a Mercury capsule named *Friendship 7*, and its astronaut-pilot John Glenn. In marked contrast to the dark secrecy with which the Russians surrounded their launchings, the Americans allowed their final preparations to be broadcast in detail all over the world, and also televised them to an estimated 135 million viewers in America.

Not only were people thus privileged to hear and see the preparations, but, during the flight,

Sailors hoist the Mercury spacecraft *Friendship 7* on board the recovery ship after John Glenn's successful orbital flight.

were able to hear recordings of John Glenn reporting his sensations in space a few minutes after the reports had been received.

". . . five, four, three, two, one, zero," listeners heard the announcer cry out the last seconds of the long countdown. A huge cloud of smoke and flame shot out of the base of the giant Atlas booster and, remarkably slowly, it started to lift. Within seconds it began to gain speed rapidly; a commentator broadcast its progress: "Height 3,000 ft., speed 200 m.p.h.;" and then, in about the time it will take you to read this: "height 25,000 ft., speed 700 m.p.h.; height 40,000 ft., speed 1,200 m.p.h.; height 75,000 ft., speed 2,500 m.p.h.; height 25 miles, speed 3,000 m.p.h.; height 40 miles, speed 5,000 m.p.h." The excitement was absolutely terrific.

As he passed through the speed of sound Glenn reported a little vibration, but all was well. At the desired height and speed the two side engines stopped and were jettisoned, and shortly afterwards, when the Atlas rocket had boosted the *Friendship 7* and its precious human cargo to a safe height, the escape rocket and its tower were also jettisoned to save weight.

Then came the tricky moment when the spaceship separated from the booster . . . Glenn excitedly radioed: "The capsule is turning round and I can see the booster during turnaround just a couple of hundred yards behind me."

Speeding across the Atlantic, Glenn loosened his chest strap and started work. First he called the various ground tracking stations and then checked the instruments inside his tiny cockpit. All was well. Apart from minor trouble with the automatic control system, all went well, until the time came for him to come out of orbit. A signal received on Earth indicated that the heat shield on the end of the spaceship was loose. To try and hold it in place if this really was so, Glenn was instructed to re-enter the atmosphere with his braking rocket pack, which is strapped across the heat shield, still in position.

This he did, and on the way down he saw pieces of molten metal fly back past his window as the rocket pack melted. "That was a real fireball, boy," he reported.

A few minutes later the heat shield was released ready for landing—it had been secure all along—and the *Friendship 7* splashed with a sizzle into the Ocean. A destroyer raced to the rescue, and soon Glenn was telling scientists all about what was undoubtedly one of the most exciting journeys the world had ever seen.

Valentina Tereshkova, who in June, 1963, completed 48 orbits in the spacecraft *Vostok 6* to become the first, and so far the only, woman to go into space.

RENDEZVOUS IN ORBIT. *Gemini 7*, crewed by Frank Borman and James Lovell, as seen in orbit by Walter Schirra and Thomas Stafford in *Gemini 6*, the nose of which is visible in the left foreground, during their historic rendezvous in December, 1965.

Richard Gordon straddles the nose of *Gemini 11* in cowboy fashion as he makes his way towards the Agena target vehicle with which it is docked.

A test flight of an early booster from which the giant *Saturn 5* rocket, used to launch America's Apollo spacecraft to the Moon, was developed.

It is difficult to realise that less than ten years separate these first short flights in space from the manned landing on the Moon by *Apollo 11* in July, 1969.

Russia followed her Vostok experiments with the three-man *Voskhod 1* and *2* spacecraft, and a series of two-man Soyuz spacecraft. It was during the flight of *Voskhod 2* in March, 1965, that another significant space "first" was achieved. Opening the spacecraft hatch, cosmonaut Alexei Leonov spent twenty-four minutes floating in the vacuum of space with just his spacesuit protecting him. This brave space "walk" showed that man could exist, suitably protected, in an airless vacuum in which his blood would soon have boiled had he ventured out unprotected.

Voskhod 2 was the last Russian manned spaceflight for over two years.

During this period America completed her entire two-man Gemini programme. Of twelve Gemini, all but the first two were manned, and all were eminently successful. During the mission of *Gemini 4*, launched in June, 1965, Edward White repeated the feat of Leonov and "walked" in space. While outside White used

a jet device called a Hand Manœuvring Unit to move about with and position himself, proving that such devices will enable later astronauts to work in space, performing jobs such as assembling space stations and repairing satellites and spacecraft.

The most significant achievement of the Gemini programme, however, was the rendezvous in orbit between *Gemini 6* and *Gemini 7*. This tricky technical feat had been attempted previously by the Russians in 1962, when *Vostoks 3* and *4* were boosted into similar orbits, but came no nearer than four miles. This was not close enough to be described as a true rendezvous. During the flights of *Gemini 6* and *7* the two craft flew in formation for several hours while separated by a distance of only a few feet. Later Geminis not only rendezvoused with Agena targets, but docked, thus perfecting another technique needed for the American Apollo programme to land a man on the Moon —and to return him safely to earth—before 1970.

TO THE MOON

These early tests and spaceflights provided experience for the most exciting and dramatic journey of all time—man's first journey to the Moon.

For this journey, America developed a giant rocket named Saturn, and a spaceship called Apollo. The spaceship comprises three separate sections; the cone-shaped Command Module, in which the three astronauts normally travel, the Service Module, containing the rocket engine needed for manœuvring in space, and the Lunar Module, the section which actually descends to the Moon.

Before attempting the landing the Apollo spaceship was thoroughly tested. *Apollo 7* was flown in space, close to the Earth, to enable experience to be gained in handling the complex craft. This test was so successful that *Apollo 8* went to the Moon, not to land, but to enable possible landing sites to be studied at close range. *Apollo 9* was used to test the Lunar Module in Earth orbit, and *Apollo 10* was the "dress rehearsal" of the real thing, with the Lunar Module descending to within 10 miles of the lunar surface.

By July, 1969, all was ready for *Apollo 11* to attempt the actual landing on the Moon. With a thunderous roar that could be heard

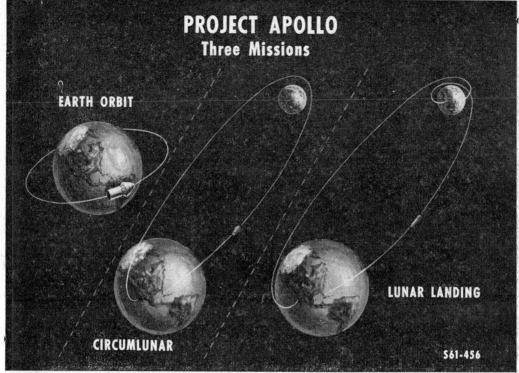

PROJECT APOLLO
Three Missions

EARTH ORBIT

LUNAR LANDING

CIRCUMLUNAR

S61-456

Three steps to the Moon. First the Apollo spacecraft was tested in orbit round the Earth. Two flights round the Moon were then made, to investigate possible landing sites and to check the vital section of the spacecraft which descends to the surface. Then came the actual landing. While the Lunar Module landed on the surface the Apollo Command Module remained in orbit round the Moon.

for 25 miles the giant Saturn rocket took off, and within minutes the Apollo spaceship was in space on its way. Arriving at the Moon the engine in the Service Module fired to slow the craft down so that it went into orbit round the Moon.

THE EAGLE LANDS

While circling the Moon, two astronauts, Neil Armstrong and Edwin "Buzz" Aldrin, crawled into the Lunar Module, leaving the third astronaut, Michael Collins, in the Command Module. The Lunar Module then undocked from the Command Module and started to descend to the surface. While separated, the CM was referred to as *Columbia* and the LM as *Eagle*, to avoid confusion between the two craft.

During the exciting descent to the surface the reports of the crew were broadcast, so that listeners on Earth could follow their progress. The LM touched down safely and then came the historic message "The *Eagle* has landed". Man had landed on the Moon, at 17 minutes past 9 o'clock, on Sunday evening, 20th July, 1969.

EXPLORERS FROM INTREPID

Such is the pace of modern technological development that within four months three more astronauts, Charles Conrad, Richard Gordon and Alan Bean, were on their way to the Moon in *Apollo 12*. The lift-off, on 14th November, 1969, was made in bad weather, and shortly afterwards the *Saturn 5* was struck twice by lightning. This caused the electrics inside the Apollo spacecraft to cut out and activated so many red warning lights that the crew could not read them all. Fortunately, no permanent damage was caused, and staging entry into orbit and the trans-lunar injection operations proceeded as planned.

The purpose of the *Apollo 12* mission was to develop pin-point landing techniques, deploy a

Intrepid in the Ocean of Storms. One of the *Apollo 12* astronauts examines the television camera prior to detaching it from *Surveyor 3* which soft-landed on the Moon in April, 1967, over two years previously. *Intrepid* can be seen on the rim of the crater, about 600 feet away, indicating the remarkable accuracy with which Conrad and Bean landed their craft.

number of scientific experiments and, if possible, examine the *Surveyor 3* spacecraft which had landed on the Moon on 20th April, 1967.

Three days after leaving the Earth *Apollo 12* reached the Moon and was manœuvred into orbit around it. When undocked the Lunar Module became known as *Intrepid*, and the Command Module, which remained in orbit round the Moon, as *Yankee Clipper*.

A smooth and successful landing in the Ocean of Storms was made in the early hours of Wednesday morning, 19 November, 1969. So accurate was the guidance, coupled with skilful piloting, that *Intrepid* was set down in sight of *Surveyor 3*, a truly remarkable example of space marksmanship.

While on the surface two EVAs, or surface walks, were made. During the first a package was deployed containing several experiments one of which recorded Moonquakes. This was so sensitive that it picked up the footsteps of the astronauts as they walked by and trans-

mitted the faint signals to Earth. A solar wind experiment was also deployed, together with the American flag. The only serious mishap was the failure of the colour television camera which prevented viewers on Earth from seeing the excitement on the Moon.

The purpose of the second walk was to survey the surrounding terrain and to examine *Surveyor 3*. During this walk, Conrad and Bean covered well over a mile during which they collected a useful selection of lunar rocks and soil. The high point of this walk, of course, was the trip to *Surveyor*, lying in a shallow crater some 600 feet from the *Intrepid*. The two astronauts removed several parts of the craft, including the TV camera, which was brought back to Earth for examination.

Subsequent examination disclosed the existence of several microbes inside one of the components—alive. These were assumed to have been inadvertently trapped inside the mechanism before the craft was launched from the Earth.

EARTH'S NEW SATELLITES

O N 4th October, 1957, Russia launched the world's first artificial satellite. The dream of Ziolkovsky, Goddard, Oberth and other early pioneers came true, when fiction suddenly became fact. The first rung in the ladder to the planets had been placed in position.

News of this momentous scientific achievement was given to a startled world in Moscow the following day, by the historic announcement:

"The Earth's first artificial satellite has been made as a result of intensive and large-scale work by research institutes and designing organisations. On 4th October, 1957, the first satellite was successfully launched in the U.S.S.R. According to preliminary information, the carrier rocket gave the satellite the required orbital velocity of some 8,000 metres per second (17,897 m.p.h.) At the present moment the satellite is tracing an elliptical trajectory around the Earth and its flight can be observed in the rays of the rising and setting sun through the simplest optical instruments."

SPUTNIK 1

The Russians first announced their intention to launch artificial satellites at the Sixth International Congress of Astronautics, held in Copenhagen, in 1955. Nevertheless, the actual launching came as a complete surprise, and was even more dramatic because of the weight of the satellite—184 lb.

The Sputnik, meaning "fellow-traveller", as the Russians called their satellite, was in fact much bigger and heavier than had been generally thought practical for this important first step towards interplanetary flight. Most British and American projects for satellites had, primarily on the grounds of economy, envisaged the smallest possible rocket. The launching rocket for America's Vanguard programme, for example, was expressly designed to be as small as possible, and the satellite the smallest and lightest capable of carrying the minimum useful payload.

Sputnik 1, the first of the Earth's new satellites, was a polished aluminium sphere with four aerials. Launched on 4th October, 1957, it re-entered the atmosphere on 4th January, 1958, and burnt up.

THE ORBIT

The satellite was launched southwards, at an angle of about 65° to the Equator. Travelling at nearly 18,000 m.p.h. and taking 96·2 minutes for each revolution, it circled the world fifteen times a day. The orbit remained "fixed" in space, while the Earth rotated inside it, so that during successive revolutions the Sputnik passed over a different part of the surface, and thus passed over almost all the inhabited areas of the world each day.

The craft looped round the Earth in a gentle ellipse bringing it within 142 miles of the surface at the lowest point (the perigee) and taking it up to 588 miles at its highest point (the apogee). Although this difference seems quite large, when considered as the distance from the centre of the Earth—4142 and 4588 miles respectively—the orbit was nearly circular, indicating precise and reliable guidance techniques.

Sputnik 1 comprised a polished aluminium sphere, 23 in. in diameter, which was lightly pressurised with nitrogen before launching as a means of controlling the internal temperature. Attached to the sphere were four aerials having lengths of 7 ft. 10 in. and 9 ft. 6 in. These were folded alongside the final-stage carrier rocket until arrival in the orbit, when they sprang out automatically at the time of the satellite's release.

This dog, a Laika, a breed akin to the Husky, was launched into space in *Sputnik 2* on 3rd November, 1957. The dog was the first living creature to go into space and survived until the air supply gave out.

The reason for the heaviness of the satellite—184 lb.—in spite of its comparative smallness was the use of heavy batteries for the two powerful transmitters, from which signals were picked up as far away as 6,250 miles. These transmitters gave out a peculiar "bleep-bleep-bleep" signal which, recorded and re-broadcast over the radio stations of the world, must have been heard by an enormous number of people.

WORLD REACTION

As can be imagined, the launching of the satellite filled the newspaper headlines of the world. All shades of opinion were expressed.

There was both scepticism and enthusiasm and also, particularly in the United States, a feeling of humiliation and disappointment that the Russians had succeeded in being "first up". Their satellite programme had received so much publicity that the Russians' unexpected success completely "stole the American thunder".

As might have been expected, the ugly idea of missile-launching manned-satellites appeared in numerous papers. One, summing up the comments of American "experts", stated: "The space station could be the greatest force for peace ever devised or one of the most terrible

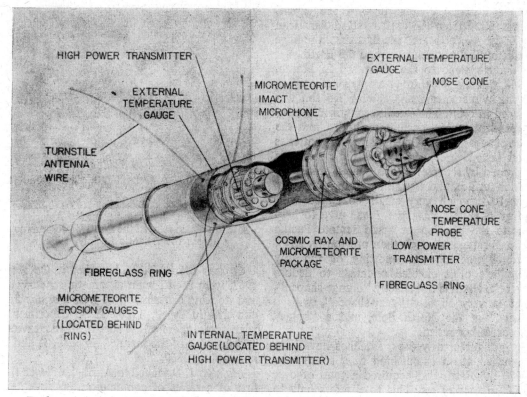

HIGH POWER TRANSMITTER

EXTERNAL TEMPERATURE GAUGE

EXTERNAL TEMPERATURE GAUGE

MICROMETEORITE IMACT MICROPHONE

NOSE CONE

TURNSTILE ANTENNA WIRE

NOSE CONE TEMPERATURE PROBE

FIBREGLASS RING

COSMIC RAY AND MICROMETEORITE PACKAGE

LOW POWER TRANSMITTER

FIBREGLASS RING

MICROMETEORITE EROSION GAUGES (LOCATED BEHIND RING)

INTERNAL TEMPERATURE GAUGE (LOCATED BEHIND HIGH POWER TRANSMITTER)

Explorer 1, America's first satellite, was small compared with Russia's Sputniks, but it discovered the now famous Van Allen radiation belts surrounding the Earth.

weapons of war—depending on who builds and controls it. A ruthless power established on a space station could actually subjugate the peoples of the world. Sweeping round the Earth, this man-made island in the heavens could be used as a platform from which to launch guided missiles."

SPUTNIK 2 LAUNCHED

Just as the world was beginning to take its new moon for granted it was announced, on 3rd November, that a second, bigger, satellite had been launched. Weighing a reported 1,120 lb. this circled on a higher orbit, reaching about 1,000 miles above the Earth at its highest point. The most spectacular feature about the second satellite was that it contained, in a pressurised compartment, a live dog. This dog, a Laika, was specially trained for the experiment and had previously been fired to high altitudes in rockets and landed safely by parachute.

The dog circled the Earth for more than a week, weightless and subjected to the full force

of the mysterious cosmic rays and other radiations, from which the atmosphere normally protects the surface of the Earth. She was the first Earth creature to stay in space for more than a few minutes and as such will always be remembered in astronautical history.

AMERICAN SUCCESS

The immediate reaction to the Russian Sputniks was an ill-fated attempt in December, 1957, to place a small test satellite into orbit using a Project Vanguard Launching Vehicle. A loss of thrust was experienced shortly after the take-off, and the 72-ft. rocket fell back on the launching pad in flames and toppled over, breaking in two.

American success came on 31st January, 1958, when the United States Army, using a modified Jupiter C rocket, placed a 31-lb. satellite, called *Explorer 1*, in orbit at the first attempt. The craft was placed in a highly elliptical orbit, varying from 200 to 1,800 miles above the surface. Although small compared with Russia's Sputniks, some clever scientific detective work concerned with the signals transmitted from the craft enabled American scientists to detect, for the first time, the huge radiation belts which surround the Earth.

Success came to the Vanguard in March, 1958, when, at the third attempt, a test satellite, 6 in. in diameter and weighing 3·5 lb., was placed in orbit. The satellite contained two independent radio transmitters, both about the size of a match box! One used mercury batteries and lasted three weeks, but the other was powered by six solar cells mounted on the exterior surface, and was still working five years later! Although very small compared with other satellites, *Vanguard 1* was used to help locate the position of some remote Pacific islands more accurately than previously. Also, careful tracking and plotting of the tiny satellite's orbit enabled scientists to deduce that the Earth is not exactly "orange-shaped", but is very slightly "pear-shaped", with a "neck" at the North Pole, and a "bulge" towards Antarctica.

Since these early days, satellites have been launched at an astonishing rate, so that by 1970 the Earth had acquired a total of over 1,000 new satellites. This total refers only to the satellites themselves and not to the final stages of the launching rockets, which also go into orbit and which are often bigger than a double-decker bus.

COSMOS BY THE HUNDRED

Russia has launched several hundred satellites under the name Cosmos. The general purpose of the series covers almost all aspects of the exploration of space, such as the investigation of the upper layers of the atmosphere; the energy composition of the Earth's radiation belts; the radiation from the Sun and other celestial bodies; and the effect of meteoric matter on spacecraft materials and different methods of spacecraft construction.

Cosmos satellites have helped to develop the Soviet Union's Meteor system of weather satellites. *Cosmos 144* and *184*, for example, were placed in orbits whose planes were at right angles to each other, to enable ground stations to receive information from selected areas twice daily. *Cosmos 206* was placed in the same orbit as *144*, but twenty minutes behind it, giving forecasters the opportunity of checking data received from *Cosmos 144*.

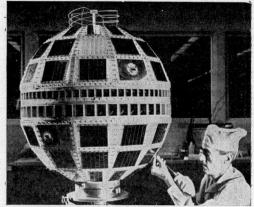

Telstar. The "private-venture" American satellite which relayed the first TV programme across the Atlantic in July, 1962.

Cosmos 186 and *188*, launched in October, 1967, were used for an automatic rendezvous and docking experiment, as were *Cosmos 212* and *213* in April, 1968. These experiments were forerunners of the successful rendezvous and docking of the manned *Soyuz 6, 7,* and *8* in October, 1969.

Molniya 1, launched in April, 1965, was the first of a series of communications satellites. The craft was placed in a highly elliptical orbit, designed to provide the longest possible communications sessions between Moscow and Vladivostok. Other satellites in this series form part of the Orbiter network, which provides telephone and colour television services to cities scattered throughout the Soviet Union.

ORBITING WEAPONS

Unfortunately, in addition to these peaceful research, weather and communications satellites, there are many military reconnaissance "spy" satellites and test vehicles for advanced weapons systems. Some are being used to help develop a particularly deadly space-borne H-bomb. This circles in orbit until commanded to re-enter the atmosphere and descend on its target.

The United States has also launched several hundred satellites. Like Russia's Cosmos, some of these are reconnaissance craft, but most of them are research satellites, on which full details have been released. Many have passed beyond the experimental stage and are now earning their keep by enhancing older forms of earth systems. Weather and communications satellites come into this category.

WEATHER SATELLITES

As long ago as April, 1960, America launched the first of a series of Tiros experimental weather satellites. Carrying two television cameras, these satellites sent back a stream of photographs of cloud formations which immediately attracted the attention of meteorologists all over the world. The pictures showed some clouds to have the form of gigantic spirals spreading over hundreds of miles. Other pictures gave meteorologists their first-ever views of complete hurricanes and typhoons, providing useful information on these terrible storms which cause such great loss of life and damage each year.

From Tiros there developed the ESSA (Environmental Science Services Administration) series of operational weather satellites, information from which is fed into the daily weather forecasts of countries in the world. The latest satellites in this series, known as ITOS—Improved Tiros Operational System—carry delicate sensors for taking cloud cover pictures in total darkness as well as during daylight hours. Previous weather satellites in the ESSA series were restricted to daytime photography only.

ATLANTIC TV

The most spectacular use of satellites, however, as far as ordinary people are concerned, is undoubtedly the high-flying communications Intelsats used to enable viewers all over the world to see exciting events such as Expo 70 in Japan and the World Cup football matches in Mexico, while they were actually taking place.

A foretaste of the great use to which such satellites would be put was gained during the transatlantic television experiments carried out with the American Telstar and Relay communications satellites in 1962. Unlike ordinary radio waves, which can be "bounced" or reflected off the ionosphere to permit long-distance communications, television signals can only follow straight lines—and thus can only extend to the horizon. To get a signal past the curvature of the Earth between America and Europe requires a relay station high enough for it to be visible from both countries simultaneously—and this is the function played by a communications satellite.

Telstar and Relay were placed in low orbits and were thus only visible for a relatively short period, but the excitement caused by the first historic transatlantic television programmes in July, 1962, was intense and kept millions of viewers in Europe watching their television sets until late at night.

From these early experimental satellites has developed the U.S. Comsat system now in daily use around the world. In contrast to the low circular orbits of Telstar and Relay, and the elliptical orbits of Russia's Molniyas, America's Comsats are in what are known as 24-hour or synchronous orbits. Placed in orbit 22,300 miles above the surface, these take exactly one day to complete each revolution. They thus keep pace with the rotation of the Earth and appear to be fixed or stationary in space above the same place on the map. Several of these satellites, placed over the Atlantic, Pacific and Indian oceans, now provide a pretty regular service between most countries of the world.

EXPLORERS, OSOs AND OGOs

For general space research the United States have launched several series of satellites with code names such as Explorer, OSO and OGO.

Explorer satellites are designed to explore space. Nearly 50 Explorer craft have been launched and they vary widely in complexity. *Explorer 14*, launched in October, 1962, weighed 89 lb. and was designed to explain some of the

Ariel, Britain's first satellite, is investigating the ionosphere, which is used for long distance radio communication.

scientific mysteries of how "space weather" affects our daily life on the surface of the Earth, and our future exploration of space. *Explorer 19*, on the other hand, was basically a simple 12-ft. diameter balloon. Inflated in orbit, the drag of the tiny particles which exist even in space, gradually slowed the satellite down, the rate of decay indicating the spatial density. In contrast, *Explorer 34*, launched in May, 1967, was an Interplanetary Monitoring Platform craft and carried eleven complex experiments for measuring solar and galactic cosmic rays at the boundary of the Earth's magnetosphere and in interplanetary space.

The OSO satellites, Orbiting Solar Observatory craft, are designed primarily to observe the Sun. Such studies are vitally important because they may help to unravel some of the mysteries which have intrigued mankind since the beginning of time: how the Sun controls the upper atmosphere of the Earth and weather; the origin and history of the solar system; and the structure and evolution of the stars and galaxies.

The Earth's atmosphere is both a blessing and a hindrance. It stops the more dangerous radiations from space—if it did not, life as we know it on the Earth would be considerably altered. But while it protects life, it hinders scientific investigation of the origin and structure of the universe because it filters out the Sun's more interesting radiations.

OSO craft, orbiting above the atmosphere, observe the Sun unhindered. OSO satellites consist of a wheel-like main "base" on which pivots a "sail" section carrying the Sun sensors. When in orbit the sail section locks onto and points continually at the centre of the Sun.

OGO satellites are Orbiting Geophysical Observatory craft designed to investigate the many influences the Sun has on the near-Earth environment and to aid the evaluation of the hazards involved in the manned exploration of space. They are among the most advanced unmanned satellites developed to date. OGOs, containing more than 100,000 parts, have space for up to 50 experiments.

America's ITOS—Improved Tiros Operational System—weather satellite carries delicate sensors for taking cloud cover pictures in total darkness as well as during daylight hours. Previous U.S. weather satellites were restricted to daytime photography only.

COUNTY OF INVERNESS
EDUCATION COMMITTEE

Bishop Eden's School

SESSION 1971 -1972

1st (equal) PRIZE

For

Class work

Awarded to

Mairietta Young

P VII Class

30/6/72 Date

W. N. Brown

Head Teacher